THINGS TO COME

Lucia's fingers hesitated over the laces, not sure whether it was gift or trap that lay beneath.

"Are you afraid to see it, then?" Theron asked softly.

She looked up at him, seeking reassurance. "But what is it? Tell me that."

"It is what makes me a man rather than a woman. It is the difference between you and me, and the source of more pleasures than you have ever dreamt of."

"Pleasures for you, or for me?"

"Both," he said, a hint of impatience edging his voice.

"All of that, under this small piece of cloth?" She tilted her head to the side, examining the area, her rational side striving to control her fear with questions. "I doubt it."

Dream of Me

Lisa Cach

LOVE SPELL NEW YORK CITY

To Clark, the man of my dreams.

LOVE SPELL®

October 2004

Published by

Dorchester Publishing Co., Inc.
200 Madison Avenue
New York, NY 10016

ISBN 0-505-52519-4

The name "Love Spell" and its logo are trademarks of Dorchester Publishing Co., Inc.

Printed in the United States of America.

Visit us on the web at www.dorchesterpub.com.

Dream of Me

ACKNOWLEDGMENTS

Special thanks to Aurelian Miron of *SoftRide Romania,* for his help in understanding how the history of his country could be turned to fictional ends; to Bill Yeaton for all his wonderful photographs of Romania; and to Kevin Friberg for creating the map.

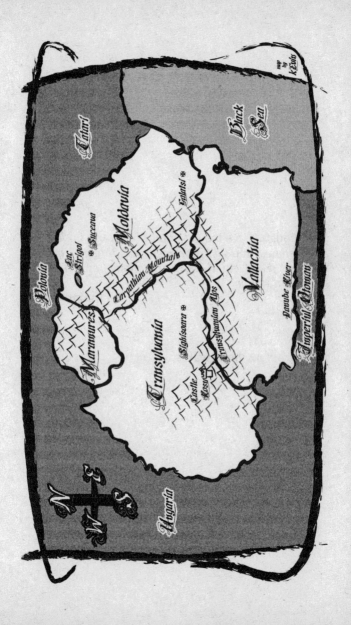

And though I have the gift of prophecy, and understand all mysteries, and all knowledge; and though I have all faith, so that I could move mountains, and have not love, I am nothing.

—I Corinthians 13

I sleep, but my heart wakes.

—Song of Solomon

Part One

Chapter One

Wallachia, Eastern Europe, 1423

"I want her."

"Wearing the crown of two countries will not be enough for you—you must have a Transylvanian princess as well?" Theron asked, in reluctant admiration of Vlad's unbridled ambition. The human would possess the world if but given the chance. He was a man after Theron's own nonexistent heart.

"Lucia will be mine: untouched, unsoiled, a virgin page upon which only I shall write."

And what a mess of that virgin page he would make, Theron thought. The man was beginning to sound as if he were a couple of stars short of a constellation. "I will ensure that Dragosh breaks the engagement between his sister Lucia and Nicolae of Moldavia, but persuading Dragosh to marry Lucia to you will be your own work." Theron raised one midnight-black, demonic brow, examining the determined man. "But I doubt you'll have difficulty."

3

Vlad was young and handsome, and despite his apparent obsession with virgins was possessed of a violent ruthlessness that Theron had not often encountered in his four thousand years as a demon. A fierce warrior and surprisingly brilliant schemer, Vlad had murdered and double-crossed his way to the throne of Wallachia. Now he had his deceptively soft brown eyes set on his neighbor to the northeast, the principality of Moldavia.

"Of course I won't have any problem. And it's not just Lucia's fresh young body I want." Vlad paused and licked his lips, a far-off look in his eyes.

"No?" Theron asked, as Vlad failed to continue.

The man blinked and came back to the present, his eyes widening for a moment in consideration of his plans. "Marrying Lucia of Maramures—I don't know what you demons understand of human politics of geography, but Maramures is a Transylvanian principality that shares a border with Moldavia—marrying Lucia will cement ties in the region that will in turn help me conquer that land."

"The only fly in your ointment being that Lucia's brother Dragosh has engaged her to Prince Nicolae of Moldavia," Theron said.

"He's trying to end a generations-long feud between Maramures and Moldavia, the idiot. There's some sort of curse on the family that he thinks he can break by marrying off his sister, and he won't listen to reason."

Theron crossed his arms over his chest and stood as if at ease within the candle circle that held him. "You must be desperate indeed, to have risked your immortal soul by summoning me."

Vlad snorted. "As if God cares about the affairs of men."

Theron shrugged. He was not going to argue human

religious questions with a man who had less idea of right and wrong than even the demons of the Night World. He casually paced the inner edge of the summoning circle, sneaking in a flutter of his black leathery wings to stretch the tension out of them. He was careful not to let their tips cross the line of the circle; a blast of pain would be the reward for such carelessness.

From the corner of his eye he caught movement: A velvet curtain across one end of the room briefly bulged and rippled, as if someone had moved behind it. Vlad was not alone.

Answering Vlad's summoning spell had been a risk. He wasn't forced to, as some human myths held; but the Night World was full of old stories of foolish demons who had been caught in the summoning circles of humans and found themselves enslaved or destroyed as a result. Theron had been waiting centuries, though, for an opportunity just such as this one that Vlad presented, and risk or not, stupid and foolish or not, he wouldn't pass it up. He only hoped his excitement wasn't evident to Vlad—and to whomever it was lurking behind the curtain.

Theron lowered his lids and cast a narrow, examining glance at Vlad. He needn't have worried on this score, at least; Vlad looked well wrapped up in his own schemes, his dark eyes wide, perspiration dampening the edges of his deep auburn hair and turning it black against his tanned skin. This was undoubtedly the only time a demon had been crazy enough to answer Vlad's summons, and the human looked on the edge of either bursting into maniacal laughter or having a seizure at his surprising success.

Theron decided to take Vlad's confidence down a notch. He subtly flexed his muscles and turned so that

Vlad could see him fully. He had a body formed by the fantasies of dreaming women: tall, broad-shouldered, smoothly muscled, and with a manhood that even at rest would make a woman dampen with desire and a man want to turn away to hide his own meager assets. Theron saw Vlad's eyes make a quick assessment of Theron's goods, then widen in surprise before looking self-consciously away.

Theron laughed silently. No human could win a size war against a demon; especially not an incubus like Theron, who had been created solely to take sexual dreams to mortal women. But Vlad needn't know that Theron was only a lowly sex-dream demon, at the bottom of the hierarchy rather than the major force of darkness and destruction Vlad assumed.

No, humans knew next to nothing of the true nature of demons, magic, and the worlds beyond their own. They fumbled with their crumbs of knowledge and thought themselves wise and wicked, but they were no more than ignorant children playing with shadows. They thought their religions encompassed all that was unseen in the universe, when in truth there were worlds and dimensions far beyond their imaginings of Heaven and Hell. One such place was the Night World.

Theron suspected that Vlad hadn't gained what small knowledge he had on his own; whoever lurked behind the curtain was probably to blame for encouraging Vlad to summon a demon. Once Theron had what he wanted, he'd have to thank the hidden helper for his foolish ignorance.

For Theron had every intention of taking advantage of that ignorance and turning it to his own advantage. He'd had enough of slaving in the Night World, never being his own master. He would rather rule as a king on earth in a brief, burning, glorious mortal life of complete power, than go another millennium in the Night World servicing lonely, sexually frustrated mortal women—a mere gigolo of dreams. He wanted an existence that *mattered*, even if it were brief.

"Lucia *will* be mine," Vlad said. "Dragosh will betrothe her to me, and give me his allegiance as well. His other sister is married to Iancu, the Hungarian-appointed ruler of Transylvania. They will be tied to me through Lucia, and together we shall crush Moldavia under our heels."

Nice fellow, this Vlad, full of brotherly love. Theron decided there was no reason to feel guilty about what he planned to do to him—assuming Theron was prone to guilt to begin with, which he wasn't. He was not a sniveling, mewling human, after all. At least, not yet.

"In return for arranging the breaking Lucia's of engagement, you swear upon your immortal soul to give me what I've asked?" Theron inquired.

"Three days in possession of my mortal body. Yes, I swear it," Vlad agreed. "But not until Moldavia is conquered. I cannot risk a demon being in control of my body until my position is secure. Come to me when victory is mine, but well before I wed. I won't have you touching Lucia through my hands."

Theron cocked a brow. "You are so certain that you will succeed?"

"Bogdan and his sons have more pride than sense, and they lack discipline. Moldavia will fall like a ripe apple from a tree. One good shake of the trunk and down it will come."

"Even if you fail to catch your apple, you will owe me my due."

"If I fail, my head will be on a pike," Vlad said, then

laughed loudly. "You may then have whatever possession of it you wish!"

Theron wondered again if the man was entirely sane. "If you do not pay me what is due, if you break our bargain, I will visit your Lucia and take from her every drop of that innocence you prize so highly."

Vlad's amusement died, and a dark light entered his eyes. "You will *not* do that."

"I hope I will not need to. Hold to our bargain and I will stay far from her. Break it and I will visit her every night until she is as educated as a whore, and I will drink in her pleasure like wine. Eventually, if you do not relent, my visits will drain the very life from her, and she will die of the pleasure I have taken from her. Your precious virgin and all her family ties will be lost to you forever."

It was the only threat Theron could make against Vlad, to force him to stick to his end of the agreement. A demon could not forcibly take possession of a human body; the human had to willingly allow the demon in. To force the issue would result in the death of both human and demon.

Once in possession of a human body, though, a crafty demon could stay as long as he liked, so long as he didn't draw the attention of Nyx, Queen of the Night, or of a meddling human exorcist. It made Theron furious even to think of a mortal priest casting him out of Vlad's body after all the hard work he would have put into getting into it. Meddling do-gooders. He hoped he never saw one.

"Very well," Vlad said. "We have made our bargain."

"Yes, we have."

They smiled, man to demon, demon to man, and a

shadow moved again in the corner of Theron's vision. When he looked, there was nothing to see, but an uneasy doubt cast itself through Theron's mind. Was Vlad planning to double-cross him, just as Theron planned to double-cross Vlad?

When one made a deal with the devil, nothing was ever as it seemed. And in this case, Theron didn't consider himself the one who was the devil.

But the bargain was struck.

Chapter Two

Theron stood in the doorway of the bedchamber of Dragosh of Maramures, watching as the succubus Samira crouched on the man's chest and sent him the nightmare that would cause him to break the engagement of his sister Lucia to Nicolae of Moldavia.

This was it; in mere minutes his end of the bargain with Vlad would be complete, and it would be only a matter of waiting for Moldavia to be crushed. Vlad's body would be his then, and he would forever leave the Night World. He would rule his own life, answer only to his own wishes, and it would be others who jumped to do *his* bidding. His whims would mean life and death. He would matter in a way that a dream demon never could, for each of his actions would leave a mark upon this real, physical world.

He would also breathe, and sweat, and feel the solid earth beneath his feet. He would age. He would have a wife, and do to her what he had only done to women in

11

their dreams. He would know what it truly felt like to touch a woman, solid hand to solid flesh. For the first time he would feel the desires and pleasures of being a man, rather than merely stealing the echoes of lust as experienced by sleeping women.

Theron looked at Samira as she crouched on the bed. She had long red hair, whereas Theron's was black, but they had the same flame blue eyes and pale, moonbeam-perfect skin. Samira had everything a male fantasy could dream up, from plump buttocks to a tiny waist, to full high breasts that jiggled but never sagged. Demons such as he had no sexual desires of their own, but Theron thought that were he human, he could do worse than to sink his sword into that bit of succubus flesh.

Maybe four millennia of playing in the passions of humans had worn off on him: He sometimes thought he could almost feel physical desires like a human. He thought sometimes of taking Samira with him onto the mortal plane; of finding her a human body to inhabit, at his side. He'd seen in her some of the same weariness of the Night World that he himself felt; seen some of the same longing for a different existence, although he sensed that she was afraid to admit it to herself.

They were breaking the rules of the Night World by meddling in the lives of princes, and would face the most severe of punishments if caught: Nyx, Queen of the Night, would likely hand them over to the Day Gods to be ripped to shreds. He'd needed Samira's help, though. He himself could only send dreams to women. A succubus like Samira could only send them to men. He'd gambled that his friendship with Samira and her weariness of the Night World would prompt her to break rules and help him, whereas the thousand other Oneroi—their fellow dream demons who were the children of Sleep—would have refused, and reported Theron to Nyx.

Dragosh moaned and thrashed as Samira perched on his chest, her hand on his forehead, sending the aging man a nightmare. Theron had left the details of the dream up to Samira and didn't care to know what horrors her imagination had created for Dragosh. Although skilled with dreams of sexual fulfillment, Samira was best known among the succubi for her virtuosity with sexual nightmares.

Dragosh's thrashing disturbed the slatternly woman sleeping next to him, half-waking her. She opened bleary, sleep-clogged eyes, and a stunned moment later let out an ear-splitting shriek. The mist of dreams still infecting her vision made Samira visible to her for the space of a moment, until she fully woke and lost her glimpse into Night. The damned wench's screech broke Dragosh's bonds of sleep, though, and he bolted up, gray hair wild about his head, mouth gaping, eyes showing white rims of terror.

Samira beat her great black wings and rose into the air, hovering above the humans with a look of annoyance on her lovely, wicked features.

The human male threw back the covers and bolted from his bed. He ran across the room stark naked, his manhood so shriveled with cold that it nearly disappeared into the grizzled hair at his loins. He rushed by invisible Theron and pushed open the door of his chamber, running past his royal guards without pause. They were too startled to do more than stare and gape and stumble back from their prince, and call out confused, alarmed questions that Dragosh did not answer. When they regained their senses, they set off in pursuit.

Curious, Theron followed, Samira along with him. "What did you *do* to him?" Theron asked, still not entirely wanting to know. Again, he was glad he wasn't ever going to be on the receiving end of one of Samira's mental works of art.

Samira shrugged, looking amazed herself at Dragosh's violent response to the nightmare.

Dragosh came to another guarded door, which he pushed open without ceremony, stopping on the threshold. His breathing was labored and rough, catching on sobs, and he stood and stared with the eyes of a madman into the darkness within. Theron, with his Night World vision, could see the room as clearly as if it were day.

A tawny-haired girl, no more than fourteen years of age, slept peacefully on a bed in the center of the room—Dragosh's young sister, Lucia.

Such a small, innocent thing, to be the cynosure of so many violent passions. Theron reached out his senses, trying to pick up some hint from Lucia of her own sexual desires. He caught a faint thread of lust—no more than a whisper through the Night World. She was on the cusp between childhood and womanhood; no longer one, and not yet fully the other. Her body had slowly begun to change, her breasts to fill, her waist to narrow, but the sexual longings that she felt were but a gentle mist compared to the pouring rain that would fall in the coming years.

He was sure that no incubus had yet visited her. It was the job of the incubi to relieve the pent-up sexual frustrations of women, and Lucia had known no time in her

14

brief life for such frustrations. Incubi gave women pleasure in their dreams when they could find no such satisfaction with their fumbling husbands and clumsy lovers, most of whom seemed to have no notion that a thing such as a clitoris existed. Incubi also, on occasion, sent sexual nightmares to women as punishment for crimes like adultery with the neighbor's strapping, horny young son—who somehow *did* know about the clitoris. Or for mocking a husband's underwhelming penis, or doing a poor job of feigning orgasm. For Lucia, though, such crimes and disappointing couplings lay only in the future.

Dragosh calmed as he watched his sleeping sister, and then, after a few shuddering breaths, turned and walked with the stiff gait of an old man back down the hall toward his own chamber. Samira turned to watch after him, then looked at Theron with both regret and accusation in her fiery blue eyes.

"Go," Theron said, stopping her before she could speak. He could see the question in her eyes, asking if his bargain with Vlad was worth what she had just done to Dragosh. Of course it was, as far as Theron was concerned, but her silent accusation was unexpected; he had never before known Samira to show sympathy for anyone, or guilt for any of her actions.

Theron touched the succubus's hair, combing his fingers through her silken red locks, and then let his hand rest on Samira's smooth, bare shoulder. A hum of sexual power flowed off her and into his hand, then coursed through Theron's body as if he were a human male she had come to visit in the night, giving him a faint taste of what it was to be a man who lusted. "You did as I asked, and I thank you. Now go." His hand tightened on her in warning. "This shall not be spoken of beyond you and me. Promise me that."

Samira shivered under his touch, then nodded. It would mean the destruction of them both were Nyx ever to learn of this. Only Morpheus, Ikelos, and Phantasos, princes of the Night World, were allowed to meddle in the dreams of earthly kings and rulers, and thus perhaps change the course of human history.

Theron released her, his hand tingling, echoes of stolen mortal desire fading away from his body. The incubi and succubi had no sexual desires of their own; they felt only the shadows cast by the lusting bodies of humans. What he felt from her must be just such a shadow from the men she had visited. It taunted him, making him want even more to feel a desire that started from his own body—to feel it for Samira, or to feel it, as Vlad did, for Lucia, as such an overwhelming force that he would destroy countries in order to satisfy it.

As Samira began to disappear, returning to the plane of the Night World, Theron turned again to Lucia's doorway. He gazed intently upon the sleeping, innocent princess, trying to sense what it was that drew Vlad so strongly to this girl above all others. Why did humans fall in love or lust with one person but not another? The differences between the choices seemed too small to matter.

Before he was aware of what he was doing, he was standing beside the bed, looking down at Lucia. Unaware that there was a demon present, one of the guards closed the door to the chamber, leaving Theron alone with the girl.

Lucia slept with one hand fisted in the sheet and drawn up close to her chin, as if she were cold. Her long honey-brown hair was a tangle over the pillow, over her neck, and over the edge of the bed. The full face of youth was beginning to show the high cheekbones of the woman to come, and the lashes that now lay so thick and innocent upon her cheeks would soon be turned to flirtation and sidelong glances.

It occurred to Theron then that if all went as he planned and he took permanent control of Vlad's body, Lucia would be *his*. When she was old enough to marry, he would have a beautiful, virginal wife on whom to play out every sex act he'd gleaned from the minds of women over the past four thousand years. It would be *her* flesh to which he put his solid hand; her virgin passage that might be the first into which he sheathed himself. She would be the one who would share his bed every night, and be his to explore as he pleased.

Vlad wouldn't be the one to despoil Lucia; Theron would be.

Without desires of his own, though, he felt no lust when he looked down at Lucia. He was achingly, miserably devoid of any desire for her at all. What he truly felt was curiosity that this young, oblivious thing could rouse such fervor in the heart of vicious Vlad.

Perhaps he could find a way to have Samira possess Lucia's body. It would be far more interesting to pierce her maidenhead if it was ancient Samira living behind that innocent face, rather than an ignorant human girl. He had seen too much of the sleeping minds of human women to be intrigued by them any longer. He and Samira, however, could rule side by side, demons over humans, and indulge in every carnal act ever known to mankind. Samira could be his equal and a challenge. A human girl like Lucia was nothing in comparison. She was only a body and a childish, simple mind.

Lucia's eyes opened.

Theron froze. Was she still asleep enough to see him and shriek? Or was she fully awake, and oblivious?

She was neither. He felt his skin tingle with a sense of eeriness as Lucia's gaze slowly traced up his body, paused at his genitals, and then drifted up and settled on his face, her own expression showing no change from the slackness of sleep, her petal-pink lips slightly parted as she breathed peacefully. Her eyes were an unusual tawny yellow at the center, shading to green and then dark brown around the edges of the irises.

"Why are you in my room?" she asked in a husky, sleep-thick voice.

He flinched, startled by the sound. He'd never been spoken to like this, never had more than a scream from a waking woman. And sleeping women did not ask direct questions! He'd seen women who walked and talked nonsense and sometimes even ate in their sleep, all with their eyes open, though. Maybe she was one such as those, only . . .

"Have you come to steal my soul?" she asked.

"I don't steal souls," he said, feeling a trickle of alarm. She was asking lucid questions and making sense, which was something sleepwalkers didn't quite manage to do.

"Are you going to hurt me?"

"Probably not." There was something strange, something truly unusual about this girl. And to a demon, unusual could mean dangerous.

"Why are you frowning at me?"

"Because you're not supposed to know I'm here. Are you awake?" he asked frankly.

"I don't know. You tell me."

He walked to the foot of her bed, watching as her eyes tracked his movement. Her body didn't stir, though, her hand still fisted and tucked beneath her chin, her chest still rising and falling with the deep regularity of sleep. It was unsettling, and the trickle of alarm turned to a full-on river, even as Theron felt the rising tide of her desire. His presence was magnifying the girl's small passions, far beyond what they should be for a child not yet a woman. But incubi derived no pleasure from such unnatural yearnings.

He should leave this place, for her sake and his own. He began to back away.

"Are you real?" she asked.

The question made him pause in his retreat. "Only as real as your dreams."

"Perhaps *I* am only as real as *your* own dreams. Tell me, demon, why have I visited your dream?"

"Demons do not dream."

"Don't they? How sad for you. Then how do you know what to wish for?"

He shook his head. Sleeping women did *not* converse with dream demons, and certainly did not pose them philosophical questions. Theron was getting a strong sense of the otherworldly about Lucia, and maybe that was what had thrown Vlad into such a frenzy over her, whether he knew it or not.

He grimaced as a thought hit him. *This* would be his wife, once he stole Vlad's body? She'd probably know that he was a demon possessing a human—the human who should have been her husband—and have him exorcised. Mortal women did not like the idea of sex with demons, and marriage to one probably didn't rate too highly on their scale of desirable matches. "Go back to sleep, Lucia, and forget you ever saw me."

She closed her eyes obediently. With a sigh of relief, Theron began to slip away into the Night World. Before he did, though, Lucia's lips curved into a smile.

"Dream of me, demon. For whether you wish it or not, we will meet again."

How did she know that?

"It is you who will not wish it," he said softly, and slipped away into the plane of the Night World.

They would meet again, but when they did, it would either mean he had succeeded in taking Vlad's body or that he had failed utterly and would be coming to her to take his vengeance.

Either way, she would not be happy to see him.

Part Two

Chapter Three

Castle Rosu, the Transylvanian Alps
Six years later

Lucia lay carefully atop the wide stone outer wall of the fortress and peered over the edge into the tangle of trees and underbrush far below. There was a flash of pale flesh, a rustle of leaves, and then the giggling of her maid, Mara.

A low male voice said something in reply, the words impossible to discern from Lucia's perch. She craned her neck, trying to find an angle from which she could see through the greenery to whatever it was the two were doing.

Mara never giggled. Laughed mockingly, yes, but never with this girlish playfulness. Lucia desperately wanted to see exactly what it was that could bring about such a change.

The spring sun was hot on Lucia's back, the pale yellow stones of the wall warm beneath her body, the heat seeping through her burgundy velvet gown. Lucia mentally cursed the bushes for hiding Mara and the guardsman so well; she couldn't stay up here all day, as easy to spot as a beetle on a sheet. Someone would catch her.

She inched farther toward the edge of the wall, her toes and hands clinging as tight as they could to the rough surface. It was a long drop from her aerie to the ledge of ground beneath, and then the nearly vertical slope of the mountainside after that, and the sight of it made her head swim. Her necklace suddenly slipped free of her bodice, the pendant swinging out and then banging back against the stonework. Lucia grasped frantically for it, nearly losing her balance, and then cradled it in her hand, her precarious position forgotten.

There was no damage, was there? Perhaps a small scratch. She frowned and rubbed the gold and amethyst disk against her sleeve, trying to polish out the mark. The disk was decorated with engraved crosses, inset amethyst stars, and archaic lettering weaving between the symbols, spelling out words Lucia could not read. It, and a small portrait of himself, had been betrothal gifts sent to her from Vlad of Wallachia, and in the letter that accompanied the gifts he had asked her to wear the pendant always, to think of him, and to keep herself pure.

Everyone had always told her to keep herself pure, but no one had clearly explained pure from *what*. She knew it was something about her thoughts and her body, though. The nuns at the convent where she had spent her childhood had impressed upon her that the body was a foul, imperfect thing, and a woman's body especially. When Lucia's menses had started, Sister Teresa herself had explained that the blood was a curse from God brought down on womankind for her sins.

Lucia didn't know what her own sins were, but surely she was guilty of a host of them, given the cramps in her lower gut that God gave her as punishment.

Perversely, the more Lucia was told that her body was nasty and unclean, the more curious she had found herself about its secrets. It was frustrating beyond words to inhabit such a fleshy well of sin, and to understand almost nothing of what depths of depravity that sinful flesh might fall into. Despite that curiosity, though, she had done nothing to explore herself on her own. She was repulsed by her own body's smells and dirt, and took care to wash herself frequently.

If she asked elderly, befuddled Sister Teresa what, exactly, it was that she was supposed to keep herself pure from, Teresa often said, "Unclean thoughts." Then Teresa would look sad and disappointed when Lucia's frustration at the non-answer made her ask how much soap it took to keep her thoughts clean, and how she was supposed to get it into her head.

Her maid Mara would laugh—mockingly, of course—if asked about purity, then give Lucia a knowing look and say that blood and pain on her wedding night would teach her all she needed to know about purity as her husband took it from her.

It was a mysterious threat that would have scared Lucia, if she didn't so strongly suspect that Mara herself had not waited until marriage to find out about purity; indeed, Mara seemed intent on giving her purity to half the guardsmen in the barracks. Lucia tucked her pendant back inside her bodice and looked again over the edge of the wall, trying to spot her wayward maid.

The giggling had stopped, but there were low murmurs rising from the bushes. There was a small level area of ground directly below the wall, the mountain slope dropping off precipitously from its edge, pine trees grasping to the mountainside's rocks with clawlike roots. The level, greenery-choked area was probably the only place on the mountaintop where Mara and her soldier—soldier*s*—could meet in secret for their mysterious activities. Neither the soldiers nor any other men were allowed into the castle proper, and the soldiers' barracks had been built just outside the wall.

A few sighs and groans later, Mara emerged from the bushes with a pouty flounce and marched highchinned along the narrow clearing at the base of the wall. She was pretty, with her dark hair and olive skin, and only five years older than Lucia, although there were times when Mara acted as if she were decades Lucia's senior.

The soldier emerged a moment later and caught up to Mara, catching her hand and forcing her to turn around and face him.

Lucia inched back until just her eyes were over the edge of the wall, but she knew from experience that people rarely looked up. The best place for spying was always from above.

"Here now, Mara, don't be like that," the soldier coaxed. His brown, dirty hair was loose around his shoulders and he had a beakish nose.

Mara said his name, "Dimitrie," and then murmured a complaint Lucia could not make out, and then the soldier put his hands on either side of Mara's face and tilted it up. He kissed her, Mara standing stiff for a moment, her hands fisted at her side, and then she relaxed and melted into the soldier, her arms going around his waist, her fingers digging into the cloth over his back then reaching down to squeeze his buttocks. The moans and murmurs started again, as the soldier pressed his hungry kisses down Mara's neck.

An aching loneliness flooded through Lucia. A yearning to herself be in a soldier's arms made her hug the warm wall beneath her, tears of longing starting in her eyes. If there were a man who would kiss her and hold her like that soldier was doing, she wouldn't care how dirty he was, and wouldn't pout or complain as Mara did. She'd hold him and hold him and hold him, and let him kiss her until the end of days, and she would give him her purity and her heart and anything at all he wanted.

Mara and the soldier broke apart, whispered a few words, and then Mara left him with an arch smile and a wave of her fingers.

Lucia climbed down off the wall, sadness darkening her spirits despite the unusually bright and lovely day. She brushed the stone dust from her gown as best she could and then felt her lower lip trembling. Her eyes stung and a tear slipped down her cheek, and a moment later she was crouching down on the walkway, blubbering into her sleeve, a furious, aching, frustrating loneliness twisting her heart like a wet rag.

She couldn't remember the last time anyone had held her. The only touch she ever felt from another human being was the fleeting, nimble fingers of Mara as the maid helped her dress and arranged her hair, and the increasingly rare pat or hug from Sister Teresa. And as for contact with men—Lucia hadn't been allowed within fifty feet of a male since her brother Dragosh had imprisoned her here in this empty castle in the middle of the mountainous wilderness six years ago.

The brother who had once fondly kissed her cheek and hugged her had become a cold and distant figure from whom she heard nothing.

She was twenty years old and she felt as if she were withering away inside, her youth wasted on the empty forests and endless, mist-shrouded mountains of the borderlands, where all who were sane feared to tread.

Her sobs slowly died away for lack of energy, and she hiccoughed herself to calmness, the strange peace that followed a good cry settling gently over her and soothing her nerves. She pulled Vlad's pendant from her bodice and held it up in the sunlight, watching it scintillate and sparkle in the light. It was her beacon of hope; her promise of release from isolation. When the wars were finished, she would be married to Vlad and begin to live. They would marry, and she would have a child. *A child.* A person all her own, to hold and to cherish.

She had met Vlad only once, briefly, and that was a year before their betrothal, when she was still a girl and had had no reason to do more than curtsy to the tall, intimidating stranger. She had been home for a visit from the convent where she had spent most of her time since her own mother had died.

That meeting had been many years ago, and she had not seen Vlad since. Indeed, as soon as she was betrothed to Vlad, her brother Dragosh had packed her up and sent her south through the country to this fortress in the desolate mountains between Transylvania and Wallachia. It was, he said, for her own protection, both from the wars that were coming and from herself. Vlad had sent Mara and several female servants to wait upon her and do her bidding. She sometimes thought they'd been sent to be more her keepers than her servants.

She hadn't understood the banishment by Dragosh, but protests and questions had been pointless, her one mewl of complaint met with a coldness from her brother that she had never known before. Not even their sister Elena, married to Iancu of Transylvania, could persuade Dragosh to allow Lucia either to return to the convent or stay with her, and Dragosh would not explain in what way he thought Lucia such a danger to herself that she needed to be locked away on an inaccessible mountaintop.

Lucia wiped the last traces of tears from her eyes and made her way back along the wall walk and down the stairs to the small garden where an apple tree was showing its white and pink blossoms, bees humming contentedly as they hopped from one flower to the next.

Sister Teresa was drowsing on a bench in front of a stone wall where a climbing grapevine was budding into green. A book of devotions lay open on Teresa's black-skirted lap, and her thin nostrils quivered with a gentle snore.

Lucia plopped down on the grass at her feet and leant back against the bench. Sister Teresa snorted, blinked, and awoke.

"Ah, there you are, my dear. Finished studying that history, have you? I shall examine you on it, you know."

"No, I haven't been reading." She had read the history in question a dozen times over already, and been tested on it twice. What few precious books the castle held, Lucia knew word for word.

Teresa frowned. "Practicing your Latin?"

Lucia shook her head. She suspected that Teresa had already taught her everything she knew and the nun was afraid to admit that she had nothing more to teach.

Or perhaps Teresa did not remember that she asked the same questions again and again.

If they had been at a convent or monastery, there would have been endless books and learning whether Lucia wanted them or not. Instead, all they had were the few books Lucia's sister sometimes sent. If not for those rare deliveries, accompanied as they were by letters and fabrics and edible treats, Lucia thought she would go insane with boredom. As it was, she sometimes thought she teetered on the edge.

Teresa sighed. "Then what have you been doing?"

Lucia smiled and shrugged, knowing that Sister Teresa would not like the answer. "Just thinking. Daydreaming. There is little enough else to do here."

Teresa shook her head. "Child, you worry me. Daydreaming is a vile habit that you must break. Pray, or show industry. But do not put yourself into those trances."

"Else the Devil may come to play," Lucia said lightly. She had heard the same scold a thousand times and more. "At least his would be a new face."

"Hush, child! The Devil will hear you! Pray for forgiveness, and please God, stop your daydreaming." Teresa put her hand on Lucia's shoulder, startling her. It was so rare that Sister Teresa touched her.

Lucia felt a spurt of guilt for distressing the nun, who was always so earnest and honest in her simple concerns. "I know you are frightened for me, but truly, I see no devils in my mind. Nothing comes to harm me."

As far back as Lucia could remember, from her earliest days at the convent school, she had lost herself in her own imaginings as a way to escape the whisper-quiet halls and the droning tedium of interminable lessons. So adept at escaping into her own mind had she become, she could lose herself in dreams with her eyes wide open and recite prayers and answer questions with only a small sliver of her awareness, while the rest of her mind scampered off to play.

"You would not recognize the Devil," Sister Teresa warned. "He would wear a handsome face and promise you your heart's desire."

And where would the evil be in that? Lucia wondered sadly. Her heart had so many unsatisfied desires, she might be willing to make a bargain with the Devil to satisfy them.

But she'd spent too much time daydreaming without ill consequence to have any belief that a devil would ever come and offer to fulfill her wishes. "In my daydreams I gallop a horse over vast plains of green; or meet fairies of wood and stream. No devils." She would not mention the fantasy of a young suitor, like the Dreamer in *The Romance of the Rose,* who fell in love with a perfect rosebud and struggled against all obstacles to possess it. Sometimes she imagined that *she* was such a rose, walled away from all who would pluck her. But the Dreamer won out in the end, possessing his rose, and someday Vlad would come and take her from this fortress, and explore all her petals as the Dreamer explored his rose. Whatever that meant. The book concluded with such confusing imagery, of a staff and a tight passage, and she had never been able to figure out what, exactly, it all meant.

"You frighten me, in your trances," Sister Teresa said, trembling worry in her voice. "You go so very still. It is not natural, to have only your lips and eyes move and nothing else. You are like a statue. If you are idle, you should be thankful for such a luxury of hours and devote them to prayer, instead of to such wickedness."

"Imagining riding a galloping horse surely cannot be wicked!" And it was a lot more fun than prayer. She would hate to hear what Sister Teresa thought if she knew about the cryptic glimpses into the future Lucia sometimes had in her trances—glimpses of events that soon after came true, albeit never in the exact form of the vision. Sister Teresa would condemn her for fortune-telling, a sin if ever there was one.

"Great-grandmother Raveca had visions," Lucia said in defense of her daydreams and of her unspoken secrets. "Everyone respected her, from the stories I hear. She was not thought wicked."

Sister Teresa made a low sound of disapproval in her throat. "Those were different times."

"Dragosh believed in her prophecies. Why else would he have betrothed me to Nicolae of Moldavia?"

Teresa frowned. "Nicolae of Moldavia? I thought you were engaged to Vlad of Wallachia."

"But first I was engaged to Nicolae of Moldavia. You can't have forgotten *that*," Lucia said in concern, looking back over her shoulder at the elderly nun. It seemed Teresa was growing more forgetful by the day. It scared Lucia—Teresa was the only person at Castle Rosu who seemed to genuinely care about her. If Teresa lost her wits, who would she talk to? Who would she go to when she needed comfort? "Dragosh broke the engagement between me and Nicolae, remember?"

"Because of a curse?"

Lucia nodded, willing the nun to remember. But when Teresa did no more than smile vaguely, she knew that the nun could not. Lucia let the issue drop, not wanting to explain it, and not wanting to acknowledge any further the nun's failing wits.

The curse—or prophecy—had been spoken by her

great-grandmother Raveca long before Lucia had been born. Raveca had been queen of Maramures and a northern area of Moldavia called Bucovina, the regions united into one formidable, mountainous country with a proud, independent people. Raveca's children, however, had split their faiths between Catholicism in Maramures and Orthodox Christianity in Bucovina. The rift had widened until what had been one country became two, with war and destruction the result. On her deathbed, Raveca had prophesied:

> "Cats and dogs will snarl and fight, and misery be their sustenance. Not until a whelp and kit bear young will lands again be one, and peace and prosperity come to the children of Raveca."

Raveca's children who had married northern Moldavians bore the Wolf of Dacia as their emblem. It was from them that the "whelp" would come. Those in Maramures, like Lucia's family, bore the emblem of the wildcat: The "kit" would be from their branch. The prophecy seemed to say that the family must reunite through marriage, and then see a birth, before there would again be peace in the northern regions and prosperity in the family.

Lucia had never seen a portrait of Nicolae of Moldavia, but he couldn't be half as handsome as Vlad. She was glad not to be the "wildcat kit" sacrificed to the enemy "wolf whelp" for the sake of the prophecy. A lifelong enemy did not seem a good choice for a husband, whereas a valiant commander from Wallachia was any woman's dream.

"How long, do you think, before Vlad comes for me?" Lucia asked. She didn't expect a true answer; she just liked to talk about Vlad and her future with him.

Teresa closed the book in her lap. "When the wars are finished, he will come."

"Sometimes I think the wars will never end."

"They don't," Teresa said, with clear certainty.

Lucia looked up at her, surprised. "Don't they?"

"One will stop, but another one always takes its place. You will see dozens of them before your life is finished, and you will forget how one was different from another. Maybe they are all the same, in the end."

The words sent a shiver up Lucia's spine. For all Sister Teresa's occasional vagueness, she still came forth with insights that were startling in their clarity.

Teresa smiled down at Lucia, but her eyes were troubled. "You will be the wife of a powerful man, Lucia. I worry that you have no grasp of how important that will make you."

"Important?" Lucia laughed. "I do not think so. I will not be making decisions, any more than I made the decision to come to Castle Rosu."

"Even if you haven't the strength to rule as your great-grandmother did, you will still be the soft voice at your husband's side. If he respects you, you may become the velvet that softens his fist of steel. A ruthless man should not rule without a beloved and gentle woman at his side."

Uneasiness stirred in Lucia's heart. "Why do you say this? Vlad is not ruthless." She could feel Vlad's pendant nestled between her breasts. The small portrait of him showed a handsome man with soft brown eyes; surely not a vicious monster. Rather a serious, courtly man who would treat her tenderly.

"The soldiers tell me that Vlad has been awarded the Order of the Dragon for his defense of Catholicism against heretics."

Lucia felt her cheeks heating with pride. "That's good, isn't it?"

"He's called Vlad Draco now. Vlad the Dragon. Or Vlad the Devil, by the peasants, the soldiers say. The peasants don't know the difference between a devil and a dragon, and the word can be the same."

Lucia's smile faltered. "Vlad the Devil?" That did not sound like the moniker of a gentle and just ruler.

But Sister Teresa smiled and shrugged, as if she had said nothing about which to be concerned. "Just ignorant peasants, no doubt. They tell tales, only half of which have any truth."

"Tales? What tales?" Over the past six years she had heard scant news of her betrothed or the battles being fought between Wallachia, Moldavia, and Maramures— or of the incursions that were the usual threat from the Turks to the south. She had been kept in blissful, bored ignorance of the outside world.

Teresa shook her head, going vague again. "I don't remember. Just tales." She patted Lucia on the shoulder. "I worry about you. You will be the wife of a powerful man, and I pray that you will do more than daydream at his side."

"I will do my best to be a good wife to Vlad," Lucia said, though she didn't know what that meant. She didn't know what the wives of rulers did. How much more prepared she would have been if she had spent these past years with her sister Elena instead of locked up here. She still could not understand why Dragosh had done this to her.

She crossed her arms over the top of her knees and rested her chin on them, looking at the flowering apple tree on the other side of the garden, but Lucia's eyes focused on an inner landscape where Vlad—appearing as perfectly handsome and gentle as in his portrait—took her hand and led her to a bench where they sat. And did what? she wondered. Kiss, yes. And? Likely they would lie down together, fully clothed. And then what? How would he explore her petals?

"I am past ready to be wed, I think. I should like to know what it is to be a wife. How soon after we wed will I bear a child?"

Teresa made a noise of distress in her throat. "Only God can answer that. Perhaps you should pray on it."

"How does the child come from my body? And how big is it?" She remembered seeing a baby when she was younger but could not trust her memory of its size, and she did not know how old it had been. "Surely a baby can be no bigger than an onion when it is born, else I don't know how it would find a way from my body without killing me. Where does it come out of me? And I will not hatch it like a chicken hatching an egg, will I?"

Sister Teresa coughed. "God will answer your questions when the time is right."

Lucia grimaced. God had proven reluctant to answer any of her questions in the past, apparently content to wait until she was wed. Certainly he had never replied to that most private of questions, of how it was that a man and woman made a child together. She couldn't figure out the workings of it, and knew already that Teresa would never tell her. Perhaps Teresa didn't know herself.

Purity played a part in it, of that she was sure. Rotten purity. She'd like to stuff it and have a taste of that giggling and sighing instead, as Mara and the soldier had done. She'd never even seen a man naked, to know how or if he was different from a woman, except for being bigger and dirtier and louder.

She'd seen a naked man that once, she reminded herself. But that hardly counted, and it had been nothing more than a dream, hadn't it? And it wasn't really a man.

She'd been fourteen, asleep in her brother's fortress, when a sound like a closing door had half-woken her. A sense that she was not alone had caused her to open her eyes.

The being who filled her dream-fogged gaze had been like nothing she'd ever imagined before. Tall and broad-shouldered, it had been a bit like a man but even more like the way she might imagine a demon, with huge shadowy wings looming behind him. He had black wavy hair that brushed the base of his neck and a silky dusting of hair over his chest in a T-shape, a narrow trail of it painting his muscled, flat belly and down to the rich darkness at his loins. And there, atop that bed of blackness, had lain something that frightened her.

She hadn't understood what that hideous appendage had been—and she could no longer clearly remember what it had looked like—but some base, instinctual part of her had reacted to it, despite its monstrousness. A warm melting had started in her loins, a tingle spreading through her body and making her yearn to feel the demon's hand on her breasts, on her thighs, and, most strangely of all, on the secret, dirty, nasty place where she was too shy to touch herself except when washing. She didn't know why she wished to be touched *there* most of all as she gazed upon the being's beastly loins.

The being was a demon, surely, else she wouldn't have such wicked thoughts, such unspeakable desires coursing through her. Evil, wicked demon.

But so familiar was she with the weird imagery of her fantasies, and so close was she to the edge of true sleep, she had been concerned in only a distant, abstract way about whether the demon might harm her. Instead, she had wished that he might try to do something thrilling and dangerous to her with that frightening appendage.

She'd talked to him, she remembered that, although she couldn't recall much of what either he or she had said. Perhaps she'd dreamt the conversation. She often could not be sure after the fact what was real and what had been vividly imagined. So perhaps she had only dreamt as well the flash of intuition that told her that it would not be the last time she saw the creature. She'd been certain that he would visit her again, and that he would play a predestined role in her life.

In all the years since, though, she hadn't had so much as a glimpse of him. She should have been relieved; he probably *was* a demon, after all. Devout women did not welcome nocturnal visits to their bedrooms by damned beings. That was what logic and reason told her.

Yet her instincts told her that the "demon" had been something from beyond the ideas of Heaven and Hell as she knew them, something outside the realm of her God and her faith. He was something *other*, with no place in her Catholic paradigm.

Even if he were a true demon, though, part of her wanted to see him again, and to again feel those dark, depraved desires flow through her body. A wicked, naughty part of her had been looking forward to such a visit for half a decade.

Sister Teresa was right: Lucia should devote more time to prayer. Surely she was too eager by half to merrily traipse her way down the path to Hell.

Chapter Four

Southern Moldavia

Theron flew through the chiaroscuro landscape of the Night World, its hues reduced to blacks and grays, punctuated by pastel bursts of color where sleeping humans dreamt vivid scenes. The landscape was formed by those sleeping minds, and it reflected their Waking World as a rippled pool reflected the sky above: the image changing with each breath of wind, distorting, fading, and returning again in a brilliant flash of clarity. In this Night World version of Earth, it was the creatures of Night who had physical substance, while the scene around them had all the reality of a dream.

As unreal as the landscape was, it was nonetheless rich in information about what was happening in the Waking World of men. Theron watched below him for signs that would lead him to Vlad. It was only the space of a sigh before he found them.

Vivid streaks of red ran through the gray shadows of a valley, the red pooling and coursing through a village where a horde of mounted soldiers raided and raped; and where the villagers resisted, the soldiers burned and killed. The violence repeated itself again and again as Theron watched, the dreaming minds of the surviving villagers struggling to release the horror of the past.

A brilliant pennant rose above the violence: a red banner with the black silhouette of a writhing dragon upon it. Vlad Draco had been here.

Dream soldiers departed to the north, and Theron followed them until they disappeared. He crossed over muddied fields of battle, strewn with the corpses of Moldavian and Wallachian soldiers alike; over towns shut tight and hunkered down in fear; and at last to the fortified city of Galatsi. Here, the dreams of the inhabitants were fractured and frantic, the Night World version of the town filled with explosions of fearful color. No one was resting easy here tonight.

The dragon pennant and a black-armored warrior with a red feather crest began to appear more frequently on the narrow streets below as Theron moved toward the center of town. The dark figure seemed everywhere at once: and he was, for Vlad had invaded the minds of the residents of Galatsi as surely as he had invaded their city and their country.

Theron perched on a tiled rooftop and stretched out his senses, carefully picking his way through the sexual emotions of the dreaming women of the town. Their inner desires rose like a hundred hushed voices from the dark houses; whispering of love and hate, of fear and loathing, of longing and resentment. Whatever the emotion they murmured to him, at its base was a sexual desire unfulfilled.

One voice cried more strongly to him than all the others: someone wounded and lost, and frightened to her core. It was the whisper of an innocent who had been taken against her wishes. He'd heard it a hundred thousand times before over the centuries, and he suspected that this cry of despair was his path to Vlad.

He followed the trail of emotion through the town and to a large corner house, its stone walls covered with stucco, the windows to its four stories shut tight against the night. He slipped out of the plane of the Night World and into that of men, where now everything was solid and real, and he was the one with no substance. He clung to the wall outside the one window where there yet burned the soft glow of a candle and peered inside.

Vlad lay asleep on the bed within, spooning a young blond woman from behind, his arm and leg trapping her securely within his sleeping grasp. The girl—no more than fifteen years old, perhaps younger—had the swollen, reddened eyelids of one who had cried herself to sleep. Her mouth looked bruised and swollen from unaccustomed kisses, her shoulders hunched as if such a small shift could break her free from Vlad's touch.

Theron passed silently through the leaded glass of the window, the solid matter sending an ache through his form but not otherwise harming him. With a beat of his wings he flew across the room and perched atop one of the posts at the foot of the bed: an angel on the head of a pin. He stared down at the sleeping couple with less than heavenly thoughts.

Vlad looked as determined and hungry in his sleep as he did when awake. He was leaner than the last time Theron had seen him, a year past, but looked the stronger for it. The man throve on war.

Theron also suspected that Vlad throve on deception. Vlad's eventual victory had been clear a year ago, but the man had insisted he was not yet secure, Moldavia not yet firmly under his heel, and Theron would have to wait for his reward.

He had waited long enough. Too long. Patience might have undone him, for he had discovered earlier in the night that Samira had been turned into a human by Nyx, sentenced to serve as a slave to a crippled prince who dabbled inexpertly in magic: none other than Nicolae of Moldavia, the man who had been promised to Lucia.

While no one in the Night World knew what Samira had done to deserve such a horrible punishment as being turned into a human slave, Theron knew that the dream Samira had sent to Dragosh must be at the root of it. If she had kept her mouth shut about why she'd sent the dream to Dragosh, then Theron might be safe. But if she had told Nyx that Theron had put her up to it . . . Nyx would be coming for him next.

He had the sickening sense that a chain of events had been set into motion and was cascading out of control, and he would have to run a frantic race to catch up and take his place if he ever wanted to rule as a king on earth. Perhaps it was too late already.

Theron leapt down from the post onto the bed, landing weightlessly, his bare feet making no indentation on the mattress. He was about to try something he never had before, and never would have now if desperation had not pushed him to the edge.

It had been a year since Vlad had created a summoning circle. Without one, Theron had no way to speak directly to the man. And without Samira, he couldn't even enter Vlad's dreams by proxy. If there had been a freshly dead body lying about, he might have been able to possess it and say a few words to Vlad: Theron had heard of young, mischievous demons reanimating the dead and stumbling around graveyards to frighten people. It was the type of lark that would get a demon's wings broken in punishment. Since there was no corpse handy, though, there was only one option left to Theron.

He turned his gaze to the sleeping girl so tightly ensnared in Vlad's grip. Good gods of the night, he hoped he was up for this. He squatted down in front of her and lay his hand on her forehead.

He was instantly in her mind, in the center of a maelstrom of emotion. All around him were brilliant flashes of recent events, overwhelming the girl even as she slept. Vlad was foremost in her thoughts: larger than life, stronger than any human man could be, and handling her with a false tenderness that scarcely concealed the brutal hunger beneath it. The few flashes Theron saw of the girl's family were tied to a deep sense of shame: She yearned to be in their sheltering midst, even as she feared they would never accept her back after what had been done to her. He found her hiding in a dark corner of her mind, shrunken into a fetal position, her arms wrapped over her head. She was keening softly with a sound beyond hope.

Theron shook his head. What a sun-blasted mess Vlad had made of the girl. He could feel the echoes of the girl's emotions, and they made him feel ill. As he explored her mind, it felt as if Vlad's attack had been on *him*. He wanted to make her feel better for his own sake. It was as if her needs were itches he had to scratch.

Theron knew from the thousands of other such attacked women he'd seen that the girl would have a hard time enjoying sex for years to come. Incubi would be paying her regular visits, trying to mend through dreams some of what had been destroyed in the space of a single waking hour. They existed to ensure proper psychic sexual functioning, and they viewed such crimes as Vlad had committed the same way an artist might view someone smearing black paint all over one of his paintings.

Worse, this had been the first time a man had touched the girl. Vlad had used her to feed his endless appetite for virgin flesh. Doubtless, now that the girl had been used, he would toss her aside like a chicken bone for the dogs to fight over. Theron wondered if Vlad had the same thing in mind for Lucia.

The thought disturbed him, more than it should have. He'd only seen Lucia the once; he had no connection to the girl as of yet, and no heart to care what became of her. She was a freakish thing outside of nature, anyway, what with the way she had lain so still and spoken to him so clearly.

Unbidden, the thought popped into his mind, *Freakish or no, she will be my wife.* With the thought came a rush of possessiveness, surprising him with its ferocity. She would be *his*. It didn't matter who she was, freak or no, hag or no—she was destined to belong to *him*, and that made her worthy of an ounce of care.

Although he'd never thought about it before, perhaps that was the reason she had stayed in his mind these past few years, creeping into his thoughts when he least expected it. She would be *his*, and no one else's. He'd never had someone of his own before, nor even the promise of such, and so Lucia had formed a pocket of fascination in his mind, tempting him even to check on her growth toward womanhood. He never had, though, and realized now that he wanted to be surprised by the adult Lucia, seeing her afresh.

He shook his head, appalled at himself. When had he grown so soft and prone to romantic fancies? Lucia didn't matter. He would still be better off getting Samira to possess Lucia's body.

He turned his attention back to the present, and to the girl sleeping so uneasily in Vlad's arms. In the girl's mind Theron found a memory of her beloved grandmother, and used the old woman's image to approach her. "Dearest, it's Nana." The old woman touched the girl on her shaking shoulder.

"Nana?" A tearstained face appeared from beneath the blonde's arms.

Theron felt the girl's yearning for comfort and acceptance and safety and gave her what she wanted. "Dearest, I know what has happened. Come, let me hold you." The old woman opened her arms.

Her granddaughter fell into them, tucking her face against the soft bosom, arms squeezing tight.

"It will be all right," Nana said, stroking the girl's hair.

"Make it all go away," the girl whispered. "Let me die."

"Shh, shh . . . You are too precious to die. But for a short time, if you want, we can let someone else be in your body. You don't have to be here, with that awful man. Would you like that?"

The girl nodded fiercely.

"All you have to say is, 'Theron, come in.' Can you say it? Say it, and you can sit safe with me, and you won't feel that wicked man's arm and leg on you. You won't feel him touching you."

"Theron, come in," the girl whispered.

The false Nana led the girl into a quiet corner of her

mind, secluded and safe, and rocked her in her arms. For a moment, an empty space was left amid the emotional chaos in the girl's mind. It was a space waiting for Theron to jump in. He hesitated, not at all certain that this was going to work.

This was the first time he had attempted what he was about to do. It was forbidden to take possession of a human body; but even more, he hadn't ever wanted to possess the body of a woman. For all that he was a demon, he was yet a *male* demon, with no wish to be female. It was bad enough that the only sexual desire he could feel was that of women while they slept. He didn't want to *be* one, too.

He gritted his teeth. There was nothing to do but try it.

Theron poured himself into the empty space in the girl's mind. His open-eyed vision of the room where Vlad and the girl slept blurred and streaked and twisted, and he felt himself falling into the face of the girl.

An instant later all he saw was blackness. His body felt grotesquely heavy, and as if it were tied down by great bands. His crotch was throbbing with pain, including *inside* his body, and his muscles all over his body were strained and aching. Then something took a warm, snorting breath beside his ear, the sound loud as a cymbal.

His eyes flew open. He was staring sideways at the darkened bedroom, a pillow squishing up around the side of his face. The warmth pressed against his back shifted, one of the bands over his body tightening, and a deep, horrified shudder went through him. *He was in Vlad's arms.* Vlad squeezed his breast. Theron whimpered.

Vlad shifted again and began to roll onto his back, and as he did so Theron felt something thick being pulled out of his new body, his flesh burning and stinging as the thing was dragged out. A gag started in the back of Theron's throat as he realized what it was: *Vlad's penis.* Good Goddess of the Night, he had a *penis* in him. It plopped free as Vlad rolled away from him, and Theron gurgled in revulsion.

How did women stand it? How?

He leaned over the edge of the bed and coughed, trying to rid himself of the nausea. His experiences of feeling the passion and release of a woman as she dreamt was *nothing, nothing* like being in a real woman's body. Stars and moon of heaven, it was no wonder the incubi were kept so busy. This was horrible.

"Come back over here," Vlad said, his voice thick. He pulled on Theron's hip, rolling him back from the edge of the bed. "I've got something big for you to choke on." He started pushing Theron down toward his groin.

Theron tried to resist the pressure of Vlad's hands, but the girl's body was too weak and exhausted. To his horror, he felt himself being shoved downward, the hair on Vlad's legs scraping against his skin and a musky scent rising up to meet his nose. Vlad's knee carelessly jarred Theron's breast, the knobby bone digging into his new soft flesh.

And then he felt *it* bump up against the underside of his jaw, and felt the damp, saggy warmth of Vlad's testicles against his collarbone.

"Open up, darling," Vlad said. "You'll like your first taste of a man."

Theron raised his gaze. Vlad had pillows crammed behind his neck, propping him up so he could watch as he made the girl fellate him. The man's large dark eyes shone with anticipatory pleasure.

Theron parted his lips.

Vlad smiled indulgently. "You're not crying anymore. You're a bad girl, aren't you? I knew you had a bit of the devil in you." He tilted his hips, nudging Theron under the chin with the head of his penis. "Go ahead."

Theron curled his lips back from his teeth, then chopped them lightly together a few times, getting the feel of the workings. The first faint line of puzzlement appeared between Vlad's brows.

"You're right," Theron said, and was shocked to hear his own deep voice come out of the girl's mouth, "I do have the Devil in me, and he has strong teeth." He grinned as he saw Vlad's eyes widen in surprise. "You shouldn't let them so near tender meat."

Theron lifted his head, opened his mouth wide, then dove for Vlad's testicles. His teeth caught the edge of one ball, nipping it hard before it slid away to the side. Vlad's scream shook the windows, and his hands gripped Theron's hair, weakly trying to jerk him away. But each pull only meant a pull on Vlad's sac, still caught in Theron's teeth.

Vlad clouted Theron on the side of the head and he let go, rolling off the bed before Vlad could clout him again. Besides, he didn't want to do *too* much damage to the body that should soon be his.

"It's so nice to see you again, Vlad," Theron said, standing up. "Do you recognize my voice?"

Vlad was beside the bed, hunched over with a look of agony on his face. He cupped his wounded crotch with one hand while fumbling for his sword with the other, all the while keeping his wide and frightened eyes on his bedmate.

"It's your old friend, Theron," he went on.

Vlad's eyes bugged even more. Theron wondered if that much bugging was doing an injury to the man's eye sockets.

There was a pounding on the door and loud voices without, drawn by Vlad's scream. "My lord! Are you all right? My lord!"

"Go away!" Vlad shrieked, sounding slightly less than a man. " 'Twas the wench's cry you heard. Begone!"

There was hesitation and the sound of milling feet, and then, "Yes, my lord." The footsteps moved away.

Theron held his new breasts in his hands and jiggled them up and down. "Huh. They're heavy." He felt something in his mouth, caught between two teeth. He ran his tongue over it, then dug around with his fingers and pulled it out and examined it. His stomach roiled as he saw that it was one of Vlad's pubic hairs. He spit on the floor, trying to clear any last traces from his mouth. "Ugh! You should do a better job of washing down there, Vlad. It's unspeakably rude to shove a girl's face into a mess like that and expect her to enjoy it. Besides, I want things clean when I take over."

"What are you doing here?" Vlad asked, his voice as cold and hard as a frozen river, cracking with strain.

"I should think you would already know the answer to that." Theron felt something warm seeping onto his thighs. Alarmed, he parted them slightly and reached between them. His fingers touched damp stickiness, and he pulled them out and looked at them. There was a shiny, viscous fluid on them, streaked with red. "Aw, Dawn take you, Vlad—bad enough you hurt the girl; did you have to leave your seed in her, too?" Theron wiped his fingers on the bedcovers, disgusted that Vlad's seed was in him at this moment. He could feel more of it oozing down his thighs. He snatched a garment off the floor and started scrubbing at his thighs.

"That's my shirt," Vlad said stiffly.

"What's going on it is yours, too. Or is it mine, since your body is mine? Because it's time to pay up, Vlad Draco." Theron stood up straight and threw the stained shirt on the bed. "Your position is as secure as it will ever be. Moldavia is all but defeated."

"All but. That's the key point, though, isn't it?" Vlad used his sword to pick up the soiled shirt and toss it into a corner. With studied, hunched nonchalance, he picked up his tunic and began to put it on.

Theron suspected Vlad wasn't comfortable with his own nakedness. He glanced at Vlad's flaccid manhood and raised a scornful brow. "I'm surprised you could do much damage with that."

"You bit its boys! Of course it's not looking its best," Vlad grumbled, pulling his tunic on and covering himself.

"I hope that's all it is. I'd like to use something of a better size during my three days in your body." He wondered if there were any size-increasing exercises mortal men could do to improve things. He hadn't thought in detail before about what it would mean, trading in his own Night World body for Vlad's. A medium-sized penis might not be the only flaw. What if he had bad breath, or worms? Or what if . . . "It's not diseased, is it?" he asked in sudden worry.

"No," Vlad said coldly.

Thank the goddess for that! "When are you going to fulfill your end of the bargain? We could do it right now."

"I am having a hard time discussing anything with

you while you're in that girl's body. Is she still in there with you?" As Vlad spoke, his eyes flicked to a second door in the room.

"She's fine." Theron, too, looked at the door. Who was in the adjoining room? Whatever help Vlad seemed to be expecting, it wasn't materializing. "She's probably the better for it, considering what she's been through."

"Don't pretend superiority to me, demon. You'd do the same to girls if you had the chance. There are few pleasures that compare to sinking yourself into a tight, fresh virgin's passage, knowing no one has been there before."

Theron snorted. Vlad seemed unaware that the prowess was in bringing a woman more pleasure than she'd ever imagined possible—and in making her beg you for more. Stuffing yourself into any helpless girl was not the mark of a confident, virile man. It was more the mark of one too weak to admit he had no skills as a lover.

"Let me draw a summoning circle," Vlad said, his gaze flicking again to the connecting door, his mouth twitching with impatient annoyance. He went to a table covered in maps and writing implements, bending over it with his buttocks hanging out from under his tunic, his balls loose and dark beneath. His buttocks were covered with hair. Theron sighed at the thought of that monkeylike rump becoming his own. At least Vlad had a handsome face.

Vlad dug around the items on the table until he came up with a piece of chalk. "We really can't discuss this with you in that girl's body. Wouldn't you rather have the circle? I can do it right here." He squatted down and began to draw.

Something Vlad had said about the girl rang a belated warning in Theron's mind. "*If* I had the chance to do the same to a girl?"

Vlad looked up from his crouch with a smarmy smile. "I'm sure you will, when I fulfill my bargain." He waddled like a short-legged troll toward Theron, his piece of chalk sketching out a circle, his penis almost dragging on the ground.

Theron stepped nimbly aside, breasts jiggling, not trusting what Vlad was up to. A summoning circle was a way for them to speak to each other without this business of possessing a body, but if he answered, it also trapped Theron in the circle until released by the summoner. "Let us fulfill the bargain now. All you need do is invite me into your body."

"The battles are not yet finished; all could still fall apart." Vlad paused in his drawing and scratched his balls.

Theron scowled. Did the human have vermin? "You're stalling."

Vlad tried getting close to Theron again with his piece of chalk, and again Theron stepped away. Vlad's nostrils flared with annoyance, and then he tossed the chalk aside and stood, his expression dark.

"Lucia's brother Dragosh is gathering his forces and preparing to come through Tihutsa Pass in the north. He'll sweep his way to the capital of Suceava, and then together we'll crush between us all that remains of resistance in Moldavia. If Dragosh does not succeed, though . . ." Vlad shrugged. "So you see, all is not yet settled."

"Yet you have nothing to do now but wait for Dragosh. It will take him more than three days to fight his way to Suceava."

· "Our enemy, Bogdan, thinks Dragosh is in the south with me. He's not expecting an army to come through the mountains. It should be a swift and easy victory."

"Still, you have at least three days. I have been waiting for six years, accepting each of your delays. The time for delays is over."

"You can surely wait a few more weeks. What are a few weeks to an immortal demon? Amuse yourself in that girl's body for a while if you are so eager to be human."

"The bargain was to have *your* body. You are putting me off, Vlad," Theron said with far more calm than he felt. The lying bastard! He had no intention of letting Theron possess his body. He could see it in the shifting of Vlad's eyes. "I begin to wonder if you have any intention at all of fulfilling your end of our agreement. I shouldn't like to have to act on my threat against Lucia."

A sly smile curved Vlad's sensuous lips and was covered by his hand to his mouth, rubbing its sides as if he'd just recalled he had bits of food stuck to them. "No, I wouldn't want you to do that."

"I shouldn't like to have to possess her, as I have this girl," Theron said. "You don't want your Lucia to lift her skirts to every man she sees, do you? I can spread her legs for any and all, until she's as used and diseased as a whore in the streets." Theron bent over and waggled the girl's bare buttocks at Vlad, then gave him a coy, come-hither look over his shoulder.

"You won't do that," Vlad said, with more calm assurance than was warranted.

"I will. Your time is up."

Vlad's eyes shifted, touching once again with a swift flash of fury on the closed connecting door. "Give me until tomorrow night. I must set my affairs in order. I must make it clear to my generals that I'm taking a rest and am not to be asked to make decisions. You do understand that I cannot let you command my armies or change my plans."

Theron crossed his arms under his breasts. What Vlad said made sense, but he didn't believe a word of it. Vlad was hoping for time to find a way out of the deal. He also seemed far more sanguine about the possible threat to Lucia than he should be. There was more going on here than Theron was aware of, and he wanted to know what it was. Asking Vlad would be no way to find answers, though. Better, perhaps, that he take the extra time Vlad asked for and find out what made him so confident.

"Tomorrow night, then," Theron agreed. "*If . . .*"

Vlad's smile of satisfaction froze like a child's caught stealing. "If?"

"This girl," Theron said, gesturing to himself. "Pay her well and send her home without further harm. You've ruined her chances for a good marriage. Give her a dowry to make up for the loss of her virginity."

Vlad shrugged. "So be it."

Theron guessed Vlad was too pleased at the reprieve he'd won to argue over a few gold coins. Theron debated for a moment whether he shouldn't leave the girl's body and stay to spy on Vlad and whomever was behind that door.

But no; he should stay in possession of the girl until she was home again, to make sure no further harm came to her. He would do what little he could to dull the memories of this night in her mind, planting dreams of the pleasure that could be had with an attentive mate. It wouldn't make this night go away, but at least the seeds of hope would be there for something different. It was the least he could do, in thanks for letting him use her body to talk to Vlad.

He'd also leave in her mind a memory, most vivid of all, of Vlad's scream of agony as her teeth sank into his balls.

The person behind the door could wait until tomorrow night. There was plenty of time for spying, and there was someone else he needed to see even more. Indeed, he'd been waiting six years to do so.

Chapter Five

In a very bad mood, Theron slipped out of the plane of the Night World and alit on the balcony outside what he hoped was Lucia's bedchamber. He had traveled a great distance through the mountains looking for this place, and hoped to the cursed sun that he had not made a wrong turn after that last fortress full of drunkards.

The whitewashed walls of the castle glowed softly in the night, a pearl set atop a blanket of mists. Heavy fogs filled the valleys between the mountaintops, making Castle Rosu look as if it existed in a world of its own, with only the night sky above and a few mountaintop islands in the distance. It was a beautiful setting, well-suited to the tastes of those of the Night World, but all Theron could see was the time he had wasted trying to find this place.

It had taken him every moonlit hour after leaving Vlad and the girl last night until now to track down where Lucia had been stashed. The beings of the Night

World had to move across the earth with the darkness of night and could not be present in a land where the sun was shining. It had meant ten hours in other countries and foreign lands, where he could do nothing to discover what Vlad was up to.

Instead, he'd listened to succubi and incubi gossiping about Samira and her mortal state. They liked spying on her in the night, watching as she tried to seduce that crippled prince whom she was sentenced to serve for the length of a month. Apparently the prince was putting up with none of her mischief.

The news had only deepened Theron's anger with Vlad and his delays. Becoming mortal had been *Theron's* plan. How had Samira ended up being the one to experiment with it first? And from the rumors, she was getting attached to that wizard with whom she lived. If Theron didn't hurry up and get his own body, Samira might not ever want to leave her prince and come live in Lucia's body as the queen at his side.

Even as he thought it, part of him doubted that was still what he wanted. He pushed the thought away. He'd formed a plan and he was going to stick to it. Vlad was *not* going to get the best of him!

Theron could already feel the call of Vlad's summoning circle, more than two hundred miles away. Vlad was waiting for him. He was glad the lying bastard didn't know the truth: that while Theron was unable to escape a circle whenever he wished, he *did* have control over whether or not he stepped into one. Yes, there was a pull to answer the summons—especially now that Vlad knew and used Theron's name—but it could be resisted.

Theron had no intention of speaking with Vlad until he'd seen Lucia. Vlad hadn't been half as worried about his fiancée's welfare as he should have been, and Theron intended to find out why.

The leaded glass windows of Lucia's chamber were open to the night air, their glass reflecting shards of moonlight. Theron climbed easily through one of the open panes and into the large room.

The walls inside had been whitewashed, and were broken up by oak beams and a few faded tapestries. Bear and sheepskin rugs were scattered over the plank floor, as well as several small chairs, a table, a mandolin, and a basket of sewing. A maid slept on a narrow pallet on the floor, her dreaming mind giving off a quiet burbling stream of sexual satisfaction. She, at least, was not a chaste woman.

He moved across the room toward the large, carved oaken bed, a sense of anticipation coming to life within him, pushing away his anger with Vlad for the moment. *Was* it her? Lucia? He reached out with his senses for some trace of the person he could see sleeping within but picked up nothing.

Nothing? How could that be?

The anticipation turned to fear as the irrational idea struck him: *Maybe she was dead. Maybe Vlad didn't fear for her because he knew she was beyond touching. Maybe he'd had his way with her already.*

But as he reached the foot of the bed Theron suddenly felt a surge of the desires churning around the sleeper; a chaotic, roaring waterfall that hovered over the slender woman. It was a cascade of unfulfilled desire such as he had never encountered before, and it left him stunned: Not only was it strong enough to almost knock him senseless as he came near but it was contained within a billowing, confused mass flowing around her. It had no direction to it, and even worse, it seemed unable to escape. It stormed around the young woman like a compact hurricane of passion. What in Nyx's name was going on?

That compactness must have kept any incubi from coming here to relieve Lucia; they would have had to be standing as close as Theron was now to even know that she yearned. There was no outward flowing stream of emotion—as with the maid, as with any other woman Theron had ever visited.

Theron leapt onto the bed, walking up the mattress to the woman's head and then squatting down, looking at her in anxious puzzlement.

It *was* Lucia. She had grown into the beauty that had been promised in the fine, soft features of her youth. Her tawny hair was still loose as she slept, tangled wildly about her head, but her cheeks were now free of their childish fullness, her features finely sculpted as if all that was extraneous had melted away.

The furs on her bed were pushed down low, only a sheet covering her to her waist. The drawstring at the neck of her loose chemise had come undone, the neckline opening and sliding down until one full, pink-tipped breast was exposed to the night. Her own hand lay across it, fingertips touching the aureole as if to give it a trace of the attention for which it longed.

Theron gazed upon her, her beauty only interesting to him in an abstract way, the curiosity that had quietly plagued him these past years only partially satisfied by seeing her physically fully grown. Oddly, he found that what he really wanted to know was whether she was still strange and uncanny, with a touch of the otherworldly. Or was she average now, grown into a dull and ordinary woman? He surprised himself by hoping for the former.

Theron remembered again the eerie way in which she had spoken to him while still partially asleep six years ago. Surely a girl such as that must have grown into someone unusual, someone who would not bore him by being like every other female he'd ever visited. And perhaps her own unusual personality was the reason her sexual desires did not flow normally.

On the other hand, Vlad might have cast some manner of spell over her, to better protect her innocence from both incubi and her own lustful intentions.

He intended to find out. He would not go to Vlad's summoning circle with only half the information he needed. He reached out his hand toward Lucia's brow.

His hand stopped against his will, inches from her, and would go no farther. He scowled and reached for her again.

Once more, some invisible force stopped him. Nothing in the quiet of the night changed. Theron felt no disturbances, no change in the flow of Lucia's unsatisfied longings, no alteration in the breathing of the maid on the pallet. Something, though, was preventing him from touching her.

Sun-scorched mother of a sunrise, he swore to himself. What in Night's name was going on?

He looked around the room, around the bed, and on the floor. He could see no circle, no symbols, nothing that should be stopping him. He climbed off the bed and looked beneath it, searching for some manner of design or object placed there to ward him off. Nothing.

He leapt up onto the headboard of the bed and crouched there, wings in a tight, frustrated furl, and stared down at Lucia. She shifted in her sleep, her hand falling free of her breast.

A pendant on a gold chain lay revealed on her chest.

It glowed faintly to his eyes, and he knew instinctively that it was more than a mere piece of jewelry. Unease tingled up his spine.

He jumped back down onto the bed and crouched beside Lucia, staring at the pendant.

The symbols that covered its surface were indecipherable to him, and he did not know what meaning the amethysts and their placement had, but now that he saw the thing he knew that *this* was the source of his inability to touch Lucia.

Damn Vlad Draco. He must have given the amulet to Lucia to protect her when Theron came to exact his revenge. Vlad must have intended all along to renege on the deal. *The sun-blasted lying son of a whore* . . .

Had Vlad known, too, that the amulet would keep Lucia's desires pent up inside her like lightning in a thundercloud?

Maybe that was what Vlad was hoping for. When he finally came to claim Lucia, she would be ravenous for sexual attention. She would still be innocent, still be completely ignorant of what to expect, but she'd be voracious in her consumption of Vlad's touch.

The double-crossing bastard wasn't going to get what he wanted. Theron would see to that. All his anger at Vlad came flooding back, Theron's gentler curiosity about Lucia forgotten as she became once again a means to an end.

He cast his eyes to the maid sleeping on the floor. He himself might not be able to touch the amulet and remove it, but the maid could.

He bounded off the bed and in two great leaps was on the maid. He crouched atop her chest, his weight as nothing to her, and with a touch to her forehead he was inside her mind.

It was filled with fornicating soldiers. The girl knew how to keep her appetites sated; he would give her that.

He found her name: Mara. And he found, too, her feelings for Lucia: envy, disdain, pity, fondness, and pockets of uneasy fear—those pockets tied to images of Lucia sitting motionless, her eyes glazed, her lips moving in answer to questions while clearly she was not mentally present.

So, Lucia had not grown out of her otherworldliness, not that it would do her any good. It wasn't going to stop Theron from what he was about to do.

He took Mara's envy and disdain, and the images and passions of her most recent lover, and began to weave together a dream.

Humans dreamt on their own, but it took a dream demon to give a fantasy of such power that it could be remembered in vivid detail upon waking, or even alter one's emotions and behavior. Normal human dreams were scattered, illogical things, bland in color. A dream given by one of the Oneroi was a powerful force that could soothe fears or arouse them, bring a sexual climax or tears, and in some cases alter destinies.

Because he was a sex-dream demon, the story he wove for Mara would be sexual in nature—though she needed it less than most women he visited. In the dream he wove for her, her soldier lover, Dimitrie, was naked beside her on one of the bearskins on the floor. Dimitrie traced his fingertips down her belly, then brushed them lightly over the lips of her sex. Mara whimpered eagerly and parted her legs.

Dimitrie dragged his fingertips back up her body and played them around one of Mara's large, dark nipples. "Not yet, my sweet."

"Shh," Mara whispered, casting her eyes over at Lucia's

bed. "Don't wake her. It is as much as my life is worth if you are caught here."

"She won't wake. I drugged her."

"Why?! You fool, if you have given her too much and she dies—"

Dimitrie licked Mara's cheek, silencing her. "Listen: She is sleeping soundly."

Theron created a sound of soft snoring, coming from the dream Lucia.

Mara relaxed. "Why did you drug her? We should have met outside the wall. If anyone were to know you were here, and Vlad heard—"

"No one will know," Dimitrie soothed, and Theron struggled to subdue the burst of non-erotic fear that had blossomed inside Mara at the thought of Vlad. He dug through her mind and deep in her memories found an image of Vlad threatening her with being flayed and disemboweled alive should she ever allow Lucia to have contact with a man or even explain the workings of sex to his betrothed.

It was an easy task to ease the fear and enmesh Mara once more in the dream.

"Lucia is drugged and will not wake until morning. You could shout into her ear and she would not know. I could have you on her bed and thrust until the bed shook and she would not stir."

A wicked thrill ran through Mara, and she shivered. Her lips curved into a delighted smile. "You could come onto her face and the twit would not know it. She'd wake in the morning and have no idea what was dried on her cheek and stiff in her hair. 'Mara, did my nose run while I slept?'" Mara laughed cruelly. "How I'd love to see Princess Daydream covered with a man's seed."

Theron winced. That last thought had come from

Mara's own dark desires, not from him. The maid apparently deeply resented the cosseting Lucia had received all her life.

"Do you know what I'd like?" Dimitrie asked.

Mara shook her head.

"I want you to take that necklace off her. I want you to wrap it around my cock, and then I want to sheathe myself in you. I want you to feel that pendant nudging up against you with every thrust, so that when you see *her* wearing it, you'll think of me and what we did with it."

Mara's heart started to race. "Take the amulet off her? I'm forbidden to touch it. Vlad had her promise never to remove it."

"All the better. She'll never know, but *you* will." He let his fingers play over her nether lips once again, brushing lightly until her hips rose to meet his touch. "Take the necklace off her. Take it off and bring it to me."

"Yes . . ." In the dream, Mara started to rise from the bearskin. In the Waking World—the real world—Mara remained on her pallet, although her hands and feet twitched.

This was the challenging part for Theron. Those who dreamt were held motionless by the power of sleep, and dream demons naturally increased those dream bonds. Sometimes the demon grip on a mortal's movements was so strong, the human half woke and felt as if a great weight was on his chest. Sometimes they even briefly sensed the presence of the demon, but despite their terror they could not move.

This time, though, Theron *wanted* Mara to move. With great care he sifted through her mind, finding the controls that kept her still while she slept. One by one he released the bonds, creating within her a state like that he'd seen in sleepwalkers.

"Remove the necklace," Dimitrie repeated. "Bring it to me."

Rise, Mara, Theron whispered into her mind. *Rise.*

Mara stirred and opened her eyes while still she slept, and Theron released her, slipping away from her and out of her line of vision. The maid rose from her pallet and slowly, stiffly, walked toward Lucia's bed. Theron caught up behind her and put his hand to the back of her head, reinforcing the dream. It could continue on its own for a short while but then might either deteriorate or go in a direction he did not intend.

Mara reached the edge of Lucia's bed, and she reached for the necklace. Her hand stopped a few inches above Lucia, and Theron felt the confusion in her mind.

He reluctantly released her, guessing that the amulet would not let a demon-controlled sleeper touch Lucia, either.

Mara grasped the amulet and began to drag the chain over Lucia's head. It caught in Lucia's hair and Mara tugged it free, using one hand to lift the girl's head.

Theron grimaced at Mara's clumsiness and watched Lucia's expression change from that of peaceful sleep to frowning discomfort.

And then the amulet and chain pulled completely free of Lucia, and the storm of pent-up desires that had been swirling around her poured outward in a torrent, washing through Theron with a force that sent his senses reeling.

Unfulfilled passion was ambrosia to an incubus. A mass of it such as this was a lure that could not be resisted, a feast that could not be denied. Lucia's confused, unsatisfied, voracious yearnings rushed through Theron, tingling through his sex, creating in him an echo of her own desire. His skin was alive all over, aching for touch. Starving for it. And what he felt was but a shadow of what raged within Lucia.

She must be half-mad with desire. The amulet had kept any incubus from ever easing her need, and now she could think of almost nothing else.

Mara stood dumb beside the bed, still asleep, the amulet dangling from her hand, and Theron could only hope that she was still dreaming of Dimitrie.

Lucia stirred and she felt with her hand for the amulet that was missing from her neck. She seemed on the verge of waking.

There was no time to waste. He reached forward and touched her brow.

Chapter Six

Theron was instantly inside Lucia's mind. He felt a flush of arousal, deliciously warm, swirling through his loins. The images in the girl's memories were a wild mix—of both Castle Rosu, and of scenes not to be found in the Waking World. Beasts and lands that did not exist populated her mind with as much substance as her true memories. Mara and a nun, and several other female servants were in her mind, but there were no men who were more than faint memories or distant glances. There was even a faint memory of Theron himself, with a cock of enormous size and bizarre shape, looking like nothing so much as a big dead fish.

Obviously his cock had been distorted by time and imagination; his penis was perfect and looked *nothing* like a trout. It was beautiful.

Lucia's memory of Vlad, too, was altered by distance, although growing from Vlad's faulty image was branch upon branch of girlish fantasy. Love, tenderness, affection, sensual kisses; Lucia thought she would get it all

69

from Vlad. She thought her life would begin the day he came for her and made her his bride.

Theron knew that her life would be as good as over if that day ever came. He saw now that she was a creature more of fantasy than of reality, and he saw nothing in her makeup that could withstand the onslaught of a man like Vlad Draco.

Not that she would ever have to, once he got his way. All he wanted right now was to steal a bit of her innocence, and to be sure she didn't put that amulet back on. While she wore it, he had no way to threaten Vlad. With it off, he was the one who was in control.

He found Lucia's sense of self wandering amid a meadow of daisies and androgynous young men. She was wearing a loose, white, flowing gown that concealed her from neck to toe, no hint of her body showing through.

He would have to fix that.

Theron erased the field of young men from Lucia's mind and gave her instead a tall, broad-shouldered, rugged-jawed warrior with the dirt of travel and battle on his skin. He was tanned by the sun and had dark hair that was long and unkempt. He wore a shirt of chain mail that clinked softly as he strode across the meadow directly to Lucia.

Lucia stopped in her daydreaming tracks—she dreamed even inside her dreams, it seemed—and stared in rising terror at the vision of raw masculinity coming toward her. Her thick gown changed suddenly to a transparent chemise and she gasped, hands going to her breasts to cover where her nipples showed through.

The warrior locked gazes with her, his intention

burning clear enough in his bright blue eyes for even Lucia to see. A sexual thrill ran through her, and her panicked virginal mind wanted to both flee and stay. She turned away and began to run.

The warrior was upon her in half a dozen paces. He swept her up in his arms and then dropped down to his knees, lowering her gently to the grass. He picked up her amulet and held it in his palm.

"*This,*" he said in disgust. "You must never wear this again." He pulled the chain off over her head and tossed the piece aside.

Lucia quivered and tried weakly to crawl backward. "It is from my betrothed. I promised to wear it always."

"You will never know pleasure for as long as it is around your neck." The warrior caught hold of her ankle, his strength too great to fight against. Lucia stared at him, her heart racing like hummingbird wings. Despite her fear, Theron could feel the girl's excitement; her anticipation as she waited to see what this unknown man would do to her.

The warrior loosened his hold on her ankle and slid his hand slowly up her leg, shoving aside the hem of her thin chemise.

Lucia watched, mesmerized. The warrior's rough hand made slow progress up to her knee. His other hand grasped her other ankle and eased her legs apart. She tried to close them against him, but her muscles were quaking and she had no strength.

The warrior knelt between her legs and slowly shoved the hem of her chemise up over her thighs, past her hips, and to her waist.

She was naked beneath it.

Lucia's dreaming mind tried to create another layer

of clothing to cover herself, but Theron tightened his control of her mind, leaving her body bare.

Lucia tried to clamp her thighs together, but the warrior was in the way, his rough clothing brushing against her soft skin. She dropped down onto her back and tried to cover her sex with her hands, but the warrior gently grasped her wrists and held her hands aside.

Theron created a cool breeze to blow across her sex, reinforcing to her that she was bare. The warrior released her wrists, and Lucia dropped her hands helplessly to the sides, submitting.

His strong hands gentle, the warrior pushed her thighs farther apart, until the lips of her sex parted.

The dream Lucia closed her eyes, her entire being quivering with fear and delicious expectation. . . .

And then Theron was jolted from her, tossed back out into Lucia's bedchamber, his hand shoved back at him with a force he could not withstand.

Lucia blinked and fully woke, her necklace pooled on her chest where it had slipped from Mara's fingers.

"Mara?" Lucia said aloud.

Her maid jerked and awoke, then stumbled as she found herself standing beside her mistress's bed. Her knees went weak and she caught herself on the edge of the mattress. "My lady?"

Lucia looked around the room, her gaze passing over Theron as if he were not there. "Is there someone in the room?"

Mara sent a panicked look over to the bearskin rug where her dream Dimitrie had been lying. Her shoulders sagged with relief as she saw that no one was there. "No, there is no one here."

Lucia frowned and sat up, her necklace sliding down

her belly. She caught it, and looked at it in confusion. "How did this come off?"

Mara blinked, her gaze shifting evasively to the side. "I don't know."

Lucia frowned and put it back on. "How very strange. Why are you standing beside my bed?"

"I—I thought I heard you stir and was afraid you were having a nightmare. I was going to wake you."

"Oh. Well, I wasn't. You can go back to sleep."

"Yes . . . I think I had better." Mara moved back to her pallet and lay down, looking confused and disoriented.

Theron watched as Lucia lay back against her pillows and picked up the amulet, letting it dangle from its chain, the amethysts catching the moonlight. There was a frown of puzzlement between her brows, and Theron didn't know if it was over how the necklace had come off or if she was remembering the dream. He didn't even know if she *could* remember the dream; there'd been no time to bind it to her memory, and human minds were notoriously poor at recalling their night-time visions.

Theron silently cursed Mara for her nerveless fingers. He could feel Lucia's desires even stronger than before, the dream he'd given her only making her yearn the more, although she probably had no idea why, or even what the feeling was. He had been planning to give her a hefty dose of orgasmic pleasure, but without that thrill bright in her mind to tempt her, he didn't know whether Lucia would ever take off the amulet on her own.

There was nothing more to do here tonight. Vlad's summoning circle was still calling to him, and as Theron slipped into the plane of the Night World, he knew just what message he was going to send to the man.

* * *

Lucia's faint, unsettling sense of someone else in the room with her suddenly winked out, and she knew she was truly alone with Mara.

She clasped her hand tight around her pendant, holding it over her heart. That warrior had said something about the necklace in her dream; something about her never having pleasure as long as she wore it.

But who had taken it from around her neck? Maybe she had done it herself, in her sleep, as she dreamed of the warrior doing it.

But what had Mara been doing, standing over her? The maid had never tried to wake her from a nightmare in the past. Neither could Lucia imagine Mara trying to steal the necklace, though.

Lucia mentally shook her head. Sister Teresa was right: She spent too much time lost in dreams. She was losing all sense of what was real and what was not.

She released the pendant and lay spread-eagled on the mattress, her hands and feet seeking out cool, crisp areas of sheet. She stared up at the cracked white ceiling with its dark beams.

A warrior had been in a field, unkempt and marked with the dirt of travel and battle, and he had been coming toward her with only one intention in his eyes. Lucia felt a warm rush to her loins, the power of it so great that it was almost pain. She caught her breath, waiting for the frightening wave to subside. As it did, the images in her mind changed without her direction, and she felt a stillness shackle her limbs.

Conscious thought fled as a vision of the future filled her mind:

Vlad was coming for her. His features were sharp and hungry, weary and determined, as he led a group of mounted soldiers to the base of Castle Rosu's mountain. His clothing and breastplate were filthy with travel and combat, his dark auburn hair tied back in a ragged tail. He dismounted from his chestnut horse and stood, arms akimbo, and stared at the beginning of the steep, stepped path that was the only way to Castle Rosu. There were 1,490 stairs between him and the castle, and he looked as if he had the weariness of 1,000 miles already on his shoulders.

He put his foot on the first step and began to climb.

The scene changed, and now Lucia saw herself, dressed in an amber and green gown, sitting on a window seat and looking out through the open casement to the sunrise in the east, the sky rose and gold, the mountains covered with a rare, soft, peaceful beauty. She wore her pendant, and she touched it as she gazed out over the mountains. A tear slipped down her cheek.

A pounding at the gate thundered through the castle, and the Lucia in the vision jumped. As male voices echoed in the hall below, she stood and wiped away her tears. She took a deep breath and began to descend the stairs.

The vision faded, leaving Lucia lying once again in her lonely bedchamber, only the moonlit darkness and Mara's soft snores for company.

She had only had a handful of such visions in her life, giving her a glimpse of what was to come. The visions felt different from her daydreams; they had a life of their own, and forced her into passive viewing as they played out before her.

Lucia rolled onto her side and pulled her furs up under her chin, a sick dread filling her chest. The visions were never true to the exact letter of what she saw, but their underlying message always was. What did this one mean? It looked like Vlad would come for her, but she would not greet him with joy.

She hoped she was misinterpreting, but she was getting a queasy feeling that she was not going to have the happiness she had been expecting. That she had been depending upon.

She threw up a fight against the doubt, struggling in its grip. Vlad was her betrothed, and her beginning. He was the man she had been waiting for for six long years. He was handsome and good and kind. He couldn't be cause for sorrow.

He couldn't. She refused to believe it.

She refused, but even so an ominous grayness began clouding her picture of the future, dousing her hopes with raindrops of doubt and misgiving.

The promise of Vlad coming and taking her away from the loneliness of Castle Rosu was all she had to keep her going. She shut her eyes tight against the despairing vision and tried to lose herself in sweeter dreams.

Chapter Seven

Vlad recited the spell once more in Latin:

> *"Creature of darkness,*
> *Come to me.*
> *Circle of light,*
> *Bind thee.*
> *Fly through night,*
> *Into sight,*
> *Speak to me,*
> *Come to me,*
> *Theron."*

He waited. Again, nothing.

He cast a furious glare to the connecting door to the next room. "He's *not* coming! Damn you, Gabriel, this was supposed to work! It's been over three hours and nothing! *Nothing!*"

The door creaked open a sliver. "Quiet! He could be here at any moment. It took a long time the first time he came, too. Your impatience is going to destroy all my hard work."

"I swear to you, if I have to go the rest of my life worried about a damned demon harassing me, possessing women in my bed while I've still got my cock in them—do you have any idea what it's like, to realize you have your cock in a *male demon*?—I will make you pay for it out of your own skin."

Vlad's brother Gabriel poked his pale, flaccid face through the doorway. His blackish-gray hair grew in uneven tufts on his strangely small head. His dark, shining eyes were as beady and crafty as a rat's, and at odds with the weirdly sagging body the door and his black monk's robes concealed. Once hugely fat, Gabriel had recently lost two-thirds of his bulk, leaving great sacks of skin hanging from his body. There was nothing saggy about his intelligence or character, however. "I should not like to see you try it, brother mine. One harassing demon would be the least of your concerns."

Vlad ground his teeth. He was never completely certain whether his brother knew as much about the dark arts as he claimed, or if it was an elaborate bluff Gabriel used to gain power he would otherwise not have.

Gabriel plainly had *some* occult knowledge, though. He was the one who had taught Vlad the summoning spell. He was also the one who had first suggested that Vlad marry Lucia of Maramures. She was the last unmarried descendant of Raveca, the legendary queen and seer of the north. Gabriel was certain that the blood of a visionary ran in Lucia's veins, and had heard from traveling monks rumors of her trances while she was living at a convent. Some of the nuns thought she had the Devil in her. Gabriel saw the promise of power.

Vlad hadn't thought much of wedding Lucia until

he'd seen her, and then his perspective had shifted radically. Even at thirteen, she'd shown signs of being a beauty. More than that, she'd had an air of innocence and purity that went beyond mere ignorance of sex. It was as if the world had hardly touched her, as if she was only dimly aware that it existed around her.

The idea of taking the blank book that was Lucia and filling its pages with himself, so that all she knew of the world was seen through him, touched a deep desire in Vlad that he hadn't even known he had. It would be as if she were his creation, and he would be her god. It made him yearn to possess her whether she had visionary powers or not, whether she was Dragosh's sister or not.

It had taken a year of planning and plotting to arrange for the betrothal, but he'd succeeded. Just as he always succeeded, and always would. This small hiccough in his plans with Theron would be taken care of soon enough.

That cursed demon had caught him unprepared when he possessed that girl's body the night before. Vlad felt a surge of anger sweep through him at the memory of being bitten on the balls. His jewels still ached, and there were the red, swollen hints of infection around one mark where the girl's teeth had broken the skin.

He glared at the closed door, where Gabriel had once again retreated.

Even caught unprepared, all might have gone to his advantage last night if Gabriel had not been in one of his drugged stupors, chasing the empty promise of poppy juice. Gabriel thought to unleash his own visionary ability through the drug, but so far had done nothing but create an insatiable craving in himself for the poppies—so great a craving that he had all but stopped eating, the appetite for food being as nothing compared to the appetite for the juice. He spent half his days asleep and the other half worrying about his supply of poppy juice. It was becoming next to impossible to get useful work from him.

As soon as Theron had gone the night before, Vlad had burst through the connecting door and dragged his brother out of bed, giving him a solid kick to the gut and cursing him with every foul word he knew. Gabriel had been too drugged to care.

Today, Vlad had confiscated Gabriel's poppy juice and only given a spoonful of it back after his brother had set to work preparing the summoning circle and the tools they would need. They planned to imprison Theron in an earthenware jug and seal him up forever—or at least until they needed him again.

He took a deep breath, checked over their implements—candles, salt, jug, wax, holy water, several herbs tied in a bundle—and recited the summoning spell yet again.

The flames of the candles burning in a circle on the floor fluttered, as if in a breeze. The room grew chill.

Vlad's gaze flicked quickly over the room, seeking out the shadows that moved in the corners of his vision. The hair rose on the back of his neck.

The candle flames flared brighter, wicks hissing and popping, and then something shiny fell into the circle, making him jump. Whatever the thing was, it lay in a pool of gold on the floor.

Vlad hesitated several wary seconds, his nerves on edge as he waited for the next movement, the next threat of attack, and then cautiously inched closer, trying to make out what the thing was. He was at the very edge of the circle before he could tell, and when he saw what it was a cold wash of fear flushed through him.

It was the gold and amethyst amulet he had given to Lucia.

Gabriel rolled his eyes as he heard his brother screaming for him in panic from the other room. Vlad had been a demanding pain in the ass since the day he was born.

"Gabriel! Gabriel!" Vlad screeched.

Gabriel silently aped his brother, then composed his features and opened the door between the rooms. "What is it?"

"He has her!" Vlad pointed at an amulet on the floor. "You said he could not touch it! You said it would keep him away from her!"

Gabriel narrowed his eyes, examining the pile of gold. He reached out with one foot and kicked over a candle. As the flame died and the circle was broken, the amulet in the circle disappeared.

"He doesn't have the amulet," Gabriel said. "It was nothing more than an illusion. She wears it still."

"You don't know that. And you don't know that he won't find a way to get it off her."

"She's safe, I tell you. He knows about the amulet, but there's nothing he can do about it." Cool and sly about everything else, Vlad was an irrational mess when it came to that unplucked bud, Lucia. Gabriel could barely keep his lip from curling in a sneer. Lately he'd been wondering if suggesting the engagement had been such a good idea. Even if Lucia had visionary abilities like the legendary Raveca, their value wouldn't be enough to make up for this hysterical softening of Vlad when his fiancée was at issue. She would weaken him if he grew too attached to her.

And a weak Vlad would mean that Gabriel's own position was weakened. In the bloody world of Wallachian politics, heads were separated from bodies with disturbing frequency, and family members were not spared.

"He probably also knows that you've no intention of letting him possess your body," Gabriel said.

Vlad's eyes were wide. "He's never going to give either me or Lucia peace."

Gabriel shrugged. "We'll keep charms around your bed. He won't be able to harm you. There's nothing to worry about."

It was the wrong thing to say. Vlad turned on him, his fear grown to fury, his lips pulled back from his teeth in a snarl. Vlad grabbed Gabriel by the throat and backed him up against the wall, pinning him there, his fingers pinching his brother's throat and squishing the extra flesh as if it were a rotten onion. "Listen to me, brother mine. You are going to put your poppy-rotted self onto the back of a horse and go to Castle Rosu. You are going to make sure that Lucia is still wearing that amulet, and you are going to stand guard against any demon who tries to attack her, or possess her, or come within ten miles of her."

Aww, crap! Gabriel silently groaned. He hated travel, especially in times of war. And he didn't like dealing with demons. He didn't *really* know what he was doing with those spells.

Vlad pushed his face right up next to his brother's, spit flying as he spoke, his eyes insane with fury. Gabriel felt a stir of alarm. His brother looked ready to kill him. "You aren't going to be muddled with poppy juice while you watch over Lucia, either. I'll send an escort with you, and the captain of the guard will control all your juice. If you perform as directed, you will be rewarded. Do nothing, and you will receive nothing. I have seen you when you do not have the juice," Vlad warned. "Do you want that?"

Gabriel shook his head, gagging, and crackling noises came out of his throat. He was starting to feel a little faint.

"I didn't think so. When I finish off Bogdan and his miserable clan, I will come for my bride, and I expect you to show me a girl who is as pure as the water from a mountain spring. A girl who has not even imagined that demons exist. A girl who has never had a thought of darkness cross her pristine brow.

"And if you fail me, Gabriel . . . I will chain you to a dungeon wall and let you watch while I take all your poppy juice and pour it down the drains, and then when you're in the throes of those visions you say torment you without the juice, I'll let loose a thousand starving rats in your cell and watch them eat the flesh from your living body.

"This I swear to you."

Gabriel gurgled, the vision of no more poppy juice sending a bolt of anxiety through him in a way that nothing else could. He couldn't live without it. He couldn't. He'd tried. He nodded what little Vlad's hold would allow.

"If you wish to return to my good graces, and to have all the poppy juice your weak and cowardly heart desires, you will capture Theron as we planned and give him to me sealed tight when I arrive at Castle Rosu. Do you understand?"

Gabriel blinked rapidly in response. The edges of his vision were going black, and he was losing sensation in his body.

"Good." Vlad released his hold on his brother's neck.

Gabriel bent double, coughing against the constriction of his throat. He hacked and spat, trying to clear the airway.

"The only thing that stops me from taking out my

sword and whacking off your head is that I have no one else I can send to protect Lucia from Theron. Which reminds me," Vlad added, walking away from him and then turning around to look back with a haughty superiority. "While you're there, give a whipping to that stupid maid, Mara. I thought she would do a better job of protecting her mistress."

"Yes, Vlad." Obsequiousness seemed called for, and the illusion of wanting to help. Gabriel would provide. "And perhaps you might send a letter to Lucia. With the wars coming to an end, she needs to make herself ready for her bridegroom. 'Twould be best if she were longing to see you."

"Hmm." Vlad scrunched up his face, and then picked with a fingernail at something in his teeth. "Yes, I should pull something together, full of the sort of blithering imbecility and cooing adoration wenches like. She'll wet herself with eagerness to have me grind her into the mattress when she gets through reading it."

Given what Gabriel had seen of Vlad's literary abilities, he very much doubted it. He wouldn't offer to help, though. Let Lucia see for herself what a horse's ass she was getting for a husband.

The thought struck him then that going to Castle Rosu might not be such a bad thing. Alone with Lucia, he might be able to worm his way into her good graces. If she liked and trusted him—or even feared and respected him—it would be one more way he could subtly exert power over his brother.

One needed as many holds as possible when dealing with a bastard like Vlad.

Chapter Eight

Mara listened with annoyance as Lucia tried once again to figure out how babies were made. The girl had a queer obsession on the topic, and Mara had long since lost her amusement over Lucia's ridiculous speculations. There were times she wanted to just *tell* the twit so she would shut up about it. Mara valued her skin too much to do so, however.

"Here in the Bible it says that Adam knew Eve his wife, and then she bore him a son. Isaac took Rebekah, and then she was his wife and he loved her. In several other places, a man 'goes in unto' a woman, and she conceives. Onan, though, spilled his seed upon the ground. So this is what I think happens when a man and woman come together," Lucia said, looking up from the Bible on her lap. "Tell me if I have it right."

Mara glanced up from her sewing, waiting for a chance to roll her eyes. She was working on the amber and green gown that Lucia had decided this morning absolutely *must* be finished; it had been lying half-constructed for several months. Mara didn't know who Lucia thought she was going to wear it for.

Sister Teresa made a despairing noise from her seat near the window, where she had been pretending to read but truly dozing.

"I think what happens is a man comes into a woman's chamber and takes her in his arms. Listen to this from the Song of Solomon," Lucia said, and translated from the Latin: " 'His left hand is under my head, and his right hand embraces me.' " Lucia looked up at Mara. "Yes?"

Mara took her cue and rolled her eyes, and looked back at her sewing. Sister Teresa made another noise like a troubled dove.

"And then, 'Let him kiss me with the kisses of his mouth.' So there is kissing. And then . . . 'A garden enclosed is my spouse.' That must be a woman's mouth, right? And 'Let my beloved come into his garden, and eat his pleasant fruits.' I think that means that a man kisses a woman, and while he does it he bites her. And when he's finished biting her, he plants his seed in her mouth. Then she must swallow it, and that is how the baby is made! And it fits with the ending of *The Romance of the Rose,* where the lover parts the rose's petals—her lips, right?—and then spills his seed within." Lucia closed the Bible in triumph. "I'm right, aren't I?"

Mara ignored the question and concentrated on her stitches, trying to subdue the resentment that prickled through her. Life was grossly unfair, to have made Lucia a princess and left Mara a maid. Mara thought that she herself would have made an excellent queen, a worthy wit beside such a schemer as Vlad. Lucia, though, would be good for nothing but breeding.

She grimaced. But that was all that most men cared about anyway, wasn't it? She sighed. Life was unfair.

Sister Teresa listened to Lucia in a mixture of confusion and alarm. What was the girl talking about—lovers and seed and rose petals? "You shouldn't be reading that," Sister Teresa said. "It's wicked."

"It's the Bible! There could be nothing more appropriate for me to read!"

Sister Teresa pursed her lips in disapproval. "I don't think it was meant to be read for that."

Lucia shrugged. "I love the Song of Solomon, with its dreaming bride and the king who finds her beautiful and beloved. Surely it is meant to be read for its description of love."

Sister Teresa shook her head, unable to find the words or wit with which to argue, knowing only that Lucia was not displaying the modesty becoming of an innocent young woman. A fleeting sense went through her that not so long ago she would have found the words to argue. She kept getting headaches, and a few times she had blacked out. She felt so very muddled afterwards. . . .

" 'Arise, my love, my fair one, and come away,' " Lucia was saying softly, repeating one of her favorite lines from the Song of Solomon. " 'For lo, the winter is past, the rains are over and gone, and the time of the singing of birds has come to our land.' " She smiled and looked at Teresa. "That's what Vlad will say to me, when he comes: 'Arise, my love, my fair one, and come away.' Away from this mountain fortress, away from the solitude, and the mists and rains, and the endless miles of black forest."

The child had a head full of foolish, romantic notions. It was all the fault of that book her sister Elena had sent, *The Romance of the Rose*. It was no way for Lucia to prepare herself for marriage to Vlad of Wallachia.

But then, neither was living here among women a preparation. What a rude awakening Lucia would have when she descended from this mountain. Teresa shook her head sadly, wishing she could protect the girl from the shocks to come.

"If the Bible tells stories of men and women conceiving children, I do not see why you cannot explain to me the specifics of how it happens," Lucia said.

"It is for your husband to tell you." Although she often felt like an aunt to Lucia, Teresa would not presume to interfere in what the girl's family wished for her. Dragosh had made it clear that she was to remain pure in body and spirit, and not even be told how the beasts of the field procreated.

Lucia sighed in defeat and set the Bible on the table. She fingered the pendant hanging between her breasts, and Teresa knew she was thinking of Vlad.

The poor child. She had no idea what she was going to get when she married a man such as Vlad was rumored to be. The poor, poor child.

Lucia looked in frustration from Sister Teresa to Mara. If neither of them would tell her anything about the conceiving of children, there was yet one source she might plumb.

It would be unspeakably wicked of her to do it, though. And it would mean breaking her promise to herself that she would never remove the necklace Vlad had given her.

A flash of memory of the vivid dream from the night before ran through her mind. That warrior had had no interest in kissing her, had he? He seemed more intent on seeing her down *there*.

Lucia felt a warmth in her loins at the very thought. Wicked, dirty warrior. She wouldn't let anyone see or touch her down there.

Although, if it were nothing more than a dream . . . She might be curious to see what would happen next. No harm would be done, and no one would ever know what had happened. It was not as if Vlad could ever know what she had dreamt.

It was her own mind, her own necklace, and she should be able to do as she wished with both of them. The warrior, if she dreamt of him again, would be her own secret, kept to herself and indulged in with the same sinful pleasure as Eve eating the fruit in the Garden. She wanted her taste of knowledge, no matter the consequences.

She held the pendant in the palm of her hand, staring down at the cryptic symbols engraved upon it. Was it more than it seemed? Perhaps Vlad had meant it as a charm of protection for her, warding off indecent thoughts that would mar her purity. It would be a mistake to take it off. She would be inviting wickedness and tragedy.

Even *wickedness* and *tragedy* seemed unreal to her, though; abstract ideas that could not touch her within the walls of Castle Rosu, with its day upon day, month upon month of dreary sameness where nothing either good or bad ever happened.

She lifted her gaze to the window, looking out at the gray sky that threatened showers by nightfall. The gold and rose sunrise of her vision seemed seasons away, the future the pendant and the vision promised more distant and unreal even than her most idle fantasies. All the same, she should be patient and good, and wait for Vlad. If she was lonely, and bored to the point of frustration, and tired even of her own daydreams, then she should pray for the strength to resist temptation.

She should.

She dropped the pendant, letting it fall again to its accustomed place between her breasts.

She should, but she did not know if she would.

Chapter Nine

Theron finished giving a dream to a young tribal bride on the opposite side of the earth from Vlad and Lucia. The girl had needed some explicit instructions on how to get satisfaction from her eager, inexperienced bridegroom. As he moved away from her, she rolled over in her sleep and sought the warmth of her new husband, cuddling up close against his back, her lips kissing his shoulder and her arm going around his chest to hold him close. The husband grasped her hand and lifted it to his lips, then held it close against him with a gentle, grateful clasp of his hand.

Theron watched the couple sleep, chests rising and falling in unison, the simple pleasure of each other's touch soothing them in their sleep. Theron felt a spurt of envy for the man, who slumbered so soundly in his bride's embrace. He had been a clumsy lover, hurting his wife through his ignorance, but still she held him as if he was more precious to her than all the pleasures of the earth. What would it be like to feel such love from a woman and to fall asleep in her arms?

He could not even imagine, except to know that it would be good.

Theron climbed out of the window and up onto the roof of the couple's new house to take in the view. The wood and thatch house was 300 feet in the air, in the high branches of a tree above a swampy, jungle-edged land that had never known any people other than the ones who now inhabited it. It was unlike anything anywhere else in the world, and Theron hoped the strangeness of it would help him clear his thoughts and see things afresh.

He stayed in the Waking World version of this far reach of the earth, eschewing the dream-rippled version he saw while in the Night World. He enjoyed indulging in the illusion that he could be part of this solid world where nothing could be altered purely by a twist of the imagination. If he had been the young husband and lost his footing while building this roof, he would have fallen, and no wishing otherwise would have stopped it. He would have tumbled and crashed through the branches, hurting his body before he hit the earth and broke it forever. Carelessness in the Waking World could mean death; what a person did had consequences that could not be undone. Life began and ended; wounds turned to scars on the body, and remained until death.

Everything was *real*. Everything mattered. Every action had an effect.

Nothing in the Night World mattered. All was illusion, and all could be changed by the twist of one's mind.

He looked up at the night sky, its blue-black meadow shimmering with a hundred-thousand white poppies, their twinkling looking like flower heads under the breath of a breeze, ducking shyly and rising again.

He liked the visions of the night sky he found in the minds of sleeping women: When they looked up, they saw the souls of their loved ones; they saw the ceiling of a sphere, beyond which the gods roamed; they saw animals and figures that spelled out their futures. They rarely saw what he did: a vast emptiness that, however coldly beautiful, went on until the edge of forever, devoid of meaning, with nothing to tell or show or express. When he looked into the depths of the night, he saw that he was nothing within its vast scope. His actions were of no consequence, his existence of no import.

If he could stand solidly upon the ground of the Waking World, and if he were a ruler like Vlad with thousands of men at his command, then he would matter. Every moment he breathed would be precious, because it would not come again, and would mark another step toward death. Yes: ten, or twenty, or thirty years living as a king in the Waking World was well worth giving up an eternity of existing in the Night World without meaning or purpose.

The simmering fury that had been beneath the surface for the past twelve hours came bubbling up again. He would force Vlad to give in. He wouldn't be robbed of this chance in which he had already invested six years of waiting.

He would not be cheated. It hadn't happened before and he wasn't going to let it happen this time, no matter what underhanded schemes Vlad had in mind!

The vision was still fresh in his mind of Vlad and his

brother Gabriel fighting after the appearance of the amulet in the circle. What galled him most was that they had been planning to capture him in an earthenware jug—a *jug!* He didn't even warrant a silver flask or a glass bottle. He'd even rather get stuck in a lamp, like that genie he'd heard about, than be corked up in a cheap jug.

He wondered if that genie had ever gotten out. Probably some human had found him and tortured him.

A doubt about his own plans flitted into his mind, breaking through the red sea of anger.

Despite seeing Lucia's amulet dropped into the summoning circle, despite knowing that she was likely vulnerable to Theron's attentions, Vlad still hadn't held to his end of the bargain and invited Theron into his body. Now, with Gabriel ordered to Castle Rosu, Theron had only about a week to do as much sullying as possible to Lucia's purity before the priest's arrival.

What if it wasn't enough? Or what if, once sullied, Vlad didn't want Lucia at all? Theron would have nothing with which to bargain.

But what choice did Theron have? None. There was no other avenue of possibility he could think of to force Vlad to heel, except perhaps . . . But no, he wouldn't go *there* for help. He shook the thought from his mind. He wouldn't.

Well, not unless he had no other recourse.

"Theron!" a shrill voice suddenly barked in his ear, making him jump. If he *had* been human, he'd have fallen off the roof, and that would have been the end of the debate.

"What?" Theron barked back. A small messenger demon, no bigger than a hummingbird, hysterically flapped her tiny black wings and buzzed a jagged path

around his head. Theron tried to keep her in his sight as she zipped from one spot to another.

"You are summoned!" She hovered for a moment in front of his face, her tiny blue eyes gleaming with delighted malice. The messengers knew that no news was good news.

Theron felt something inside him shrink. *Son of the night . . .*

"Nyx, Queen of the Night, Supreme Ruler of the Night World and Goddess Without Compassion does hereby summon you, Theron, miserable scum of an incubus, to her presence."

Sun-blasted . . . Good goddess, did Nyx know all? He was done for, if so.

Theron narrowed his eyes at the messenger, looking for clues to the truth. "Is that how she described me, as scum?"

"She did not deign to describe you, you miserable smear of demon booger."

Theron made a feint at the messenger, as if to snatch her out of the air. She shrieked and zipped away.

"She'll hear about that!" the messenger screeched. "You know the messengers are not to be touched! You know—"

Theron didn't listen to the rest of the high-pitched rant. If not for Nyx's protection, the messengers would be batted out of the air like flies on a regular basis. Everyone hated them.

And everyone hated a summons to Nyx's presence.

Moon and stars protect him, he could think of no other reason for the summons than that Nyx knew everything.

He took one last look at the solid earth around him, not knowing if it would be his last chance to see it. A depressed frustration twisted inside him: it was all so *close*. It should have been his. How cruel was fate, to take away the possibility before he could taste of its pleasures.

With one last mournful glance around him at the vast panorama of the true world at night, he slipped away into the Night World.

When Nyx called, there was nothing to do but answer.

Chapter Ten

In the Palace of Night, Theron followed a pair of obsidian-skinned female demons down the long corridor to the throne room. His escorts were so dark that he could see them only by the silhouettes they made against the star-studded walls. The corridor—indeed, most of the palace itself—was formed of the substance of space, cut and bent and warped to build Nyx's residence. It changed shape and location at her will, and was no more solid than a whisper, except when and as she wished it to be.

There was no power in the Night World greater than Nyx, and even the human gods of old had feared her. Not even Zeus had ever dared cross the Queen of the Night.

A pair of immense doors opened before him, brilliant white light spilling forth. Theron winced against it, and felt an instant's panic that it might be sunlight, but it hit him without harm. As he came to the entrance of the room he saw that the light came from the floor; or, rather, from the moon, whose brilliance made up the illusion of a floor, albeit one with no surface. The palace was floating above the moon, and in a great arching cathedral window behind the throne Theron could see the distant earth, half covered by the shadow of night.

Nyx herself lounged nude on an immense white-light throne, the better perhaps to show off her dark splendor. She, like her palace, was formed of the blackness of space and the stars and galaxies that swirled within it. She appeared twice the size of Theron, but he knew that giving her a size was impossible: she *was* Night. Any form she took was but a chosen illusion. Her body right now was long and slender, with high, pointed breasts topped by nipples like small moons.

Her eyes were coalesced clusters of stars, and they turned to him in lazy, half-lidded boredom as he entered. A cloud of darkness was concealing her loins, but at a flick of her fingertips it swirled away, revealing her sex. The cloud spun into a pillar and then took the form of a man: Darkness, Nyx's chief consort, and the father of several of her children.

Nyx trailed her fingers down Darkness's front, then let a sly, starry smile part her lips. "Would you stay and meet your newest competition?" Nyx asked Darkness.

A deep wave of sound that Theron could not comprehend was Darkness's answer, and then he was gone.

"Your Majesty," Theron said, coming forward and going down on his knee, bowing his head, his wings folded low behind him. He had no idea what Nyx had meant by "competition." He hoped to the stars that he wasn't going to have to *fight* Darkness as part of his punishment. Darkness would blot him out in a wingbeat.

"Theron. It's been a while since we have talked."

"About two thousand years, Your Majesty." There'd

been a small incident about a Norse girl, rival chieftains, and too much knowledge for an *innocent* young lady. It had been an honest mistake on his part, that time.

"Ah, yes. And have you been up to mischief since?"

He didn't know how to answer. Was it a test, to see if he would confess and throw himself on her mercy? She was regarding him with clear, unreadable eyes. For all he knew, she could see right into his head. "There is always mischief in the work of an incubus," he hedged.

"None so damaging as that last time?" Her gaze continued steadily on him.

"I . . . have tried to be more cautious."

"An interesting answer. One would almost say evasive."

Could he be absolutely certain she knew? He felt his wings begin to shake and struggled to control the telltale sign of fear. If there was any chance she didn't know or wasn't certain, any chance at all, he mustn't give himself away. "I endeavor to be as honest as I can be."

Nyx laughed. "Spoken with the glibness of a true demon. You have a honeyed tongue when you choose to use it, Theron. I think I would like you to use it on *me*." She parted her thighs wide, the star-glistening folds of her sex exposed.

"Your Majesty?" he squeaked, and stared, stunned, at the invitation.

"You are one of the older of the incubi still sending dreams to mortal women, Theron. Not the oldest, no, but one of the elder. I've found that the incubi generally make it to five or six thousand years before they start becoming infected by humanity's idiosyncracies and lose their effectiveness. They become mired in their own thoughts, you see. Their own wants. Their own 'personalities.' At that point, an incubus has to be destroyed, and poor Sleep has to have another child to replace the lost one."

"Is that what you think has happened to me?" Theron asked, barely managing to keep the fear out of his voice.

Nyx put her long elegant legs back together and stood, then stepped down from her dais and walked a slow circle around Theron. "You may be on the verge, but it would be such a pity were you to get to that point. Instead, I'd like to make the best use of your four thousands years that I can." She trailed her fingertips over the top of his head, disarranging his hair.

Theron subdued the urge to reach up and comb it back into order. "What use would that be?" he asked, but he was beginning to get an idea of what it was, and he didn't like it. No, he didn't like it at all.

"My harem needs a new member. They have nothing *interesting* to do to me; they've run out of ideas. Not even Darkness can do anything to please me." She stood in front of him and tucked her chin down, taking on an almost petulant expression. "No one gives me satisfaction."

His throat was dry. "You think that *I* can?"

The sly smile returned. "Oh, I'm sure of it. That streak of mischief in you—you might be willing to dare things that others never would. I think they fear me, you see. They don't feel free to express their art upon my body. You won't fear me, though, will you?" She lifted his chin with one long, midnight finger.

"Not if it displeases Your Majesty." *Midnight sun!* How was he going to get out of this? "When, ah . . . are my new duties to commence?"

"'Duties,' Theron? This is an *honor* I am bestowing upon you. You will no longer visit the earth. You will never again put wingtip into the Waking World. No more slaving to mortal women, no more listening to their boring frustrations. You belong only to me now."

With each word, Theron felt his stomach sink lower and lower. He knew about the harem; everyone in the Night World knew about the harem. Most everyone wanted to be in it.

Theron did not.

The demons in the harem had their wings shrunken to one quarter their natural size, and the hair permanently removed from their bodies. When not servicing Nyx, they played games and bragged about their past exploits, and generally lay around the palace doing nothing. Most of them had their own rooms, made to resemble whatever bit of earthly or unearthly fantasy they desired. Theron thought of the rooms as dressed-up dog kennels.

The biggest bone Nyx threw to her dogs of the harem, however, was to alter her pets so that they could feel her pleasure while she was awake. Nyx did not sleep, nor dream. The demons in the harem pleasured her with their hands and mouths, and felt whatever satisfaction she did. But just as before, they would feel no lusts of their own; they would not climax unless it was an echo of Nyx's climax. They would still be but a mirror for a woman's passion.

A hundred years ago, Theron might have leapt at this chance. But not now. Not when he had his own plans in the works, and was getting a taste of trying to control his own fate. He didn't want to sit around playing games and talking. He wanted to *do* things, alter fortunes; he wanted to *matter*.

Neither did he want his first true sexual experience to be with Nyx. Aside from the fact that she was his grandmother, the thought of putting his member inside that cold, starry slit made him shudder. Nyx's flattery didn't fool him, either; she had been with hundreds of thousands of demons and wouldn't give a gaseous star for Theron. He would be but one of many, and she would tire as quickly of him as she had of all the others.

It was so unlike the way it would be were he to have someone like Lucia as his first. To her, everything they did together would be new, and it would mean the world to her.

"Your Majesty, may I beg a small favor of you before I accept this great honor?"

Nyx tilted her head, hair flowing in a black waterfall around her. "You may beg."

Theron tried to smile but feared he must look like a resentful hound baring its teeth. Nyx *had* to give him this; had to allow one small window of chance. He couldn't go into the harem; he'd rather be blasted to nothingness by the sun. "May I have a month in which to make my farewells to my old life?"

She raised her brows in an astonishment that he could not tell whether was false or real. "You are so fond of being a dream demon?"

"There is much of beauty on the earth," he said carefully, hoping he sounded sincere. "I would see my favorite places again, and perhaps visit a dreamer or two before I gratefully take my place in your harem and accept this great honor."

Nyx traced her fingertip down the ridge of his nose, and then to his lower lip, resting it there. She pursed her mouth and slowly tilted her head from side to side, as if considering. His body roiled with anxiety, waiting for her answer.

She lifted her fingertip off his lip and tapped his nose. "Come back in a month, then, dear Theron, and do not make me fetch you. I am not one with patience for coyness, and I find it most unbecoming in a demon."

"Yes, Your Majesty." The dog would give every appearance of obeying, as long as the mistress was watching.

He had only one month to bring all his plans to fruition. After that, his chance at a mortal life would be gone forever.

Chapter Eleven

Lucia waited until Mara was snoring, and then she carefully lifted the necklace from around her own neck. She held it for a long moment, her heart beating with nervousness, and then with a shaking hand set it on the bedside table.

She scooted down beneath the covers, eyes wide, body tense. Her breasts felt full and tight, and there was a restlessness in her thighs, making her want to rub them together.

The minutes ticked by, but nothing happened, her anticipation keeping her from falling into a natural sleep.

The minutes wore on toward an hour, and she began to think herself a silly fool. What was she doing, lying here with eyes wide open, waiting for a dream lover who did not exist? The necklace was just a necklace; it had no power to control her thoughts and dreams. She'd probably dreamt of that warrior because she'd been spying on Mara and the guardsman. It meant nothing, and would teach her nothing more than she already knew.

With that rational thought, her eyelids lowered, feeling the weight of the late hour.

Then she was asleep. A small part of her was aware that she was, but it was too small a part to do more than watch from a distance, barely noticeable to the rest of her slumbering mind.

Confused images of the day jumbled around her head, then found nonsensical order, woven into a story that made no sense. Lucia drifted through the strangeness, knowing it for the routine, nightly organization of her thoughts.

And then she was in her amber and green gown, walking down the stairs to the great hall, where male voices were echoing against the stone.

She had never heard male voices inside Castle Rosu.

She came around the last turn in the stairs. Vlad stood with several of his men in the hall.

No—not Vlad. His features subtly changed to those of the warrior in her dream from last night.

She would prefer Vlad's face. She tried to turn the man back into him.

She couldn't.

She stopped on the last step of the staircase, puzzled. She could always control her dreams. Most people could not, but she had long ago mastered the technique.

She wanted Vlad.

The warrior narrowed his blue eyes and put his hands on his hips and remained a stranger.

Lucia felt a shiver of fear run through her, telling her that she was not the one in control of what the warrior would do.

"Welcome to Castle Rosu," she said, as the warrior continued to stare at her. "Have . . . have you come far?" What did one say to an unknown man who had arrived without invitation at one's home? She had been given no practice. Sister Teresa had not covered the situation in her many lessons.

"I have come many hundreds of miles and would have you welcome me as if I were your husband."

"Er . . ."

Sister Teresa and Mara appeared. "I'll take care of the rest of them," Mara said, and she winked at a soldier.

"You must take care of *him*," Teresa said, nodding her head toward the warrior. "You are mistress of this castle, and it is your duty to welcome and entertain him, however he pleases."

"Really?" It was a little hard to believe. "But I'm not supposed to be alone with him, am I?"

"You are mistress of the castle," Teresa repeated. "Welcome him as he wishes."

Lucia shrugged. "All right, if you say so."

"Ready a bath for me," the warrior said.

"As you wish." She turned back up the stairs and gestured for him to follow. She didn't know what room she was going to give him—one of the larger ones? Perhaps the one with the view to the east, if she could find a maid to make up the bed. She wasn't sure whether the mattress had been infested by mice long since, unused as it was. "May I ask your name?" she inquired over her shoulder.

He hesitated, as if caught by surprise by such a simple question. His blue eyes blazed more brightly than any she had ever seen before, his gaze intense upon her. "Theron. Call me Theron, frequently and with passion, and remember my name long after I have gone."

"Yes . . . uh, if that's what you want."

"I don't want to stay in a room with mice. Take me to your own chamber."

He didn't know what she was thinking, did he? "I really shouldn't—it wouldn't be proper. I have purity to protect," she said, feeling it was the right thing to say.

"Your purity be damned! You are to entertain me as I see fit. Your bedroom. Now!"

A maid passed by on the stairs, and Lucia touched her on the arm and ordered a bath brought up to her room. She turned back to Theron. "You're terribly insistent. Are men always like this?"

He scowled at her.

She shrugged, and her lips curled into the hint of a smile. Maybe he would be as intent on mischief as he had been in the meadow. She shivered in anticipation.

As they reached her door, she had a sudden fearful thought: She hadn't left any of her undergarments strewn around, had she? Plates of half-eaten food, clothes, music for her mandolin, sewing projects half-done; she could be a bit of a pig at times. He might find it unappealing.

When she opened the door, though, all was neat within, and there was already a bath waiting for Theron. It was twice the size of any she'd ever seen, the barrel-slatted sides encircling enough steaming water to wash a horse.

Well, the warrior *was* large and dirty. Perhaps it would take so much.

"There you are," she said, gesturing to the tub. "I expect that someone will bring you food shortly. I'll wait out in the garden. Let me know when you're finished."

"You will stay, and wash me."

"I beg your pardon?" she asked in shock.

He kicked the door shut and strode quickly up to her. Her heart raced, a flush of panic and excitement rushing through her as he approached. He stopped when he was but inches from her, glaring down at her from his great height; he was at least eight inches taller than she. Theron seemed to assume that he was the one who would give all the orders, and that they would be obeyed without question.

Her heart tripped in excitement. Yes, she wanted him to tell her what to do. She wanted him to take her places she had never been before.

"Take off my clothes."

"What?" That was proceeding a bit too swiftly.

"Take off my clothes."

"You aren't going to try to kiss me, are you?" she asked anxiously. "I'm a virgin, and it would be a disaster if I were to conceive a child before I was wed."

"Kiss, conceive . . . ?" He shook his head, as if shaking off the thought. "I promise that no matter what I do, you will not conceive a child. Now undress me!"

She had a flash of doubt about his trustworthiness, and he was too impatient by half. "Do you swear it?"

"By the moon and the stars, I swear it. Enough of this talk!"

Such a rude man! But she admitted she liked it. She closed her lips over the hundred questions that were eager to spill out of her mouth and decided to learn by doing, not talking.

She gingerly reached for the top wrought-gold button of his tight-fitting *pourpoint*—a sleeved outer garment that ended at the tops of his thighs. Her slender fingers struggled with the large ornate button and the thick brown material, unable to undo it. She forgot that there was a man underneath the garment and started jerking on the stubborn fabric, using the heel of her hand to jam the button through the narrow opening.

The small sound of a weary sigh emerged from some-where in his throat.

"I'm *sorry*," she said crossly, "but I haven't done this before. If I had my way, the thing would fall off you and we'd be done with it."

"Aren't you excited to undress me?"

"It would be a lot faster if you'd do it yourself." She bent the edge of her nail on the button, winced, and then attacked the thing with angry, renewed fervor. She'd throw the button off the balcony, she would, if she could just get the blasted thing *undone!*

"But then there's no thrill of anticipation," he complained.

"I've been anticipating my entire life. I don't need any more."

"Trust me. I know what I'm doing. You're going to enjoy this a lot more if you undress me."

She scowled at him but went back to work on the buttons. "I *know* I'm dreaming," she grumbled. "And I should be able to have exactly what I want in my own stupid dream. . . ."

"Maybe what you want," he said softly, "is not to have your way."

Her fingers stopped on a button and her gaze lifted to his. His brilliant blue eyes were looking directly into hers, and it felt as if their gaze went right into her soul. A thrill of submission raced through her veins, making her thighs weak.

"Maybe what you want," he went on, "is to be told exactly what to do, whether you like the task or not."

"I don't think so," she lied, and licked her lips.

His mouth showed the faintest whisper of a smile, and she knew he was aware she was lying. Warmth flooded her loins.

"Undress me," he said softly.

She bent her head down and worked the buttons with shaking fingers, finally getting them all undone. He wore a linen shirt underneath, and linen braies over which his hose had been pulled. The hose were held up by tabs tied to cords inside the *pourpoint*. She carefully untied the first set, the warmth of his body tangible in the warmth of his undergarments.

She moved around him, lifting up the hem of the *pourpoint* to untie the cords in back. She could see nothing of his skin as of yet, although her eyes did not rise from the folds and creases of linen that concealed it.

Back around in front, the last piece to untie was a triangle of cloth, covering the place in front where the hose were not joined. A silken cord laced the eyelets on either side of the triangle. Under the triangle, there was a bulge unlike anything she had ever seen on her own body. It was in the same place as the demon's strange appendage.

Her fingers hesitated over the laces, not sure whether it was a gift or a trap that lay beneath.

"Are you afraid to see it, then?" Theron asked softly.

She looked up at him, seeking reassurance. "But what is it? Tell me that."

"It is what makes me a man rather than a woman. It is the difference between you and me, and the source of more pleasures than you have ever dreamt of."

"Pleasures for you, or for me?"

"Both," he said, a hint of impatience edging his voice.

"All of that, under this small piece of cloth?" She tilted her head to the side, examining the area, her rational side striving to control her fear with questions. "I doubt it."

"Am I going to have to stop you from speaking?"

"I should like to see you try." Ha! This was *her* dream.

111

Theron made no move, but suddenly Lucia found that she could not speak. Her throat did not move, her lips did not open.

"And do I have to stop you from thinking, as well?" he asked. A moment later her thoughts started becoming fuzzy.

Panic pumped through her blood. To lose control of her mind was to lose control of herself entirely. It was to lose her *self*. It was to be vulnerable to every fear that lurked in her heart. She whimpered.

As quickly as it had come, the fuzziness was gone. She turned away from Theron, her delight in his presence destroyed, the fluttering of fear making her sick to her stomach. She crossed her arms over her midriff, holding herself.

This was not enjoyable. This had been a mistake, and she wanted it to stop. She should have behaved herself; she should have kept the necklace on to begin with. Vlad had been protecting her. What was she doing here, frolicking with another when she had such a kind and good bridegroom waiting for her?

Her gaze lit on her necklace, piled in a heap of gold on the table beside her bed. The small part of her that was still awake and aware remembered that the real necklace was only inches from her, as her real self slept in the bed. Just as leaving it off had brought this dream, she intuitively knew that taking hold of it would banish this warrior. Lucia closed her eyes and concentrated on making her real, sleeping body lift its hand and reach—

"I swear I will not do that again," Theron said behind her. "Forgive me, Lucia."

She felt his hand on her shoulder and opened her eyes. She knew her real hand was hovering above the

112

necklace. She didn't need to stay in this dream if she didn't want to.

"But you do want to stay," he said, and he gently brushed the hair away from the back of her neck. A shiver went down her spine as she felt his breath, warm and moist, on her nape. And then, soft as the brush of a feather, his lips touched her skin.

Her eyes closed of their own will, her shoulders relaxing as if the strength had gone out of them.

His hands clasped her shoulders in their strong warmth, and then his fingers gently pulled at the neckline of her gown. The ties and lacings had somehow come undone, and the neckline slipped over her shoulders and halfway down her breasts. Theron's lips moved from her nape to the bend between neck and shoulder. His hands moved to her collarbone, tracing as lightly as air the ridge and the slight hollow beneath, and then his fingertips met over her breastbone.

His hands slid down, slowly, his rough palms lightly grazing her delicate skin, the edge of his hands pushing the neckline of her gown lower and yet lower, until it barely covered the peaks of her breasts.

Her whole body waited for him to complete the descent. Instead, one hand went around her waist and gently pulled her back against the hard solidity of his body. The other rose up again, gliding up the front of her neck, his fingers spreading out to raise her chin and turn her head until she was leaning back against him and he could bend forward and meet her mouth with his own.

He did no more than let his lips graze hers, so that it was the softness of his breath that she felt more than the bare touch of him. His hand on her waist moved lower, pressing over her belly, the slight pressure somehow awakening her body until she thought she could feel every point where his body touched her own.

Then he released her, stepping back, his hands gliding over her and away. "Will you stay?"

She grasped the neckline of her gown, keeping it from falling to the floor and trying to keep herself from gladly letting it. Although this was but a dream, everything was feeling a little bit too real, a little too deliciously sensuous, and surely such pleasure must be sinful.

She felt again that this was a betrayal of her betrothed. Even in her most private thoughts, she should be true to him. She shouldn't be seeking another's touch.

She looked back over her shoulder at Theron, her hair shielding half her face as if it could provide some promise of protection. A wicked streak of perversity was stirring inside her. The strong need not to betray Vlad was creating in her a powerful temptation to do just that. She didn't want to betray Vlad; she didn't want to do the forbidden and imperil her future, for surely if he ever knew of the wickedness of her thoughts, he would break their engagement and all her hopes for a husband and a child would be dust. But it was like walking on the edge of the high fortress wall and looking down at the rocks below: She didn't want to step off into the nothingness and fall to her death, but there was an almost unbearable temptation to do exactly that.

Perhaps if she just dangled one foot over the edge . . .

"You will not cloud my thinking," she ordered. "You will not silence me. You will not hurt me."

"I swear it."

"And you will not tempt me to lose my virginity, even though this be but a dream."

Theron shook his head. "That I will not promise. If your love for your betrothed is so great, it will surely hold you strong against any temptation I may put in your path."

"It is my own honor I rely upon to keep me from temptation." And then, softly, "I am not so confident of its strength. There has been nothing against which to test it."

"Take me as your test, then. See what you can resist, and know that you will do nothing except by your own will. No touch will be forced upon you, if you refuse it. Your desires will be as my own."

She pulled the edge of her gown back up over her shoulder. She didn't want so much control over what he did; she wanted him to be unpredictable, like before. Only not so frightening.

"There is always fear in what we cannot control. You cannot have the one without the other."

"You know my thoughts," she said, finally accepting it as the truth.

"The strong ones. And some that you have hidden away. I am, after all, part of your dream."

"Are you? I have never had dreams like this before. I have never been unable to control all parts of one. Are you truly only part of my own thoughts?" She walked a wide circle around him, feeling far more naked and vulnerable than a slipping gown could account for. This warrior must know how she had wished to have him touch her in that darkest, most wicked of places. A flush of embarrassment went through her, making her flinch. She glanced up, meeting his eyes.

"Nothing you wish is shameful. Unless, of course, you enjoy the shame," he allowed, and the smile curling his lips was beyond wicked.

He was only a figment of her imagination, a part of her

own fantasy, and yet . . . he wasn't. He was something other, something that had not been revealed for all the years she wore Vlad's gift. Just as that demon—whether he was real or imaginary—had stayed away from her.

She sat down on the end of her bed, her knees held tight together to keep them from quaking and betraying her nervousness.

"Do you think your honor is up to the challenge?" he asked. "Can you resist whatever temptation I may throw into your path? Are you willing, dearest Lucia, to test how close to the edge you can walk without tumbling over?"

She tilted her head, staring at him, her frightened mind trying to work out the logic and therefore control this dream that was beyond control. "I cannot tumble over. If you are only part of my own imaginings, then you can show me nothing that is new to me, and therefore there will be nothing that I have not faced before. If you have something more to show me than is in my mind already, then you yourself are not of my mind. You are . . . other. And I don't know who or what you are. Who are you, Theron?"

He scowled. "You think too much."

She laughed. "That is not something I have been often accused of. Rather they say that I lose myself too much in idle fancies."

"Lose yourself now, and leave off your questions. Save them for the daylight, if you must think upon them at all. The hours of the night are short, and there is so much you have yet to learn." He walked up to where she sat on the edge of the bed, his hose staying up by some miracle of dream work. The triangle of cloth over his loins was square in front of her, begging to be untied.

"I shouldn't," she whispered. She wasn't at all sure

that Theron was only a phantom of her own imagining.
What if he truly *were* something other? Then she should
not touch him. She should don the necklace and send
him away, and count herself fortunate for having escaped whatever evil he had planned for her. Vlad
wanted her to wear the necklace, and she should obey
her betrothed's wishes.

"This is too frightening for you, isn't it?" Theron said,
his hand brushing once over the triangle of cloth at his
groin. "You, who have been locked inside these white
walls." He raised a patronizing brow. "They have caged
you even in your dreams."

"Never that," she swore, looking swiftly up at him.
"My dreams are my own."

"Are they? Or are they Vlad's, and your brother's,
held *pure* by them because that is how they wish you to
be? I promise you, the landscape of your dreams is as
poorly furnished as these white walls, compared to what
it could be."

She felt a spurt of anger. "My dreams are rich!"

"But only half as rich as they should be. You know
nothing of men, and those who people your dreams are
but sexless mannikins, showing you know nothing of
what is real. They are the dreams of a girl, not of a
woman."

"Why are you here?" she demanded angrily. Who did
he think he was, to say such things to her?

"Here?"

"Here in my dream. Why have you come to me now?"

"Because I can."

"Surely there is more to it than that," she argued, dis-
believing.

"There would have been dozens before me who came

117

to your dreams, if you had not worn the amulet. Dozens to touch you and teach you, and to relieve some of that ache you feel inside."

Some of her anger with Theron died away as she was confronted with this new idea. She struggled to make sense of it; struggled to shift her paradigm to fit this outlandish concept. "Is that the way of the world, then? Does every woman have such men in her dreams?" Had she truly been missing out all this time? "The men are even, say, in Sister Teresa's dreams?"

"Sooner or later, yes. Even in Sister Teresa's."

So Vlad's necklace had kept her sheltered beyond even the ignorance of a nun. Lucia felt a flame of fresh anger put torch to a bonfire of resentment inside her, its wood piled on piece by piece during the years of her stay in Castle Rosu. She had been locked away and kept *pure* beyond anything that was natural. Not only had she been isolated from any family who loved her, like her sister Elena, but she had been kept to the knowledge of a child. It wasn't fair. It wasn't normal!

" 'When I was a child, I spoke as a child, I understood as a child, I thought as a child,' " Lucia recited from memory, and then paraphrased the rest in a low, angry voice: "But when I became a woman, I put away childish things."

She said in a determined voice, "I *would* put away childish things."

She reached for the ties on the cloth triangle, and thus stepped over the edge of the wall and into the empty air. Just this once, she was going to feel the fall from the high wall. She would throw herself into this one dream, and then leave the necklace on forever after. Theron was a serpent beguiling her, she knew it, but she was a woman and expected to taste of the forbidden fruit. Vlad should never have left her alone for so long if he expected otherwise.

With that rebellious thought she yanked loose the tie, and the triangle and hose fell away. Underneath them was a short linen pair of braies, gathered at the front into a pouch. Lucia could see Theron's flesh and dark hair pressing against the linen, whatever was in there supported by the fabric. The garment tied at the top with a thin cord emerging from two eyelets. She grasped the end of one of them, careful to keep her skin from actually touching the pouch of the garment.

Before she could pull the cord, Theron shrugged out of his *pourpoint*. "Would you like to take off my shirt first?" he asked.

She felt her cheeks color at her own overeagerness. "Yes, of course." She stood, and tugged the hem of his shirt out of the braies, and then lifted it up over his chest.

And lifted and lifted, her arms stretching high and her face confronted by a broad expanse of bare, muscled chest, astonishingly flat and free of visible softness. She paused, arms still high, Theron's own arms lifted and waiting for her to peel the garment off him. His face was hidden by the lifted shirt.

Some atavistic instinct made her lean forward and smell him. He smelled faintly of sweat and leather, horse and linen. She brought her face so close to his chest that she could see nothing else, and the slightest sway would have brought her lips into contact with his skin.

His nipples were small but turning hard with the cold just as hers often did. She resisted the sudden urge to nip one with her teeth.

He cleared his throat. She was brought back to herself with a start, and realized she'd been breathing in the scent of him for far longer than a moment. "Bend down," she said. "I can't reach."

He obeyed, and she pulled the shirt off over his head, the neckline catching for a moment on his chin and then his nose, coming loose only after a sharp tug. "This should be going more smoothly," she complained.

He shook his head. "You want it this way. You don't want it happening too quickly."

"Yes, I do."

He shook his head again, and moved away from her, toward the tub. "You don't even want to see this yet." He untied the braies, and with his back to her he dropped them, then stepped out of the undergarment and into the basin.

She watched his backside, wide-eyed. He had firm-looking, rounded buttocks that rode atop muscled thighs, without so much as a spoonful of fat to mark the transition. Dark hair lightly coated his legs, and she caught a flash of moving shadow up between his thighs as he stepped into the tub.

Her heart thundered in her chest. His backside did not look anything like the soft, girlish backsides her imaginary princes sported. Theron's whole body was larger and harder than she had thought a man's to be.

And it was also far more appealing. She wanted to run her hands all over his body. She wanted to feel those planes and ridges, those sleek muscles, that tanned skin. She moved toward the tub and reached it just as he sank down into the hot water with a sigh.

He raised a brow, a knowing look on his face. "Wash me."

She unpinned the tops of her sleeves, untied the ribbons under her forearms, and slid each of them off. She rolled up her chemise sleeves and knelt by the side of the tub.

"You look as if you're ready to scrub a floor," Theron said.

"I didn't want to get my gown wet."

"Delays, delays . . ." He leant back against the side of the tub and spread his arms along the rim, presenting himself in open invitation.

Lucia pressed her lips tight together and picked up the sea sponge and cake of soap and dunked them in the water, splashing about until the sponge was wet and soapy to her liking.

Theron watched her without moving, his eyes cerulean gems between half-closed lids.

She took a deep breath and faced the expanse of his chest, sponge poised. She tentatively dabbed at it.

"Ohhhh!" he groaned, as if in extreme pleasure.

She jerked back, sponge clenched to her chest.

He grinned. "Just teasing."

She threw the sponge at his face. It bounced off, and before she knew what was happening he was dragging her over the edge of the tub and into the water. She was dunked under, the warm water seeping quickly through her clothes, and then her face was again above water, and she found herself clinging to his shoulders, her body slightly buoyant and drifting sidesaddle just above his thighs.

He dug his hand into her wet hair, his palm brushing against her cheek as he cupped her head and pulled her down to meet his kiss.

He took possession of her mouth before she could think to protest, and then the movement of his lips, so unexpectedly gentle and soft, chased thought from her mind. She held herself motionless, her hands still on his shoulders, and let him caress her lips with his own. It was a slow, damp massage of mouth against mouth. His lips grasped her bottom lip and pulled gently, his tongue painting her flesh. Then he nipped her lightly with his teeth.

Her eyes went wide and she jerked back. "No! You will not eat of my fruits!"

"Eat of your— What? Fruits? You mean your lips?"

"Don't deposit your seed in my mouth."

"Not if you don't want, but some women like that. Not many, but a few. We won't try that until later."

"You promised that I would not conceive a child with you," she protested.

"You won't, no matter what . . ." He trailed off, and looked into her eyes as if looking into her thoughts. He shook his head. "Lucia," he sighed, "you have very strange ideas. Nothing we do with our mouths could ever make you pregnant."

"Really? Damn," she cursed under her breath. "I thought I had it figured out this time."

"You're right on top of the answer, my frightened princess." He bounced her upward with his hips. He was lumpier than she would have thought.

"I'm close, am I?"

"Very." He bounced her again.

She remembered, belatedly, that while she was fully clothed, he was nude. A bolt of alarm shot through her as she realized that that lumpiness she felt was not a roll of hose. In a sudden panic of realization she shoved away from him, splashing and lurching her way to the other side of the deep tub, her lumbering sending a wave of water sloshing over the brim to splash on the floor.

"Do men have something different at their loins than women?" she panted, heart racing as if there were monsters lurking under the surface of the water. A faint imagining of something like a big fish flitted through her mind, almost as if it were a memory.

The demon. That was where she'd seen such a trout-like thing at a man's loins. But surely Theron would not be built like that?

Theron slowly began to stand, the water sluicing off his body like rain down a windowpane. His chest rose out of the water, and then his muscled, ridged belly.

And then something broke the surface of the water a couple of inches from his body—a purple head like a turtle's, peeping up to stare at her. She shrieked and pushed back against the edge of the tub, trying to escape the thing before it swam at her and attacked.

Theron continued to rise, and the turtle head rose above the water, revealing a thick fleshy neck that went on and on and on, widening into a great stiff snake seeming as thick as her forearm. Black curly hair shining with droplets of water concealed the base of the monstrous thing, although it did little to cover the deep reddish sacs that hung free beneath, like bags of cheese.

"Mary Mother of God, protect me," Lucia whispered in horror, and crossed herself.

Theron scowled at her. "It is magnificent!"

"By all that is holy, where did it come from? It was not there before, behind that bit of cloth."

"It was. It gets bigger when a man is ready to make love to a woman."

Her eyes widened even further. "It will get even *larger*?"

"Well, no."

She gaped at him. "Do you mean that you are ready to make love to me?"

He grinned.

She scrambled backward and flipped out of the tub, splatting on the floor in a heap of wet gown. She rolled over and tried to get her feet under her, desperate to escape, but they kept catching in the heavy hem. She whimpered, and frantically tried to crawl away from the tub, her knees pinning her gown to the floor, her long hair getting caught under her palms. She heard a splash of water behind her and looked over her shoulder.

She yelped. He was getting out of the tub! The mammoth *thing* seemed to have its narrow eye pinned on her, seeking her out with the deadly intent of a serpent. The eye started to widen, opening up, and revealed a ring of sharp teeth. It growled at her and snapped its jaws, growing larger and larger—

"Lucia, stop!" Theron ordered. He smacked the crotch monster on the side of its snarling head. It screeched and nipped his finger and he smacked it again. It suddenly turned back into the slit-eyed snake it had been when he first emerged from the water.

"No, no, no . . ." She resumed her frantic crawl, then tripped on her gown and banged her elbow on the floor. "Ow!"

"I won't come any closer."

She looked over her shoulder again. He was still standing by the tub.

"Those teeth aren't really there. You imagined those. Your fears took control of the dream."

She turned around and sat, watching both him and his snake warily. "Just what is it that happens between a man and a woman?"

"If we were to make love, I would put my cock"—here he gestured to the serpent—"inside you."

"That's a *horrible* thing to say," she said. She stared at the thing, and it seemed to throb with life. It was just waiting for a chance to get at her, she knew it. But then, as she continued to stare at the crotch monster, she began to calm. It was an intriguing thing, really, and if *all* men had such a beast . . . "I would choke on it. It would never fit."

"While surely any man enjoys having a woman try to take it in her mouth, that is not what I meant. It goes between your legs, into that place where your blood flows."

Her jaw dropped open, and she felt light-headed. "Into . . ." she started, and couldn't finish, imagining that thing touching her *there.* "How much of it?" she asked, her mouth dry.

"All of it, to here." He touched the base of the snake.

She knew there was a small slit in her flesh from which the blood flowed, but how could this thing ever fit? She remembered Mara's words: pain and blood. Yes, the thing would force its way into her like a battering ram; it would lance her halfway to her heart and kill her.

No wonder Vlad wanted her pure and free from knowledge! He was protecting her from such terrors. She should never have taken the necklace off; never!

"It may hurt you a little, the first time, but you will grow to love it," Theron said. "It will bring you such great pleasure, you will yearn to have it inside you again and again."

As he spoke, she felt her body responding. Her loins tingled, as if eager for that devilish thing to force its way inside her. That cock was the serpent beguiling her, tempting her to her doom. She felt a pulse in that secret place between her legs, as if it were reaching for him, as if it would betray her and make her commit horrible acts.

She wanted her purity back; she wanted to spit out the taste of knowledge that had brought such wickedness to her mind and body.

Theron took one step toward her, and she saw the head of the serpent grin and give a happy hiss. It was coming for her!

And she wanted it.

"No!" she screamed in a hysterical panic, fighting against herself, and suddenly she broke the bonds of sleep, her own cry startling her awake.

She opened her eyes to a huge naked man squatting on her chest, his cock inches from her face. He stared down at her with eyes a brilliant burning blue that glowed with their own light against the darkness of the room.

Lucia screamed.

The man spread great black wings and lifted into the air, and then in a blink was gone.

Lucia screamed and screamed, and even as she recognized that the man creature had been the one who visited her when she was fourteen, she screamed still, until Mara came and grasped her by the shoulders.

"My lady, what is it? What is it?"

"*Cock,*" Lucia gasped. She felt her eyes roll back, and then all was darkness.

Chapter Twelve

Theron flew in distracted confusion over the Night World version of the Transylvanian Alps and Carpathian Mountains, traveling from Castle Rosu in the southwest to Lac Strigoi in the northeast, the swampy lake where some of the other incubi had told him Samira was serving her sentence as a human.

He could barely keep his attention on following the directions the others had laid out for him; he couldn't remember if he was supposed to turn east before or after the gorge where the gypsies were camped. Their dreams full of music and silver shimmered in the night, while their darker nightmares sent ghosts and evil spirits creeping through the mountain forests and lurking in dark caves and shadows.

He flew over their camp, ignoring the strains of sexual yearning coming from some of the women, and turned east, into Moldavia. He'd sworn he wouldn't go to her for help, but now it looked as if Samira and her crippled magician might be his only hope of overcoming Vlad.

Good goddess of the night, it was humiliating to go to them for help. Could he accomplish *nothing* on his own, not even forcing a lowly human to stick to his end of a bargain?

Seducing Lucia into letting him despoil her nightly with orgies of pleasure plainly wasn't going to work. Lucia would likely have that blasted amulet welded shut around her neck after the scare she'd gotten.

Nothing had gone as he'd planned. Even while she dreamt, Lucia was not fully asleep. Part of her remained aware—far more aware than any woman he had ever visited. He'd been unable to make her forget for more than a moment at a time that she was dreaming. Her awareness made it difficult for him to read and control her thoughts and emotions, and she had instinctively, unconsciously begun to build barriers against him in her mind. She had even managed to change parts of the dream—turning the warrior's cock into a snarling beast had not been *his* idea. Her fears had done that.

If she had been a normal woman, he would never have so misjudged her as to frighten her right out of her dream with the sight of an erect penis. As it was, though, he wouldn't be surprised if even without the amulet Lucia would soon be able to withstand whatever control he exerted in her dreams.

She was uncanny, and she was trouble. He wouldn't be the least surprised if she recognized him in Vlad's body and had him exorcised. She was too scared to take a chance on anything else.

If—goddess forbid—he failed to possess Vlad's body, then being wed to Lucia would be punishment enough for Vlad. All those questions! All the bargaining and compromising! She might be a creature of daydreams and fantasy, but she was a stubborn, controlling thing once she got the bit between her teeth.

Theron had seen stubbornness win out over intelligence, brutality, common sense, talent; at the end of the day, whatever the opposition, the stubborn were the ones who got their way. Or they got themselves killed. Either way, Vlad would get more than he bargained for with Lucia.

Yes, Theron could see it. She'd seduce Vlad with her big adoring eyes and sighs of fear and pleasure. Even tyrants could be seduced. Once Vlad was in her thrall, she'd start on the pleas and complaints, until Vlad wouldn't know which end of his sword was for stabbing himself in the gut and putting himself out of his own misery.

Ha! It would serve him right.

But Theron didn't want Vlad to be the one to challenge Lucia in the flesh. She was *his* battle to fight and win. And what a prize it would be, to see her lay down her verbal arms and part her thighs in trust. If she could be coaxed to allow the enemy inside the gate, she might then gladly cling to him with every inch of her soft flesh.

An incubus flying by startled him out of his imagined scene of Lucia, body laid out before him like an offering, her eyes full of loving acceptance as he knelt between her knees.

He might have retreated for a time, to think of another plan for forcing Vlad to hold to their bargain, only Nyx's threat of the harem gave him no time to waste. He needed to do something that would work, and to do it now. He had no time for ineffectual dreams and warnings.

Up ahead, Theron saw a ruined fortress on an island in the middle of a small lake. A flock of incubi and succubi were gathered around the tower of a church in the center of the fortress, peering in the windows as if at a great curiosity. This must be Lac Strigoi.

He joined the other dream demons at one of the windows and peered inside.

Samira, wingless and wearing human clothes, sat at a table with a black-haired man with a burn scar down the side of his face: Prince Nicolae of Moldavia, Theron had been told. Both Nicolae and Samira appeared to be studying books. Minutes crept by.

Theron turned to a succubus hovering near him. "How long have they been doing this?"

She shrugged. "Hours."

"Do they ever do anything else?"

"Samira tries and fails to seduce Nicolae, and sometimes they fight."

"I assume she sleeps, too," Theron said.

"Toward morning. But if you are thinking of invading her dreams, you won't have any luck. See the book by her elbow?"

Theron nodded.

"She sleeps with it. No demon can so much as lay a finger on her while she holds it. They've tried."

Blast! Did *everyone* have charms against demons these days?

Through the window he could see that there were more dream demons inside, resting on the rafters above Samira and Nicolae. The roof of the tower was pyramid-shaped, extending upward another thirty feet past the lowest rafters, the dark space criss-crossed with several layers of beams. Even if the demons were visible to the waking eye, they would not be seen up in that vast darkness. Theron crawled through the window embrasure and jumped up to one of the beams.

"Time to go!" he ordered. "Out! Begone!"

The dream demons turned and glared at him. One of the incubi snarled. "Begone yourself."

Theron grabbed him by the hair and the base of his wings and heaved him through the wall. Another incubus came at him, and a succubus from behind, and he unleashed his strength on them. He beat and threw and bent demon bodies, twisted and whacked and kneed in a whirlwind of violence that quickly cleared the tower. He was one of the oldest of the dream demons still around, just as Nyx had said, and he knew a thing or two about how to hurt his fellows.

He looked to one of the windows. The demons peering in jerked back and disappeared.

Theron settled onto the beam, and he watched Samira and her human master down below. They were still quietly studying the books, but sooner or later Samira would fall asleep. He doubted she would keep a grip on that book all through the night; it wasn't the way of mortal sleep. And when she released it, he would pay a visit to his friend in her dreams.

He forced a smile to curl his lips. This should prove much more entertaining than his visit to Lucia. Samira was a much better match for him. Much.

He wished he believed it.

Chapter Thirteen

In Castle Rosu, Lucia paced the covered gallery above the small inner courtyard, afraid to lie down in her bed and close her eyes even though it was the middle of the day. She had been awake since reviving from her faint, and had insisted that Mara light the candles and oil lamps and keep them burning until dawn broke.

Rain softly pelted the roof above the gallery and leaked through the places where shingles had slid loose, the dripping sound of water far too soothing for her tastes. She wanted lightning and crashing thunder, blowing winds and torrents of rain. She wanted to be kept wide awake, to not risk closing her eyes and being squatted upon again by a demon.

She held her pendant over her heart, hoping it would protect her from both the demon and herself. The worst part about the night had been awakening to find that creature atop her, but a close second had been remembering that she had enjoyed the kisses of the stranger in her dream, and had been willfully untrue to her betrothed in her heart.

A heavy, rushing sense of dread and shame washed down over her. Vlad would never know, would he? No one would want a bride who was visited by demons in her sleep and kissed strangers in her dreams. No one wanted a wife whose purity could not be trusted, who might bear a bastard child. She understood that much at least!

But she couldn't bear waiting another six years to marry and have a child. She couldn't bear the loneliness. She *couldn't*.

On the other hand, marriage would mean facing the crotch monster. Lucia shivered as the memory rose huge and threatening in her mind. She wasn't certain, though, where her fear stopped and a wicked, shameful excitement began, that place between her thighs growing damp even at the thought of the thing.

Perhaps the dream had been a lie, and nothing about it true, not even that fearsome appendage. She could have made up such a strange thing out of her own imagination, couldn't she?

Maybe she had imagined the demon squatting on her chest, just as she might have imagined him so many years ago. None of it need be real. She might still be innocent, her mind pure, her ignorance blissfully complete. She might! Wild hope burst forth in her heart. It was all a dream; none of it was true!

Mara appeared in the courtyard below, wearing a hooded woolen cloak to protect her from the rain as she went to the well and struggled to lower the bucket down the deep shaft to the spring in the mountain. The winch had a habit of jamming.

"Mara!" Lucia called. "Mara! Come up here. I must ask you something."

Mara scowled up at her, squinting against the rain. "Ask me from here. I'm busy." She jerked on the handle of the winch.

"I need you to come up here!"

"I'm too tired, *my lady,*" Mara complained, apparently in one of her bad tempers. "I'm worn out from tending lamps for you since the early hours of the morning! I haven't had a wink of sleep. And now this blasted thing isn't working!" She jerked angrily on the handle. "This place is falling to pieces without men! Leaking roofs, uneven floors, cracking walls. Even the privies are rotting! They're going to fall off the side of the castle one of these days."

Lucia knew of what she spoke. She herself was afraid to go into the small wooden water closets that extended beyond the outside wall of the castle, clinging like snails to the high sides of the castle and dropping their waste through the air and down the steep mountainside. She used a chamber pot instead.

"I know you're tired, but I don't want to ask you from up here," Lucia complained back. There were only fifteen feet or so separating her from Mara, but the question she wanted to ask didn't seem appropriate to the open air.

"Ask me now or leave be!"

Lucia glanced around. There was no one in sight, the other servants huddled indoors away from the damp chill. So be it, then. "Do men have things called 'cocks'?" she called down. "Big, scary, snaky things at their loins, with a knob like a turtle's head at the end, that may or may not have an eye or a toothy mouth? And do they split a woman between her thighs—"

"Hush! My lady, hush!" Mara cried, releasing the handle to the well's winch, the chain suddenly rattling free

135

of its jam, the bucket plummeting to the water far below. "Who has told you these things?!"

"So they *do* have cocks? And have they red sacks that hang beneath?"

"Quiet! My lady!" Mara cried again, and made a hushing motion with her hands. "Say no more, I beg of you! I am coming inside. Meet me in your chamber."

"All right," Lucia said, alarmed and secretly a bit delighted at Mara's dramatic response to her questions. So there might have been something real to the dream, after all. She shuddered—and shivered. That might mean that that demon had been as real as he looked. Somehow, he and the dream were tied together.

She met Mara back in her room, the maid going from door to door, checking that they were all closed and bolted. She was still wearing the wet cloak.

"Are you cold?" Lucia asked.

Mara turned to her, her dark eyes wide. "Cold?"

"Your hands are shaking."

"Shaking with fear."

"You aren't afraid of cocks, too, are you?" Lucia asked with a rising hope. Perhaps her fear was normal for women!

"Of course not!"

"Oh. Then what frightens you?"

"*You.* Who told you those things about cocks?" Mara demanded.

"No one."

"You didn't find any of that in the Bible. Who told you? Did one of the soldiers sneak inside the castle?"

"No. There was no one."

"You're lying."

Lucia bit her lips. "Not really."

"For mercy's sake, my lady, tell me who!"

"I dreamt it."

Mara looked ready to slap her. "Don't lie to me!"

"I'm not lying. I dreamt that a warrior came to me, and he showed me his cock and told me that a man puts it in a woman where her blood flows."

"God's blood, he'll have my skin," Mara said under her breath, and sank down onto a chair. "He'll never believe you dreamt it. He'll blame *me.*"

"You do believe me?"

Mara shook her head as if denying it, but her words said otherwise. "When you woke last night I thought you said 'cock,' but I hoped my ears were playing tricks on me. I convinced myself you were just choking, and it was nothing to worry about."

How comforting. "Who is the 'he' you speak of? Who won't believe I dreamt it? Your lover, Dimitrie?"

Mara gaped at her, her face draining of color. "Is that where you saw it, then? You saw Dimitrie and me together?"

"I saw nothing but a kiss."

Mara dropped to her knees on the floor, her face ashen. "My lady, I beg of you, never tell Vlad Draco that I had a lover. Not when he comes for you, not even after you are wed, or even ten years from now. He must never know."

"I don't know why he should care. It is nothing to do with me."

Mara laughed, the sound bitter and harsh. "As usual, you understand nothing."

"Seeing a kiss is no harm to my innocence. Even the Bible describes kisses. He cannot protest that."

"He can and will. Before I was sent to this godforsaken castle, your betrothed threatened to . . ." She shook her head. "Never mind."

Lucia frowned. "Threatened to what?"

"Never mind! It won't affect *you,* so never mind!"

"You don't mean that Vlad threatened you in some way?" She shook her head. "I could not believe that. He is a gentle and fair man."

Mara rolled her eyes.

"He was awarded the Order of the Red Dragon," Lucia said with pride.

"Yes, I know. We all know."

"But does that not suggest that he is a good man?"

"Just promise me that you won't tell him," Mara pleaded. "If you never do anything else for me, do that. Will you?" Mara swallowed thickly, looking as if she had the taste of bile on the back of her tongue. "Please?"

Lucia couldn't understand what was making Mara so desperate. Why should the maid fear her betrothed so much? Was it just because he was a ruling prince? "If it means so much, then yes, I promise."

"Thank God." Mara shakily got up and sat again in the chair.

"I want a favor in return."

Mara's cheek twitched, as if with nerves. "What?" she asked ungraciously.

"Can you tell me if all I saw in my dream was true?"

Mara pressed her lips tight together, then burst out with the answer, as if trying to get it done with and in the past as quickly as possible: "It's true."

Lucia put her hand to her mouth, appalled. "And . . . and have you done this thing with a man?"

Mara nodded.

"It did not kill you," Lucia stated.

"Apparently not."

"But surely you don't enjoy it. Do you?"

"It's better than listening to Sister Teresa's snoring or

to your prattling." Mara shrugged out of her wet cloak and folded it into a tight wad. "I go half mad from boredom here. At least I can talk to the soldiers, and they treat me well."

"You could talk to me," Lucia said in a small voice. What she would have given, to have a friend. In all the years they had been together here, this was the most honestly and openly she and Mara had ever spoken to one another.

Mara laughed. "Talk to you about what?"

"We could talk as we are talking now."

"This is only because you hold my life in your foolish hands, you stupid goose. You don't even know the power you wield."

Lucia let the insult slide past her, though it stung in the going. "I have no power."

Mara shook her head in disgust and rose from her chair, then moved as if to leave the room.

Lucia saw her chance at making a connection with Mara disappearing, and she made one last try, feeling like a beggar as she did so, her pride lower than the bucket in the well. "I know you don't like me, but I've never understood why."

Mara sighed, and stopped. "You don't want an answer to that."

"Tell me. Maybe I can change it, whatever it is." God help her, was this what loneliness was doing to her? Making her beg a maid for insults? She saw how pathetic she was, even as she could not stop herself from reaching for some connection with Mara.

"You can't change it. It's what you *are.*" Mara tossed her wadded cloak onto the chair and put her hands on her hips. "Heaven knows I'm tempted to say more, but I won't."

"No one ever tells me anything. Why can't you tell me this one private thing? It is only between you and me, and I promise I will not hold it against you."

Mara snorted.

"Why am I so despicable?" Lucia asked. "Tell me, please." She felt tears start in her eyes as her loneliness welled up from deep inside and spread like a flood through her soul. There was obviously something about her that people found unlovable. She was so despicable, her brother—who had been like a father to her, since their own had died—had sent her away to this castle; so despicable, her betrothed had not sent one word or gift to her since their engagement; so despicable, her own maid sneered at her, demons were drawn to her, and her only companionship was to be found in dreams with a man who frightened her with his crotch monster.

Perhaps she had been born bad; tainted somehow. Maybe that was what Dragosh had been referring to when he said she needed to be protected from herself. He'd seen that she would get into trouble if given half the chance.

And look at her: Given no chance for mischief, she'd still managed to draw a demon to her bedroom.

"You're not despicable," Mara said. "You're just . . . nothing. You know nothing, you understand nothing, you see almost nothing of what goes on around you or how hard everyone has to work to keep you clean and fed and safe. You're like a child, ignorant and unaware, with nothing of intelligence to say, and yet you babble and expect others to listen. And we have to listen, because you are a princess and will one day be a queen."

"I didn't know I was boring you," Lucia said faintly, Mara's words burning deep and scorching her heart.

"What have you done to deserve all this?" Mara went

on, gesturing at the room around them. "Nothing but be born to the right family. The only thing asked of you has been to remain pure and innocent, and yet you won't even do that. You constantly pester both me and Sister Teresa, seeking the knowledge that you know is forbidden.

"If I were in your shoes, I should thank God that I did not have to scrub someone else's floor and wash someone else's dirty linen in order to keep myself fed. I would sit quietly, embroider my linens, play my mandolin, and be grateful that God had allowed me to be such a spoiled, empty-headed princess. I wouldn't spend all my energies trying to do the one thing I had been told not to."

Lucia ducked her head, the words pelting her like hail, stinging her with each hit. She struggled against the assault, trying to fight her way clear of the accusations that were beating her down, one by one. "You yourself would never have been able to stand this place without your soldiers. You can't blame me for seeking a little bit of what you have."

"*I* am not betrothed to the ruling prince of Wallachia. You're going to be a queen, for God's sake. There is more expected of you."

Mara narrowed her eyes, looking Lucia up and down, then continued: "You're never going to survive being Vlad's queen. No one will respect you. People sense weakness and attack it like a dog attacks meat. Even if Vlad decides he likes you well enough, those at his court will despise and destroy you."

Mara picked up her wadded cloak and tucked it under her arm. "That's why I don't like you. It does not matter what your noble descent might be: No one likes a weak and useless woman who is nothing but a burden to others. If I were you, and had extra energy after putting down my mandolin and eating the dinner that someone else had cooked for me, and after someone else had washed me and combed my hair, then I might think about how I could make life a little less miserable for those who hadn't been so fortunate in their birth. But I'm not you, so if you'll excuse me, *my lady,* I must return to my work. Your linens need washing, and I must see to your dinner." Without waiting for a reply, Mara turned her back on Lucia and left the room.

Lucia felt all strength leave her body, and she stumbled to her bed, collapsing across its fur covers. Her eyes wide, she stared at nothing and felt a soul-draining emptiness spreading inside her.

She was despised, and deserving of it. No one was ever going to love her, for she was unlovable. Only her own child might, before it knew any better.

Mara was right: She was weak and useless and spoiled.

The demon might as well have her. No one else ever would.

Chapter Fourteen

Theron lay belly-down on the beam and sighed in impatient boredom, annoyed with Samira and her studious prince. He let his arms and one leg dangle over the edges of the beam like a lazy cat and swung them idly in a way of poor amusement as he waited for Samira to go to bed down below.

He'd been here several nights, watching, wasting his precious time, waiting for the chance that had not yet come. His impatience was firing an annoyance that he had to tamp down with increasing frequency.

Even while deeply asleep, Samira had held tight to that demon book as if her very life depended upon it. Theron didn't know why she was so anxious about one of her fellows paying her a visit. He would think she'd be glad to talk to her own kind, and even more glad to ease her sexual tension. Somehow the demon book seemed to be magnifying the unfulfilled passions she felt, sending a thick river of lust out through the Night World. Theron had nearly had to rip the wings off several incubi who had come to relieve her of her misery. If anyone was going to ease it, it would be him.

Instead of welcoming such a chance, however, Samira appeared to be interested only in Nicolae. Her eyes went to him with sickening regularity, like a dog seeking its master's approval. It was as if she had forgotten what she really was, forgotten there were so many better possibilities for her than were presented by that scarred, limping prince.

It was as if she was *enjoying* being human, she who had protested such before.

Theron ground his teeth in frustration. How had *she* ended up with a mortal body while he was still struggling so hard to steal one for himself? Look what poor use she was putting hers to. She had gained no power for herself, made no allies, established no position of strength—not that there was much opportunity. This Prince Nicolae only had five soldiers at this burned-out fortress. But Samira hadn't even managed to seduce Nicolae, the one task Theron would think could be accomplished without any effort whatsoever. She was a succubus, for Night's sake. She knew what men wanted.

Below, Nicolae pulled the demon book across the table and opened it. Theron stopped his limb from swinging, holding still lest Nicolae look up and somehow be able to see him. Theron didn't know what the powers of the tome might be, and didn't want to take any chances.

Samira yawned. She looked at Nicolae, who was engrossed in the demon book.

Another ten minutes went by. Samira yawned again, and her eyelids drooped. She sent another glance Nicolae's way, a small frown between her dark red brows.

Then she looked up into the rafters and the shadows, obviously searching for any sign of demons. Her human eyes must have shown her nothing but empty darkness, for she lowered her gaze back to Nicolae.

At last she got up from the table and went to her pallet, crawling under the covers and wrapping them tight around her. When she had rolled away from the light of the candles on the table, Nicolae raised his own gaze and looked at her, although what he might be thinking Theron had no idea.

Half an hour later, Nicolae shoved aside the demon book in favor of another.

Samira was still awake, if only barely. Theron could feel the irregular waves of her desires as she dipped into sleep and then back up to the surface of consciousness. And then, finally, she went completely under.

He leapt down to the wooden floor of the tower, landing soundlessly beside her. She made an attractive human woman, but it was strange to see her without her wings. Strange, too, to see her hair tightly braided and her body covered with clothes. It was as if she was denying what she had been.

He'd have to remind her.

He stepped weightlessly onto her chest and squatted down. He could feel her unfulfilled sexual desires coursing through her—not with the strength she had when she held the book, but strong enough to let him know that Nicolae had done nothing to ease her. What was wrong with the man? Perhaps his cock was as crippled as his leg and arm.

Theron reached out and touched Samira's brow. He was immediately in her dreaming mind, surrounded by images of Nicolae and feelings of longing. He found her sense of herself and formed it into a copy of her *real* body, sleeping on the floor of the tower. He re-created the tower as well, so that it would seem as if they were talking in the Waking World, instead of in her dreams. He sat down beside her on her dream pallet.

"I thought you'd never fall asleep," he said.

Samira's eyes fluttered open, then widened in shock as she saw him. A moment of confusion clouded her gaze, and then understanding cleared it. "My eyes aren't really open, are they?" she asked.

"No, and you're not really speaking either. Nor do you have to look like a serf." He stripped her of her ugly clothes and sat her on Nicolae's bed, her great black wings again on her back as they should be. He sent her hair flowing around her in shining garnet glory. Much better!

"Theron, don't!" she complained.

"You *like* being a peasant?"

"I *like* being in control of myself."

He shrugged, although he was in truth a little disturbed. How could she prefer looking like a mortal serf, even in her dreams? "Very well." He returned her to human form, although this time her clothes were of soft silks and velvets. "You're not going to complain about the garments, are you?"

"No, they're an improvement," she conceded. Rather ungraciously, he thought. "What are you doing here?"

"Such a welcome you offer your friend, and this after I've been trying for so long for a private chance to talk to you. Why for the sake of Night were you clutching that book every night?"

She crossed her arms over her chest, as if protecting herself. "I could have spoken to you while awake if I was touching it. Why didn't you show yourself?"

"Because of *him*," Theron said, tilting his head toward Nicolae. "It was a private chat I was seeking, but he's always with you at night."

"He is, isn't he?" she said with some pleasure.

Theron rolled his eyes. He was beginning to get the sense that whatever friendship he and Samira had shared, it had been replaced by her attraction to Nicolae. She didn't seem at all happy to see him, and yet she had known him for most of her three thousand years. Was he so easily replaced? "You've attracted hordes of incubi, too, each time you slept with the book," he said, "but I've scared off most of them."

"Have you been coming here every night?" she asked, not sounding at all appreciative of his efforts. She sounded disturbed and unhappy.

"Are you afraid I've been spying on you?" He didn't know what she could possibly be afraid of him seeing; she had done nothing but read and sleep every night. She was proving herself to be spectacularly boring as a mortal.

"Theron, why are you here? I never told Nyx your name; don't attract her attention now by visiting me."

He sensed that she was feigning concern. She wanted him gone, that was all. "She'll think nothing of it. Rumors have been flying through the Night World about your temporary humanity, and you've become a bit of a curiosity—an amusement to be peered at. Most of your audience is quickly bored and moves on, you'll be happy to know."

"Delighted."

He got up and joined her on the bed, finding a place where he could stretch out his legs and make himself comfortable on the pillows. His manhood lay large and half tumescent in the valley where thigh met hip. Her gaze drifted down to it, and her unfulfilled desires made it grow and harden. She met his eyes, hers large and alarmed.

He grinned, although it was anger that he felt. She wanted nothing to do with him; in all but words, she was telling him to go away. And for what? For a mortal man she'd known for only a few weeks.

"You have quite a river of pent-up human lust, Samira. Your Nicolae hasn't been helping you with that." He looked down at his erection with exaggerated pleasure. "You know what a good measure this is of your frustrated desire. Wouldn't you like me to take care of it for you? I promise I'll make it good. I'll even look like *him,* if that is what you want." And so saying, he transformed himself into Nicolae, only without the burn scars.

He flexed a muscle in his loins, making his erection bob. "Come take a ride," he leered.

"Theron, stop it," Samira said angrily, but he could feel that she was affected. Part of her could not help but be aroused, whether she liked it or not.

He changed back to his own form and sat up, wanting to hear her admit the truth. "You've been afraid I *would* come visit, haven't you? You wish I'd go away. I can see it in your mind."

"This isn't fair."

He touched her chin, tilting her face toward him, and looked deeply into her eyes. "Nothing ever is." If she had abandoned him in her mind, then he wanted her to remember that she was in the mortal world now, and he was still a dream demon. She was at his mercy.

He felt her tremble. "What do you want?"

"I know you feel that you've already done far too

much for me," he said lightly, releasing her chin and affecting an attitude of nonchalance. "I need you to do something else, though."

She shook her head. "No, Theron. Nothing more."

"But this time it will help your precious Nicolae. Indirectly, of course."

"I suspect that it will help you more."

He shrugged. "Naturally. Why else would I do it?"

"Why else, indeed?" she echoed.

He heard the rest of her thoughts, unspoken and hidden though they were: She pitied him. She thought she had evolved beyond him, understanding deep truths of humanity of which he was unaware.

What a load of nonsense. Her ability to think had obviously deteriorated just as much as her ability to seduce. Her doglike adoration of Nicolae had turned her into a condescending half-wit.

"Vlad has reneged on his deal with me," Theron said, cutting to the chase.

"You tried to collect?"

"It's time."

Her lips parted in shock and she shook her head in denial, plainly understanding the implications. Her Nicolae's country was all but under Vlad's heel. "What has happened? Where are Vlad's forces?"

"The southern half of Moldavia is his. He is called Vlad the Devil by the peasants, did you know that? He was made a Knight of the Red Dragon for his defense of Catholicism, but *dragon* and *devil* are the same in the language of the peasants: *Draco*. They can't tell the difference, and neither can I, frankly. The man is wicked. Vlad waits now for Dragosh to finish the job of conquering Moldavia."

149

"Dragosh?" she asked on a gasp.

Theron nodded. "Dragosh and his army are preparing to head through Tihutsa Pass and sweep their way to the capital of Suceava. They should be passing through here in about ten days' time. The days of Bogdan and his clan of Dacian wolves are all but over." Ha! Let her stew on *that* when she looked at her precious prince.

He fluttered his wings. "So there Vlad sits, nothing to do but hold his ground and wait, his victory as secure as any victory ever is in this war-mad place. But will he fulfill his end of our bargain? No. He refuses. I don't think he ever had any intention of fulfilling it."

Samira gave him an I-told-you-so look and asked smartly, "What do you want *me* to do about it?"

"Have your fledgling wizard cast a spell for me."

"Nicolae?"

"That demon book must have a spell for allowing a demon into a human. Have him find it and then go to Galatsi, where Vlad has made his headquarters, and cast it on Vlad. Once he's done so, I can take over Vlad's body." He waited, hoping she would agree. It wasn't so much that he was asking, after all. Nicolae should be delighted at the chance to hurt his enemy.

But Samira shook her head. "You've aided in the destruction of Nicolae's country. Why on earth would he want to help you now?"

"In exchange for the information I've just given you, of course. His father doesn't know that Dragosh is going to attack from the west. Bogdan thinks Dragosh is with Vlad, in the south."

"It's not much of a deal. Instead, I want you to swear that when you take over Vlad's body, you will withdraw his forces from Moldavia."

Theron laughed. Who did she think she was bargaining with? "Samira, my darling, what would be the point of being a king if I had to give away half my kingdom?"

"You won't be a king at all if you can't possess Vlad's body."

"Be reasonable," he cajoled, although he knew he would give her what she wanted if he had to. He was still angry, though, that she had abandoned their friendship so easily. It especially kinked his wings that she had abandoned him in favor of a weakling like Nicolae. "You know this is what I've been working toward for years. I'm not going to give it up for the sake of a scarred, banished princeling with an army of five. Look at him! He has no future. He barely has a present. Better that Moldavia—or at least the southern regions—be in my hands than in faltering ones such as those."

As Theron spoke he felt Samira digging in her heels in resistance. She didn't want to listen to reason. She wanted, instead, to lie at Nicolae's feet and snarl at anyone who came near.

"There will be no bargain," she snapped. If she'd had hackles, they would have been raised. "I will not ask him to help you."

Theron looked at her in surprised amusement. She thought of this useless male almost as a god. It took but a moment, then he realized what was happening to her and started to laugh. "You're falling in love with him!"

"Succubi do not love, you know that. I do see that he is a good man, though, with the potential for greatness within him. He—"

"You see what your little human heart wants you to see. You can't hide it from me, Samira. I can see right into you. You're falling in love with him." She was in love and she didn't even know it! But then, perhaps it was not such a powerful emotion, as they had always believed. The creatures of the Night World, from Nyx down to the lowliest demon, did not love or weep, for they had no souls.

Samira shook her head. "The succubi—"

"You're not one right now, though, are you? But really, I thought you had higher standards than to fall for a dabbling trickster, a one-armed warrior."

"You thought I could fall for one such as yourself, perhaps?"

He *had* thought so, and realized his pride was offended. It made so much more sense for her to like someone like him; they were from the same background, and were both strong. Or had been. He wasn't sure about her anymore.

"You don't want him," Theron said, nodding toward Nicolae. "You think you do, but only because he's the only male you've spent any time with as a human woman. You can't help yourself. Think, Samira: Get Nicolae to help us and then I'll take over Vlad's body and come fetch you. I'll have all of Wallachia *and* Moldavia, and you can rule by my side!"

"Isn't Vlad to marry Lucia of Maramures? Dragosh won't approve if the betrothal is broken."

"He won't be strong enough to complain. Moldavia would rather side with a Wallachian ruler than one from Maramures or Transylvania. And if worse comes to worst, we can do the same to Lucia that I do to Vlad. I'd be willing to take you in Lucia's body."

Even as he said it, he wondered if it was a lie. Compared to this new version of Samira, Lucia was the more interesting woman by far: the more challenging, the stronger. At least Lucia could exert some control over her dreams, whereas Samira—for whom it should have been second nature—was lost. Almost everything in

Samira's mind was tied to Nicolae, and it had made her weak. He could do whatever he wished to her right now and she wouldn't know how to stop him.

"You're not going to take me in any body at all!" she protested, her mind still saying, *Nicolae, Nicolae, Nicolae.* "You've lost your dream-fogged mind, Theron! You can't steal lives like this. You are a dream demon; you have no place in the Waking World."

"You've found one. Why can't I?"

"It wasn't my choice! I don't belong here!"

"But you want to stay."

"I do not," she said, and he knew it for a lie.

"You want him to make love to you and whisper your name in your ear. You want him to forget that you were ever a demon. You want him to love you as a human woman, and to ask you to be at his side for the rest of his days."

She shook her head in denial.

A furious frustration made him want her to see the truth. He wanted to rub her nose in it until she saw what a disgrace to her former self she had become. He wanted her to turn back into the Samira he had known, who would take risks in order to help him. *Him.* Her friend. Not Nicolae. "He'll never forget what you were, Samira. He'll never love you. He can't even bear to have sex with you, and what could possibly stop a man from having sex with a willing, beautiful woman?"

"It's not me, it's the past." She looked on the verge of tears and repeated more softly, "It's not me."

"He'll never love you," Theron said more gently. "Why try to help him? Help me instead, and I can give you the life and the love you want."

She shook her head, tears spilling down her cheeks. "You can't. You don't understand anything."

"I understand you better than you understand yourself. I would suit you just as well as him. Better, for I understand you in ways he never could."

"I don't want you, Theron. And you don't want me—not truly, not as a man would. You don't have a heart."

He wouldn't admit to her that she was right: He *didn't* want her in the way she wanted Nicolae. And thank the goddess of the night for *that!* When he got Vlad's body, he'd be careful never to fall in love and make himself into such a witless creature as Samira had become. But he still needed her help and would use whatever persuasion he could to get it. "You would do well enough with me. At least I would give you the sexual satisfaction you so desperately need." He reached out and stroked his fingertips over her breast, and made her clothes disappear.

"Theron, don't," she said, looking frightened. "Please don't."

"You're still a virgin. Don't you want to know what it's like to feel a man inside you?"

"Not you. . . ."

"Then how about like this?" He changed back into Nicolae, this time as naked as she was. He spoke with Nicolae's voice and said what he knew Samira wanted most to hear. "Let me make love to you. I want you, Samira. I've wanted you from the very beginning."

"You're not Nicolae," she whispered.

"Samira," he said softly, and gently touched her cheek. "Don't be frightened." He bent his head forward and kissed her, although it was only her own pleasure that he felt. The dream version of himself had no real substance, no real way of feeling a touch. It was all an illusion in her mind, and only through her could he feel any of it. He slid one hand around her waist while the other softly stroked the outside of her thigh.

"I want to be inside you, Samira," he said softly, and lay her back on the furs of the bed. His hand moved between her thighs, and they parted as if her body was not hers to control. He stroked his fingers expertly over her feminine folds, playing over her with just the right amount of pressure, arousing her until he could use her own dampness on his fingers.

"I'll give you want you've wanted," he said, and plunged his tongue into her mouth at the same moment he slid his finger deep inside her, the perfection of the dream leaving no space for pain.

She arched her back, moaning, his fingertip pressing inside her on a sensitive spot that made her want more and more. She was as malleable as clay in his hands, giving in with nary a whimper or a struggle.

How different from Lucia. And how strangely disappointing.

"Get off her!" Nicolae suddenly shouted at him.

Theron looked up in surprise, his hand still on Samira's forehead in the Waking World, his feet still planted on her chest as he squatted atop her. Nicolae was standing above him, holding the demon book and looking pale with anger or fear. Theron smirked. "He speaks! And he sees. But he does nothing."

"Get off her, now!"

Theron made a mocking, sad face. What did Samira see in this dolt, anyway? "But I'm having so much fun, Nicolae, and so is she. Don't make us stop now, just when things are getting interesting. She had to lose her virginity *sometime,* after all."

Nicolae looked as if he'd just been punched.

"Theron," he hissed. So Samira had told the princeling about him. Probably all bad, of course.

Theron half-closed his eyes for a moment. "Ohh, she's liking this part."

Nicolae stepped closer and met his eyes, the fear gone now and a deadly determination in his dark brown eyes. "One last time: Get off her."

Theron smiled. "No."

Nicolae dropped to his knees, gripped the book in one arm, and lay his hand on Samira.

An explosion of pain and energy shot Theron in a screaming ball up through the roof. He could see nothing as confusing images and emotions overwhelmed him, submerging his own thoughts beneath a tidal wave of memories and feelings that were not his own:

Flames and battle; clashing swords, bleeding bodies; pain and solitude; faces of men looking at him with an absence of faith; with embarrassment and shame; loneliness and humiliation; injured pride and struggling hope; candlelight, books, and Samira; protectiveness; curiosity; anxiety and energy; determination.

And then, spreading outward from his chest with deep, consuming warmth, came an emotion he had never experienced. He didn't know what it was, but he felt it pushing through his limbs to the tip of every extremity, and up through his neck into his mind. His ability to think evaporated, and he could feel the alien emotion filling his head, altering all that it touched. Panic exploded in his chest as he felt the unknown warmth somehow *changing* him. He struggled to find himself beneath the borrowed emotions, and when he regained a trace of control his vision cleared.

He was high above Lac Strigoi, his wings beating slowly, holding him in midair. The alien warmth began to recede, but it left behind a sense that something had been done to him; he had been invaded and altered.

Fear and fury mingled, and he set his eyes on the church tower far below. He dove downward, with the speed and deadly intent of a hawk after a rodent. He barely flinched as he passed through the roof of the tower and the beams that separated him from Samira and Nicolae.

She was gripping Nicolae's arms, a look of panic on her face. "He bore terrible news, Nicolae! He said—"

Theron dropped down in front of them, furious. "I said what? Are you going to spill secrets not yours to share, Samira? Perhaps I shall do the same for you. There are things your precious Nicolae should know, don't you think?"

"Leave us!" Nicolae ordered.

"I don't think so," Theron said, and walked slowly around them, well out of arm's reach. Those cursed images were still flickering in his mind. Had they came from Nicolae? Flames and pain, and tortured desire . . . and then flashes of that sun-baked warmth, still licking at his mind as if prepared to devour it in suffocating softness. He tried to shut it all out, focusing on Nicolae, who had somehow done this to him. He leapt lightly up onto the table and squatted, looking down at them with a bravado he did not feel, trying not to show that he was still half-stunned. "You shouldn't be so eager to see me gone, Prince Nicolae. There is much I could tell you, about Dragosh and about that little demon clinging to you so prettily. We might even be able to work out a bargain, you and I."

Samira whispered something up to her darling, and he tightened his arm around her, holding her against his chest. Nicolae began to chant.

A new flame of fear flickered to life inside Theron. "What are you up to now?"

Nicolae kept chanting, acknowledging Theron's words with only a small lift of the eyebrows. "*Aska ma douska, ooska ma diiska!*" he finished loudly, with a look on his face like something dramatic had happened.

Theron looked down at his body. Nothing had changed. He looked back up at Nicolae and grinned. "Very good, wizard. You've accomplished absolutely nothing."

Nicolae smiled back and slowly turned his head toward the window on the east side of the tower. "Have I not?"

Theron followed his gaze. When he looked at the window his eyes widened in horror, and he scrambled backward on the table. Dawn was creeping over the landscape, the edge of the sun appearing over the horizon.

Sunlight was destruction to a creature of the Night World: one touch of it and Theron would be burnt. If he remained in the daylight world even if shaded or underground, he would be torn apart by the force of the day. He would cease to exist.

But it had been the middle of the night when he arrived, and Nicolae was but a dabbling half-wizard, not possessed of such powers, he was sure of it! "You can't have—"

"You don't know of what I am capable. I've learned from Samira how fogged is the vision of those of the Night World. Nothing you think you have seen or understood compares to what is seen in the clear light of Day."

Theron gaped at the window. A yellow shaft of sunlight suddenly pierced it, shooting past Theron and burning a bright target on the wall behind him. "Damn you!" Theron cursed; arching away from the shaft. The danger was too great; too much that was unexpected had already happened to him here tonight, and he didn't want this to be the end of all his nights.

He ducked out of the Waking World and into the safety of Night, then flew as quickly as possible away from the dawn and from that book of demon lore. Away, too, from the betraying Samira, who had tossed him so easily aside for her mortal beloved.

As he gained some distance from Lac Strigoi he slowed, realizing he had unthinkingly set his course for Castle Rosu and Lucia. That weird warmth that was still flickering through his body and taking residence in his head seemed to be pushing him to go there.

What was the point of it, though? Lucia would be wearing the amulet, so he couldn't invade her dreams. And she had screamed the moon down out of the sky when she'd woken and seen him in his natural form. She wouldn't welcome his visit any more than Samira had.

There was no point to going, but still he flew onward toward Castle Rosu.

Chapter Fifteen

Lucia dabbed a piece of bread in her bowl of tripe soup and tried to stay awake. She was too tired to eat; too tired to do more than watch as a chunk of her bread got too soggy to hold together and fell off into the broth. A strip of tripe, disturbed from its slumber on the bottom of the bowl, bobbed to the surface. For a moment Lucia was stirred to wakefulness, reminded of the horror of the crotch monster as it emerged from the bathwater.

"Are you feeling well?" Sister Teresa asked from across the table, where she was finishing off her own bowl of soup.

Lucia forced a smile to her lips. "I'm fine. Just tired."

Teresa's watery blue eyes blinked with concern. "You look pale, my dear, and there are shadows under your eyes."

"I haven't been sleeping well." Lucia spoke through a yawn that was stretching her mouth, "I . . . just need to . . . take a nap."

"Perhaps you should go to bed."

"It's the middle of the afternoon."

"Is it?" Teresa asked in some surprise. "I thought it was later. But you should get some rest. You'll grow ill. Go to bed, child."

Lucia smiled and nodded, although she wouldn't follow the reasonable advice. She might take a nap in the garden or on a window seat in the great hall, but she would not lie down in her own bed when she was so weary. To do so would be to risk falling asleep, and remaining so through the night. She had other plans for the night.

For four nights now she had removed the necklace from around her neck before crawling into bed, and then stayed awake through all the hours of darkness, forcing herself to keep her eyes open lest the demon should come. She wanted to talk to him, and to find out what part he had played in that terrible dream. She wanted to know why he had come to *her*, of all people. She was certain that the answer would have something to do with the necklace.

So far, though, she'd neither seen nor sensed the demon, and as night followed night without a sign of him, she began to wonder if he would be returning at all.

Not even the demon wants to spend time with me, a lonely part of her said.

If she was completely honest with herself—which she didn't want to be, though she could hear the truth whispering within her—she would admit that it wasn't really an interrogation she wanted with the demon. She didn't want to tell him to keep away, either; that would be easily enough done just by donning the necklace.

No, what she really wanted from the demon was a bit of companionship.

Crazy, to want companionship from a demon! Yes, she was crazy. But after Mara's harsh words, she didn't feel fit for human company. She was self-conscious around the servants in a way she never had been before, and wondered each time they spoke to one another whether they were whispering about her. There was no one else: Mara hated her, and Sister Teresa . . . well, Sister Teresa's main interest of late seemed to be taking naps.

Lucia saw that Sister Teresa had dozed off once again. Her chin was resting on her chest, and a bit of tripe clung to the front of her black robe. Lucia felt a surge of longing for the way Teresa used to be: alert and attentive, and possessed of a simple wisdom that drew others to her. Teresa was a thoroughly good person.

The demon was bad. He was evil; he was no good. He probably thought that that was a fine way to be, too. Unlike Lucia, he wouldn't lie on his bed and moan about no one liking him. He wouldn't feel lonely and unloved. What did he care?

She wanted not to care, either. If she didn't care, she wouldn't hurt inside, and she wouldn't feel such a miserable stew of self-loathing.

A sigh escaped her as she recognized how foolish she was being. She wasn't going to find friendship with a demon. It was a sign of how desperate for companionship she was that she would even consider it. Sister Teresa would be horrified if she knew that Lucia was welcoming a devil to play.

Besides, with each night that went by it seemed more and more likely that her mind had been playing tricks on her, and there was no demon after all. Cocks might exist just as she had seen in her dream, but that didn't prove that a demon had told her about them.

She'd like another dream of that warrior, Theron, though. The very thought made her shiver with a mixture of fear and delight, and aroused a wicked, determined streak of rebellion. One snippet of their conversation in particular had stuck in her mind, replaying again and again over the days:

"My dreams are my own," she said.

"Are they? Or are they Vlad's, and your brother's, held 'pure' by them because that is how they wish you to be?"

Why shouldn't she be as bad as she wanted to be, in her own dreams? A flame of anger lit again within her, at what the wishes of her brother and Vlad had meant for her: solitude for six years. She needn't be pure and alone in her dreams, though, need she? Especially when the dreams weren't *completely* under her control, as Theron had shown her. She shouldn't be held responsible for anything that happened. Nothing was a sin if it was beyond her control, was it?

Lucia yawned and looked again at Sister Teresa, the nun softly snoring now. They were, the two of them, a sorry pair, muddled with sleepiness and only half in touch with reality.

Lucia spooned up a piece of tripe, the pale strip of flesh quivering in its bath of creamy broth, and wondered if tonight would be the night the demon returned.

Chapter Sixteen

Theron landed on the balcony rail outside Lucia's bed-chamber, a steady rain piercing through him with zings of pain but wetting him not at all. There was neither a moon nor stars in the sky, a thick layer of clouds blotting out all heavenly light, and the darkness was so absolute that even he, with his Night World eyes, saw the landscape only in murky shades of gray.

To his surprise, he could feel a steady stream of Lucia's desire flowing from her chamber. What in Night's name was going on? Had something happened to the necklace? It was a good thing no other incubi had stumbled across Lucia's desire while he was gone; he'd have to do violence to any who did and tried to invade her dreams. No one would touch her. No one but *him*.

The windows to Lucia's room were shut tight against the weather, although a hint of yellow candlelight shimmered in the small, wavy panes of leaded glass. Theron hopped down from the rail and walked across the stone balcony to one of the windows and peered in.

Lucia was sitting up in bed, her head canted awkwardly to the side, her eyes closed and her lips parted. A candle burned low on the bedside table, illuminating a shimmering pile of gold and amethyst at its base.

Good mother of the Night, she had taken it off. Even after what had happened the last time?

He turned to the left and the right, face close to the glass, scanning the room for signs of anything unusual. Mara slept in her accustomed place on the floor. No one else was to be seen; nothing else looked different, and the only hint of movement came from the dance of the candle flame as it was buffeted by drafts through the room.

He looked back over his shoulder, half expecting to see Vlad's brother come lurching out of the shadows of the balcony with his clay jug and a crucifix, reciting a spell to capture him. All that met his ears, though, was the patter of the rain on the balcony and on the tiles of the castle roof, and the only movement was the rain on the rippling puddles that spread like a flood over the slate flooring of the balcony.

Gabriel wouldn't have arrived yet anyway, not unless he'd ridden at a breakneck pace, and he didn't seem the sort to do that, no matter the fierceness of Vlad's threats. It might be another few days before Gabriel reached the foot of this mountain, and perhaps much longer if he encountered any difficulty or became distracted by his poppy juice.

After one more check of the room, Theron slipped through the wall. He stepped over Mara and cautiously made his way to the bed, carefully watching Lucia's face for any sign of wakefulness or even half-wakefulness. She was sitting propped up as if she had been intent on staying awake through the night—there were three more candles lying beside the candlestick, enough to light her through the darkness to dawn. It looked as if she had been afraid to fall asleep or face the darkness.

But why then had she taken off the necklace?

He stepped up onto the bed and squatted down near her, muscles tensed and ready to flee. She looked exhausted: Dark circles were under her eyes, and her breathing was loud and deep.

Could she have been sitting up, waiting for him to return? If this was not a trap, then removing the amulet seemed as clear an invitation as she could possibly give.

Perhaps desire had outweighed fear. She had so much lust flowing through her, she might indeed invite a demon into her bedroom if it meant she would get some relief.

Still, it seemed unlikely.

He crept on hands and knees to the head of the bed. Lucia looked more vulnerable than he remembered. Younger, too. He glanced at the amulet on the bedside table and felt something unfamiliar flicker in his chest. Lucia had some idea of what he was, and still she invited him to visit her.

What a contrast to Samira, who had seemed to be his friend but who now clung to a magic book in order to keep him away.

If he had a heart, he might have been affected by Lucia's show of faith and trust. Being a demon with far too much experience of sexually frustrated women, he'd have to assume it was her craving talking, not her fondness for him as a demon.

He'd still have to corrupt her innocence, of course, but it was nice that she wanted him, even if for this basic purpose. He'd make a special effort to be gentle this time, and to go as slowly as she needed. Maybe that way she wouldn't fight him, and would relax and enjoy herself.

He'd create a different persona than the warrior for this visit. If Lucia didn't recognize that it was he who was giving her the dream, she might fall more easily under its spell. He'd create someone less threatening, to soothe her deepest fears and make her believe that anything done to her body, however odd the act, was good and right.

Don't lie to yourself, a dark voice said inside. *You're a coward; you're afraid she'll grab that amulet and be rid of you the moment she figures out it's you, and then you'll know for certain that you're unwanted. That's why you want to hide behind an unknown face.*

He pushed away the thought. It was nonsense, doubtless caused by that encounter with Nicolae that had scrambled his brain.

No, the truth was that if he was going to debauch Lucia in her dreams, there was no reason they couldn't both have a good time while the deed was done. No one else seemed desperate for the company of either of them; they might as well amuse each other.

He reached out and touched her forehead.

Exhausted from several nights without sleep, Lucia's eyes drooped shut despite her best efforts to stay awake, and she fell into a deeper sleep than she had known for years. She dreamt, and for once was too lost in slumber to be aware that she dreamt:

She sat on a garden bench in the warm, soft sunlight of late spring, the fruit trees in pale, full fresh leaf, and roses fragrant with honey and spice climbed the walls and scattered their red petals on the ground. She was alone with the lazy drone of bees and the songs of the birds, and beyond the garden walls the occasional distant clang of a cow bell or baa of a sheep.

Beyond the garden rose the tall towers of a castle, but one unlike any she had seen before. This one seemed as much concerned with beauty as defense, and colorful pennants flew from atop the ramparts. It was a place of peace, beyond the world she knew.

Her golden brown hair was loose down her back, and flowers twined into a crown sat atop her head. Her gown was of golden silk, trimmed in bands of rose velvet, with velvet ribbons tying her sleeves onto the bodice of her gown. Her fine linen chemise showed through at the joinings, and the delicate embroidery of its edges peeped out over the low neckline of her bodice.

She picked up her mandolin and began to play a light, airy tune of her own devising. Her mind was not on the melody, however; instead, she was thinking that she must make a marvelously charming picture, sitting on the garden bench with the roses in the background, playing her mandolin. She was looking her best, what with her hair nicely arranged and the sun picking out the gold in her hair, and she'd never worn such a pretty dress. She even felt as if her breasts were a little higher and plumper than usual, and her stomach was delightfully free of bloat.

What she needed now was for a handsome prince to come by and notice. If one did, surely he would come speak to her, eager to find out who this beautiful creature could be, his heart set on winning her so that he could take her away with him and love her forever and ever and—

"What a lovely picture you make," a gentle male voice said.

She struck a sour note on the mandolin and it slipped from her hands, falling to the stone path with a hollow twang. She looked up to see a slender young man dressed in white velvet trimmed in gold. His features were fine, but soft, almost feminine. He had blond hair and lightly tanned skin, and bright blue eyes that rivaled the clear sky for intensity.

"Please, don't stop playing," he said.

With a trembling hand she picked up the mandolin and turned it over, examining the damage from the fall. "I think its playing days may be over."

"I shouldn't like to think that I had caused that. Here, let me see it." He sat down beside her on the bench and reached for the instrument.

She handed it to him, too overcome with shyness to do more than meet his eyes for a moment, then look down at her hands, clasped nervously in her lap. No one ever seemed happy to listen to her play the mandolin. That he apparently was happy to do so made her like him already.

"It's no more than a scratch, but I shall have a new one sent to you. A perfect creature such as yourself should never have to touch a flawed instrument."

"I'm not perfect."

"Let me see." He set down the mandolin and then reached over and touched her clasped hands, gently untangling the one closest to him. The unexpected contact startled her to stillness, and she watched as he lifted her hand, laying her long fingers over the side of his own.

With his thumb he lightly stroked her knuckles, and then down over the tops of her fingers, making her heart flutter. "*These* look perfect," he said. He played the edge of his thumb softly against the sensitive tips of her fingers, sending sensation swirling through them. The hand against which hers rested slid away just enough that he could turn it slightly and then stroke the soft flesh of her palm.

She drew in a breath, the innocent touch tingling over her skin and rousing echoing sensations elsewhere in her body. She pressed her thighs tightly together, trying to stem the feeling, and pulled her hand away.

"I have traveled through a hundred countries, seeking a perfect princess to be my bride. Might you be she?" the young man asked.

Lucia shook her head and turned her face shyly away, using her hair to shield her. "I am no creature of perfection, and I am already betrothed."

"Betrothals can be broken, and you may be the one I have been seeking for so very long. Won't you let me see if you are?"

She peeked back at him. He was as handsome as Vlad was in his portrait, but in a much gentler way. He seemed a kind man, one who would not frighten her. He would not force her to do things she did not want to; he wouldn't chase her across a room with his crotch monster like the warrior Theron.

Betrothals could, as he said, always be broken. She cocked a brow in interest. Perhaps he would be a better husband than Vlad. He, at least, was here right now, whereas Vlad seemed to exist more in her imagination than in reality.

"How will you know if I am the one?" she asked, turning a bit more toward him. It wouldn't hurt to *listen*, after all.

He knelt down on the ground, his pristine hose risking stains and dirt. "I must see your toes."

"What?"

"I see your shoe peeping from beneath the hem of your gown. May I touch it?"

This was a very strange thing for a prince to do, she thought, but if it was what he wanted . . . "Very well." She pulled her skirt up by the fabric in her lap, revealing her slippers. They were much nicer than any slippers she remembered owning, these being made of cloth of gold and studded with gems. Their pointed toes curled up at the ends, and a tiny bell tinkled from the tip of the curls.

He lifted her foot into his hand, and carefully eased off the slipper, revealing her foot clad in white silk hose. He let the arch of her foot rest in the palm of one hand, and with the other he softly stroked the sides of her ankle. Her toes curled in pleasure and she sucked in a breath.

"You should not be touching me so."

"I touch you no more closely than did your slipper. Surely you would not say your slipper did more than was proper?"

His fingertips left her ankle and traced lightly over the top of her foot, down to her toes. Her foot arched as if of its own accord, seeking his touch as if she were a lonesome cat. "No, my slipper is blameless," she whispered.

"As am I," he said, and his fingertips brushed back over her foot and upward, his warm hand curling around her ankle and grasping it firmly for a moment before releasing and then gliding lightly, quickly, up to her knee. His fingertips found the tender place behind her knee and played there, massaging gently.

Muscles deep inside her contracted in surprised pleasure, and she stared in shock at her skirt, the fabric concealing from her view the prince's hand on her leg. "I . . . I think you should take your hand down now. My slipper never ventured so high."

"No, but your garter did." As he said so, his questing fingers found the band of her garter, tied tight above her knee. With a few tugs it was undone and falling away from her. His hand, large and warm, lay against her bare thigh, and then it slid with the hose down over her knee. The woven fabric of the hose dropped easily without the garter to suspend it. The young man's hand followed it down the front of her leg, and then he grasped her ankle again, a brief shackling that sent a bolt of sensation up her leg.

"What are you doing?" Lucia whispered, and her breath caught on a gasp.

"I must see your foot if I am to know if you are the perfect one I have been seeking." The look he cast her was not entirely guileless. He eased the hose off her foot, leaving her toes bare in the sunlight.

"Is it perfect?" she asked, peering over her knee. This was a little too strange to be thrilling.

"I'm not sure yet." He lifted her foot up to his face as if he were smelling a rose.

She leant back, forced to by her rising leg, her hands bracing her on the bench. With her leg lifted up, she could feel the cool air of the day drifting up under her skirt, and she fretted about how much he could see. A moment later she had something else to worry about: He was raising her toes toward his mouth.

Her eyes widened. "What are you—"

173

"Just a kiss. My princess will taste perfect everywhere, from her lips to her toes."

"No, no, no," she said, and this time did try to jerk her foot out of his grip. He held tight, with more strength than she would have guessed resided in such a slender, gentle-looking man. "Feet are *dirty*," she cried.

"Yours are perfect." He parted his lips and sucked her second toe into his mouth.

Lucia yelped, and tried again to jerk away. But again he held fast, and as she struggled his tongue went to work, swirling around her toe and dabbing down into the space between it and its companions. She laughed once in embarrassment, and then ceased her struggles for a long, stunned moment, his tongue and the gentle suction doing strange things to her body. It was wrong, what he was doing: dirty, obscene and unnatural, ludicrous . . .

And it felt so good.

She weakly tried again to jerk away, and he looked up at her from under his brows, her toe still in his mouth. She felt another laugh begin to build in her throat, but then he ran his soft yet rough wet tongue deeply between her toes, and the laugh turned into a soft moan of pleasure.

With a long, slow suck he drew her toe out of his mouth and then lowered her foot back to the ground.

"Are you sure my toes are perfect?" she asked, wishing he hadn't stopped.

"Your toes are perfect," he assured her, "but there are other places I need to check." Still kneeling, he reached for the ties of her bodice.

She clasped her hands over the velvet ribbon and over his own hands. "No, I can't."

"If you are to be my betrothed, I must know that you are perfect. We will see all of each other on our wedding night, so there is no sin in seeing each other now." He plucked at the ribbon, and her hands on his were no hindrance at all.

"But—" she protested, although she did nothing more to stop him. She liked the feel of his hands at work above her chest, and wanted him to glimpse her breasts, even though she knew she should not.

"I take no more liberties than does your chemise. You do not accuse *it* of being wicked, although it presses itself against your body and lies over your breasts." The tie at her neckline came undone, and he slowly pulled the ribbon loose from the eyelets.

She felt the relief of the pressure from the garment, her breasts unconfined. She closed her eyes, too shy to watch as the young man tugged the neck of her chemise down low. She felt her nipples pop free of the fabric, and a wave of embarrassment swept through her that was as much arousal as it was shame.

She waited for a touch to her breasts, but instead she felt his hand again sliding up her leg, this time lifting her gown and chemise up above her knees. His hand slid along the top of her thigh, easing the fabric upward, until she was bare from the tops of her thighs down. He shifted, finding a place between her knees, his body moving closer to hers. The width of his body forced her thighs apart, leaving her most intimate area all but exposed.

She murmured in protest, but he ignored her, his hand still moving higher on her thigh until he came to her hip. He splayed his fingers over the top of her thigh, his thumb pressing into the crease where leg met body. His other hand, outside of her gown, went to her waist, sliding around to the back and holding her steady.

Lucia opened her eyes. The man's face was close to hers, no more than a few inches separating them. He wasn't looking at her face, though; he was gazing at her breasts.

She sat motionless, his gaze almost tangible on her skin. She glanced down at her breasts and watched as her flesh tightened, her nipples puckering as if with cold, although she knew that it was the prince's gaze that was affecting her so. Waves of desire ebbed and flowed through her, and she silently urged him to touch her.

"Are they perfect?" she managed to ask, as she swayed with the force of her desire. Oh, how she wanted them to be perfect for him.

"I shall have to taste one to see." He slowly bent his head and took a nipple into his warm mouth, his tongue circling around and then flicking against its tip. His hand on her lower back pulled her closer, until she could feel the velvet of his *pourpoint* against her secret place. The hand atop her thigh moved around to her buttocks, squeezing one cheek even as his mouth pulled harder on her nipple.

Her breath seemed to leave her, and Lucia found herself falling slowly backward. The man was supporting her, lowering her down and turning her so that she lay along the length of the bench, with her legs over the end, her knees bent and her feet on the ground. He was still between her legs, and the hand under her skirt slid even higher, until he could splay his fingers across her lower belly.

He rolled her nipple between his lips, and then with a pulling suck released her. She glanced down at herself and saw that her aureole had turned bright pink, her nipple long and erect.

"Your breasts *are* perfect," he said.

"Then am I the one? Will you take me away with you?"

"There is still one more place I must see."

"Where is that?" she asked with trepidation.

The hand splayed on her belly moved downward, and his palm covered her *there*.

"Oh, oh, no . . ." she said, and tried to close her thighs.

His body blocked her efforts, and then he moved his palm lightly over her. The sensation was unlike anything she'd ever known, sending tingling arousal through her like heat, but he was touching her *there*, in the dark, dirty place, and she couldn't enjoy it. "Stop, you mustn't . . ." *He* couldn't be enjoying it, either. Surely it was like touching a filthy animal.

"Shhh," he soothed, and pushed her skirts up past her thighs, past her hips, until they were at her waist and she was revealed to him in her entirety.

Lucia rolled her head to the side, eyes closed tight in humiliation. He *couldn't* want to look at her there. She was beastlike down there, overgrown with hair and damp folds of flesh. Every dirty function of her body had its outlet down there. It was as if the light of day was shining on her deepest, most shameful secret, and he was right there witnessing it.

"There is no perfection there," she said softly, still ineffectually trying to squeeze her thighs shut.

She felt his fingertip brush down over her, his touch

like a rivulet of cool desire licking through her shame. "I see nothing but perfection. You are beautiful."

"No . . ."

"Beautiful, in all your parts."

"Not *there*."

"You are a garden enclosed," he said reverently, and she recognized the words as borrowed from the Song of Solomon. "'A spring shut up, a fountain sealed.' I would unseal you, if I could," the man said.

"I can't; it's not right," she protested feebly, his touch still stroking lightly upon her. "Please, cover me." She reached down with her hands, trying to lower her skirts, but she stopped at her lower belly, too embarrassed to touch his own hand while he did that to her.

"'Awake, O north wind; and come, thou south; blow upon my garden, that its spices may flow out,'" he said softly, almost singing. "'Let my beloved come into his garden, and eat his pleasant fruits.' Let me taste of you, and know that you are perfect."

Lucia forced herself to open her eyes and meet his gaze. His brilliant blue eyes were unwavering, telling her without words that he *would* continue, whether she gave permission or not. As their gazes held, a dim recognition flickered to life within her. Hadn't she seen—

But before she could complete the thought he lowered his head, and she felt the soft, damp touch of his mouth upon her. Her thighs shut tight against him, trying to make him stop, but then the intimacy of his cheeks pressed into her soft thighs was even worse, and she parted them again.

She did not know what he was doing down there, but his lips and tongue seemed to be everywhere at once, swirling and stroking. His touch was inescapable, and was beginning to draw a response from her despite herself; there was one spot that he touched upon again and again that made her weak, and drained from her the will to protest.

A part of her was still weltering in shame, though. Did he not *know* that he was putting his mouth upon a place so dirty and foul? He could not be enjoying it, he could not think it pleasant. He must be wishing he could stop and leave her, now that he knew how nasty she was there. She reached down and gingerly touched his hair. "Leave be; I am not perfect, I am not the one you seek."

He lifted his head and rose up so that he could see her face. "You are as a lily; you are a flower in the field, and you are perfect. You are beautiful. The only imperfection," he said, and reached forward to touch her forehead with one fingertip, "is in the vision here. You do not see that you were created with beauty in all your parts."

She had no answer for him. *He* did not see her as dirty and foul. *He* truly did find her perfect and beautiful in every part.

"I will show you how beautiful you are," he said, and lowered his head once again.

She closed her eyes, overwhelmed as a delicious tension tightened the muscles of all her body as his tongue did its work, worshipping her with its caresses. Each lick and stroke felt reverent, as if he were bowing down before a goddess and seeking her favor, begging for it with each touch of pleasure he gave her.

She felt his tongue trace over the slit from which her blood flowed. She wanted to roll aside in shame, but the steady stroking kept her motionless, showing as it did no hesitation, no revulsion, nothing but a constant purpose. The tip of his tongue forced its way into that small opening, a soft and warm invasion that had her clenching her fists. She wanted it *more,* and she wanted it not at all.

The tip of his tongue pressed in and out against her slit, and he used his thumb to stroke her higher, up in the sensitive spot he had found before. Of their own volition her thighs parted fractionally more, as if her body could encourage a deeper thrust of his tongue.

For she *wanted* that. She wanted to feel something thicker and more substantial pressing its way inside her. She wanted . . .

Her eyes opened to the bright light of the garden as she realized what she wanted. She wanted *it,* the thing, the crotch monster. She wanted this man, this blond prince with his intense blue eyes, to untie his *pourpoint* and lower his hose and braies, and release the snake-like creature within. She wanted to feel it force its way inside her, parting her, filling her, reaching deep inside her in a way that his tantalizing tongue could not.

In the same moment she thought it, she remembered where she had seen those eyes of such a brilliant blue before: the warrior. And with that thought she realized that she was dreaming.

And if she was dreaming, then the demon must be in her bedroom, his own eyes shining like blue flame in the darkness.

The prince's tongue delved within her, his thumb stroking expertly over her place of pleasure, her body enthralled to his touch. Her loins were captive to him, her hips rocking in sync with the thrusts of his tongue and the strokes of his thumb. It felt as if her flesh was swelling and becoming more sensitive with each moment, pursuing its own end no matter what her mind was thinking.

And the demon was probably crouched atop her at this very moment.

The prince left off with his tongue and replaced it with his finger, the tip sliding into her opening, gently stretching her and tracing a small circle just within her. She arched her hips up against him, urging him to do more, to press harder.

Instead, his mouth took hold of her sensitive place, sucking the tip of it between his lips and stroking the captured flesh with his tongue. His finger kept circling within her entry, never quite deep enough to give her all that she wanted.

Perhaps it was actually the demon himself who was crouched between her legs right now, in disguise; perhaps it was a demon mouth that laved her loins. The thought perversely excited her, increasing the pleasure coursing through her. It was building, her need for it to continue growing stronger with each rock of her hips.

This was a demon, and he thought her perfect. He said so, and she could sense that it was true. Yes, it made sense, it fit, for she was loathsome in the eyes of her human companions. To a demon she would be beautiful. Let him have her, then!

"Theron," she said softly, arching her back. "Is that your name?" she knew it was. "Tell me your name. *Theron,*" she moaned.

"Yes."

She tilted her head up to see him. He had stopped his caresses and was looking at her, his eyes blazing. "You are the dark-haired warrior," she said. "And you are the demon crouching on my chest."

The statement hung in the air, the silence between

them interrupted only by the incongruous, innocent sound of birdsong, her pleasure hanging as suspended as the accusation.

At last he said again, "Yes." As he said it, he slid his finger deeper inside her, stretching her, the feeling unlike anything she had ever tried to imagine. His fingertip found a new place of pleasure within her and massaged it, the touch sending sensation echoing out to the peak of her folds, as if the two were connected. His hand rocked against Lucia's loins, his finger thrusting gently now. She arched her head back, her eyes closing, unable to do anything else.

She hadn't truly believed that there was a way for a man to come into her body, but now she finally understood. *This* was part of the secret of what happened between a man and a woman. It was forbidden knowledge, as it should be. She felt his mouth lower once again to her folds, his finger still deep inside her.

"What . . . what is happening?" she asked between breaths, as she felt her body tensing and her heart begin to race. It was as if she were running some great distance, only she was not moving at all.

He didn't answer her, except to slow his tongue and use it to circle with delicate precision her most sensitive spot. His finger inside her stopped its thrusting and instead pressed firmly on that hidden place.

Her whole body tensed in response, and it was as if she was poised on the brink of some great chasm. He flicked his tongue once more against her and she went over the edge, falling weightlessly into wave after wave of contracting pleasure. She could feel her flesh around his embedded finger pulsing, muscles she hadn't known she had gripping him again and again. The contractions grew farther and farther apart, diminishing in size, and as her legs started to shake she closed her thighs against him.

Her heartbeat slowed, and a warm languor stole through her body. She felt him slowly slide his finger out of her body, and she let her thighs fall away from him, not caring now that she lay exposed to all the world. With her eyes closed she lay beneath the warm sun, feeling as if she were floating, feeling for this moment as if it was good and right that her body be bare, her most intimate areas exposed. The use to which her body had just been put was beautiful, in a way that a mirror could never tell her.

The blissful exhaustion stayed upon her for a few minutes more, and then her mind found its powers of thought and she remembered who she was with.

She blinked her eyes open. With that overpowering need for pleasure released, every thought and feeling that her need had overwhelmed came bobbing back to the surface. *Mother Mary protect me, did I just let a demon lick my loins?*

The thought was enough to jerk her out of her lassitude, and she quickly sat up, shoving her skirts down over her legs. Her breasts were still exposed, and with a small yelp of surprise—she'd forgotten they were bare—she pulled the necklines of her chemise and gown back up, tying the ribbon of the gown.

Theron was standing a few feet away, apparently studying the roses climbing the stone wall. His white clothes were spotless.

But they would be, she reminded herself; this was a dream. "This is not your true form," she said aloud, stating the thought as it occurred to her.

He turned away from the roses and walked back to her, looking down at her where she sat on the bench.

He arched one dark blond brow. "Questions again?"

"Yes." She crossed her arms over her stomach, as if she could cover up now all that had been so thoroughly exposed a few minutes before.

"I am not here for questions, Lucia." He reached down and stroked the side of her cheek. The touch sent a tingle down her neck, and incredibly she felt her body respond. He let his fingertips follow the trail of that shimmering sensation, as if he knew exactly where it was in her. "A woman can have her climax again and again. You are satisfied now, but the potential for passion is still burning within you. I can stoke your fires and quench them, over and over again."

She leant away from his touch, although she wanted to lean into it. "Why? Why have you come?"

His fingertips trailed down over her collarbone and then back up her neck. He held her chin in his hand, and with the pad of his thumb softly brushed her lower lip. "To fulfill your every secret desire."

Her lips parted, and she felt the hunger begin once more in her body.

No. She didn't want to succumb again, not without some answers first.

But he forestalled her by saying, "There are no questions that need their answers so quickly. There is always time for pleasure." His hand slid around to the back of her head and he slowly lowered his mouth to hers, laying his lips gently against Lucia's own and kissing her softly.

Her heartbeat quickened, and she was aware not only of the kiss but of Theron's male body looming over her smaller one. And, too, she knew now some of what he might persuade her to do.

No. She clenched her fists, digging her fingernails into her palms, trying to keep her senses. If she let him continue, she would learn nothing about the demon behind the illusion. She had to regain control of herself.

But it felt so *good*, his kiss . . .

His tongue stroked her lips, reminding her of what it had felt like when it had stroked her elsewhere. Her body reacted as if it were her nether folds he was laving and not her mouth, and she felt a clench of desire in her loins.

What would it matter if she let him do as he wished with her once more? There would be time for questions afterward.

No!

Against all the urgings of her hungry body, and still caught halfway between sleep and wakefulness, she forced herself to open her real eyes, in her chamber at Castle Rosu.

The demon filled her vision.

Chapter Seventeen

The demon's hand was stretched out and touching her forehead. It made everything solidify, become terrifyingly real. A rising shriek of horror rose up inside Lucia, a hysterical need to flail and escape. She wanted to scream; she tried to scream. She couldn't.

The realization made her terror all the worse, for she knew that the demon had control of her.

Theron was squatting on her thighs instead of her chest this time, as she was sitting upright in her bed. She couldn't feel his weight on her, although her limbs felt strangely heavy. She tried to move them and could not. Nor could she turn away from his touch to her forehead.

She felt as if she couldn't breathe, as if she needed to gasp for air, only her chest wouldn't move. Panic flooded through her, and the dream still stumbling along in her mind faded to nothing, the prince in white disappearing. Theron finally noticed her diverted attention and dropped his hand from her forehead.

The breath came back to her, and she suddenly felt as if she could move again, if she wished. She realized that she was not fully awake; she was, instead, in one of those trances that she had spent her lifetime practicing. Fortunately, her trance state—which was not a true wakefulness—allowed her to force the shrieking part of herself back behind a wall. The only way to deal with having a huge naked man with bat wings squatting on her thighs was to remain as outwardly calm as possible—to show weakness was to be crushed.

"Please get off my legs," Lucia said as calmly as she could, trying to keep her voice from squeaking or quavering.

"I know I'm not hurting you."

"Please get off."

He shrugged and stepped down off her thighs. "Very well."

The shrieking part of her paused in her noise-making, Theron's willingness to do as bade doing a bit to ease her tension. She let out another short yap of a shriek anyway, like a barking dog giving warning that while partially pacified, she was still on her guard.

Theron rustled his wings, rearranging them so that they would not interfere as he sat tailor-fashion on the bed, facing her. The position left his genitals fully exposed. Lucia blinked and shifted her gaze up to his face.

He was a handsome creature, with masculine features that were almost too perfect. His black, glossy hair hung in waves down to his shoulders, and his jet brows were perfect, smooth arcs over his brilliant eyes with their thick black lashes. A hint of beard shadow tinted his jaw and chin, nicely setting off the graceful, subtle curves of his lips. She could see in his features hints of both the warrior and the blond prince; they could have all three been brothers.

"I have many things I need to ask you."

Theron sighed dramatically. "Women. You always need to talk, don't you?"

His exasperation was an act, though, meant to cover the unease that was creeping up his spine. He studied Lucia as she sat in the last flickering light of the candle flame, her face eerily calm and composed. He did not know exactly what was going on behind that lovely facade, which both alarmed and, perversely, excited him. He hadn't been in full control during the dream, either: He had only been able to seduce her to a degree, and at a speed, which she wished to be seduced.

It was proving an unexpected pleasure to match wits and wills against her, using his best wiles to circumvent her barriers, digging through her thoughts and finding the exact recipe for her seduction. She was a challenge, and it had been thousands of years since he had faced any challenge in a human woman.

It had been thousands of years since he had faced any true challenge at all, for that matter. At least in his work. That was why he'd been so miserable: The existence of a dream demon had seemed to have nothing new left to offer him. What a gift, then, to be so unexpectedly intrigued and entertained, even if it was en route to a greater goal. And even if that entertainment carried with it a wary uneasiness. He didn't know of what Lucia might be capable.

"I will answer your questions," Theron said, deciding on a game, "but for each one I answer, you must answer a question of mine."

Lucia's eyelids fluttered in surprise. "You've seen all that is in my mind already, haven't you?"

"Not all." With her, he suspected vast stretches of her mind had been yet concealed from him. And with her strong imagination, even he had not always been certain if what he saw in her mind was real or fantastic. "So ask your questions with care, because you will have to give to me as much as you receive." He was curious if she would limit her questions in fear of what she might be asked in return.

He hoped she *would* limit her questions, now that he thought about it. He didn't want to answer some—but then again, part of him liked the idea of someone at last showing interest in *him*. In his personality, in his desires.

"Will you tell the truth?" Lucia asked.

"Demons always tell the truth."

She blinked at him, doubt filling her golden brown eyes. "But you bring dreams that are lies."

"True." He shrugged, thinking of his lies to Vlad when making their bargain. "Perhaps we lie sometimes, in extraordinary circumstances, but for the most part, no."

Although he knew that in her trance state she could not frown, he felt the force of one in the stare she gave him.

"All right, all right. I promise not to lie to *you*," he gave in. "Are you satisfied?"

"Neither will you give me tricky answers."

He muttered but did not respond. He liked tricky answers.

"And you will cover yourself. I do not wish to speak to you with *that* staring at me." Her gaze flicked to his groin.

His penis bobbed in response and started to thicken and grow. It was her own attraction to it that was causing the change. "Now who is lying?"

"It's distracting," she complained.

He laughed. That, at least, was not a lie. "I have nothing with which to cover it."

"A pillow."

He passed his hand through the bedding on which he sat. "I cannot move solid matter. You can see and hear me, but you cannot touch me. It is only for comfort that I appear to use the floor and bed as you do."

"Then turn away. I will not stare at the thing!" She said it with more force than he'd yet heard from her in one of her trance states.

He smiled. "It seems to me that you can hardly take your eyes off it." Nonetheless, he unfolded himself from his tailor-fashion position and stretched out on his stomach beside her, propping himself up on his elbows. "My wings need space," he said, and nodded his head once in the direction of his back.

Her eyebrows twitched, and as her gaze traveled over his great black wings he thought she looked frightened.

"I'm not going to leap upon you," he reassured her.

Lying like this, he was closer to her, and he liked the forced intimacy of it. Of course he'd been as close and closer to thousands of women, but they'd all been asleep. Never had he spoken to one like this.

He wanted to reach out and touch her. *Really* touch her, as a human man would touch a human woman. And he wanted her to see him with eyes that were not entranced.

Her eyelids fluttered nervously, and there was a quiver in her voice. He might be imagining it, but it seemed as if more of her emotions were showing through her trance state. "You have such big wings. They are quite impressive. And you yourself are so very . . . long."

He grinned again. "Say the exact same things about Vlad's cock on your wedding night and you'll be well on your way to a happy marriage."

She shook her head infinitesimally. "I don't think Vlad would like that."

"You would be right."

"You haven't truly met him, have you?" she asked, sounding surprised.

"Is that your first question?"

"Is that *yours?*" she countered.

"And a second question for you."

She pressed her lips together in a tight, annoyed line.

"All right. Just the one. Yes, I have met him," he admitted, and wondered if it was a mistake to do so. He had said he wouldn't lie, though, and there seemed far more potential for amusement if he played by the rules. "And now my question for you: Why did you take off the amulet tonight?"

"Amulet? You mean the necklace?"

He nodded.

"I . . ."

"No lies."

"I wasn't going to lie," she protested.

"A long pause sounds like someone preparing a lie."

"Well, I wasn't going to. That's a demon's way of thinking."

"It's the thinking of experience. And you are not answering the question."

"If you'd stop distracting me—"

"Answer."

She blew out an annoyed breath, the effect strange given the relative stillness of her features as she did it. "I took the necklace off because I wanted to see you again."

"Obviously. But why?"

"It's not your turn."

"But—"

She stared at him.

"Very well," he groused, and then muttered under his breath, "*Sun-baked daughter of a—*"

"I *can* hear you."

"I know."

"Did you meet Vlad before or after you met me?" she asked.

"Before. Why did you want to see me again?"

"I wanted to talk to you and find out who or what you were. I had been waiting to see you again since I was fourteen. I knew you would come back. Or I—"

He felt the hairs rise on the back of his neck. "You *did* know. I remember now: You told me we would meet each other again."

"Did I? I don't remember that."

"What did you mean when you said it?" he asked. Had she meant they would meet as they were now, or would he get Vlad's body and see her again that way? What did she know?

She shook her head. "I don't recall what I meant. Sometimes I know things but cannot explain them. I have . . . visions."

"I hope you don't tell people about them," he said quickly, feeling a spurt of concern.

Concern? Since when did he feel concern for humans? But there it was: He didn't like the idea of what would happen to her if she started proclaiming herself

193

a visionary. Some people in the area had a great fondness for burning those they thought were witches. He
didn't want that to happen to her.

"No, I don't tell anyone. My turn to ask a question:
What are you? Don't just give me one word. Explain."

"I'm a dream demon, of course," he said with some
surprise. "I thought you understood that."

"Dream demon?"

"We are the Oneroi, the one thousand children of
Sleep. The grandchildren of Nyx, Queen of the Night,
who is herself the only child of the vastness of the beginning: Chaos."

A small frown forced its way between her brows. "Do
you exist only in dreams, then? Or half-dreams? And
this question is part of my original one, so don't try to
count it."

"We exist in the Night World, with all the rest of Nyx's
descendants. We visit your mortal dreams, though—
when a human mind is in need of more help than its
own imagination can provide."

"So this is *help* that you give?" she asked incredulously.

"Yes, of course. I am an incubus: The dreams I give
are of sex. Many, many women need dreams of good
sex. They have such poor experiences in their waking
lives—precious few of them even know what it is to
climax—and they cannot imagine on their own what it
feels like to be properly taken by a man."

"So you do this to hundreds of women."

"I've given dreams to tens of thousands."

"Oh."

"That bothers you?"

"No, not at all."

He frowned. It sounded like a lie. An outlandish notion hit him: "You . . . you aren't jealous, are you?" He felt like an idiot for even asking.

"Of course not!"

"Those others didn't mean anything. It was just—"

"I'm not jealous! You're a demon, for heaven's sake, not a man! And not my fiancé!"

Those words shouldn't have affected him, but they did. He didn't think it was just because they touched on Vlad's breaking of the bargain, either.

Son of the Moon, what was wrong with him? Theron rolled his shoulders, feeling strange, and trying uselessly to stretch the feeling out of him. He hadn't been feeling himself all night, since that encounter with Nicolae. Something had infected him, altered him, and now he was almost *hurt* that she was saying she didn't care what he did. How odd, and . . .

"I didn't talk to any of those other women as I talk to you, if that makes any difference," he assured her. He wanted her to care.

"I said I wasn't jealous."

"I *couldn't* talk to them. You're different."

"Am I?" she asked, softening a bit, caught by the promise of flattery.

"You must know you are. This—what we are doing here—it isn't even possible with anyone else. You have rare talents, Lucia. And a rare courage. I don't know of anyone else who would seek to speak with one such as myself without ulterior motives."

"I am not impressive."

"You've had no chance to show all that you are. Why do you spend so much time in daydreams?"

The corners of her lips turned down, and he thought

he caught a sudden sheen in her eyes. She breathed deeply, and her breath was jagged. "I daydream because I have no one and nothing else. How else am I to fill my days until Vlad comes for me?" She looked away from him, staring into nothingness for several moments before she spoke again, this time even more softly. "My world is empty, and worse than merely boring. There is nothing in it to which I can aspire, nothing new to do, no challenges."

Her words resonated inside him, voicing as they did what he himself was feeling. *No one and nothing else.* How sad.

"My turn," Lucia said lightly, as if trying to break the newly somber mood. "Why did you visit me when I was fourteen?"

"I . . ." *Dawn,* he silently swore. He didn't want to explain all of *that.* She wasn't ready for that much truth. She would loathe him if she knew that he was indirectly responsible for her being here at Castle Rosu.

"No lies," she warned, and he almost feared for a moment that she could see his thoughts.

"I was watching a succubus visit your brother, Dragosh, and when he woke up and went down the hall to check on you, I followed. I was curious." That was the truth, as simple as he could make it.

"Curious about *me?*"

"Many events have revolved around you. Lives have changed course because of you."

She shook her head, the movement barely discernible. "No, that can't be right. I have been stuck away at convents and in this castle. I have done nothing of any import and can mean nothing to anyone."

"You are the eye of a hurricane, the silent place of still air around which the violent forces blow."

"But why me?" she said, in almost a wail.

He shrugged. "Destiny, perhaps. Or an effect of those uncanny abilities of yours. Yours will not be a quiet life."

"It's been deafeningly quiet up until now," she remarked bitterly.

"You'll hear the howl of the winds soon enough."

Her bitterness gave way to fear. "Don't say things like that. They scare me."

"You wanted the truth. It is not my fault it is not as pretty as you wish."

"I begin to feel as if no truths are pretty, demon."

"I'm sure that some must be. Just don't ask me what they are. And now it's my turn to ask a question. Wasn't there more to why you took off the amulet than curiosity?" The question burned at him. *In* him.

"Like what?"

He shrugged one shoulder, wing fluttering slightly. For some reason, he was terribly anxious to hear the answer. Anxious, even, about asking the question. A hint of . . . was it embarrassment? vulnerability? was tingling uncomfortably through him. "You tell me."

She opened her mouth to answer, but it never came.

Chapter Eighteen

Mara woke to the sound of Lucia's voice. At first she hoisted her blanket up over her ear, trying to shut out the soft sounds of her mistress's speech; but then, as her sleepy mind woke completely, she realized that Lucia shouldn't be talking to *anyone* at this time of the night. Who was here? Mara was facing the opposite direction and was afraid that if she rolled over, whoever was there might notice she was awake. Instead, she pulled the blanket down from her ear and tried to listen.

"I have done nothing of any import and can mean nothing to anyone," Lucia said. A long moment of silence passed, and then Lucia spoke again. "Why me?"

Mara carefully rolled over, trying to make no noticeable movement. It sounded as if Lucia was having a conversation, only no one was answering.

"It's been deafeningly quiet up until now," Lucia said.

Mara felt a chill run up her neck when she saw the girl. The guttering candlelight revealed her sitting up in bed, her face composed in an expression of unnatural peace. As she spoke, her gaze seemed fastened upon the empty space beside her on the bed, as if there was someone there who was listening.

"Don't say things like that. They scare me."

Holy Mother of God, Mara silently swore. This scared her, too! Who or *what* was Lucia talking to, and was it answering her back? Mara had seen her mistress in trances many times before, but she'd never held one-sided conversations while in them.

Strange things had been happening at night this past week. There had been her own weird dream about the necklace, and then waking to find that she had gotten out of bed and removed it from Lucia's neck. Mara had no idea why she had done that. Then there had been Lucia's screaming fit, ending with the word *cock,* and now this conversation with no one.

She huddled down deeper in her blankets, her skin crawling with gooseflesh. She wanted no part in whatever wicked thing was going on. Even as she huddled down, though, she felt a stab of guilt. She'd been feeling bad ever since she'd told Lucia exactly how she felt about her. It had all been true, but it had been more than anyone should have to hear about themselves.

"I begin to feel as if no truths are pretty, demon."

Mara shivered, Lucia's words strangely fitting to her thoughts. But . . . *demon?*

Ohhh. Oh, no. Mara peered over the top of her blanket. Surely there was no one there, not even a demon? It didn't look like it.

Still, she should wake Lucia from her trance. She knew she should. It was the right thing to do.

She clung more tightly to the blanket, and realized she was trembling. She didn't want to risk it; didn't want to find out too late that there was a demon on Lucia's bed.

She knew what Vlad would do to her, though, if it turned out that a demon had been visiting Lucia and she, Mara, had done nothing about it. She wouldn't count on her fellow servants at Castle Rosu not to tell tales about her to Vlad, once he came. They did not seem to like her much. They were jealous, of course, of both her beauty and her position.

With the prospect of an angry Vlad more frightening than even a demon, Mara quietly crawled out of her nest on the floor and approached the bed.

"Like what?" Lucia said to no one, staring at her bedcovers as if there was someone lying there, talking to her. The barest shadow of a smile showed on the girl's lips. Mara felt her skin crawl and was overcome with a sudden need to break Lucia's eerie trance. "I suppose if I was to be honest, I'd say—"

Mara dashed the last few feet to the bed and waved her hand in front of Lucia's face. "My lady! My lady! Wake up!"

Lucia blinked rapidly, but her flat expression did not change.

Mara grabbed her shoulders and shook her. Lucia was stiff for a few shakes and then suddenly her muscles relaxed and she collapsed onto the pillows.

"My lady? Are you all right?"

Lucia looked confusedly about her, as if seeking someone who was not there; then her gaze settled on Mara's face. "Mara? What are you doing awake?"

"I would ask the same thing of you. You were in one of your trances, but you were talking to someone. I thought I had better wake you."

Lucia looked around her again, seeming agitated. "I'm quite all right." She sounded annoyed.

"I heard you say . . ."

Lucia's gaze snapped to Mara's face. "What did you hear me say?"

Mara's heart tripped, and she realized with a start that she was suddenly intimidated. In the hard focus of Lucia's gaze Mara could see hints of the future queen the girl might possibly become. In the past any of Lucia's attempts at imperiousness had been tempered by her vague good humor and overall air of weakness.

Mara realized the disappearance of the good humor—at least as directed at herself—was her own sorry fault. She'd done a thorough job of burning that bridge.

Lord preserve her. What a stupid thing to do.

"I . . . thought I heard you say 'demon.' I was worried for your welfare and thought I should wake you."

"Did you see a demon?"

"No, but—"

"And do I look as if any harm has been done me?"

Mara bowed her head. "No." *Damn.* She could see her future dimming. Now that she'd finally revealed to Lucia all her pent-up annoyances of six years and could see past them, she saw that in the process she'd done a good job of ensuring that she would be left to fend for herself as soon as Lucia married. The girl would find a more friendly maid, and Mara could forget about living at court.

Instead, she'd probably have to marry a sheep farmer and break her back over the work of a farm wife. *Damn. Damn, damn, damn.*

"I'm sorry, my lady. And if I could, I would apologize

for those cruel things I said to you. You didn't deserve them."

Mara waited, her eyes lowered, not daring to check Lucia's reaction and give herself away as less than perfectly sincere.

Moments ticked by, and then at last Mara felt Lucia touch her hand. "We won't speak of it again," the girl said.

Mara looked up. The forgiving, accepting expression she had hoped to see on Lucia's face was not there. The girl looked, instead, like someone who might not speak of the injury but had not given up thinking about it, and who had not given up considering what Mara's motives might be for apologizing.

Damn.

Chapter Nineteen

He had come. Lucia dozed in a window seat, her head tilted back against the stone wall, the gray light of the rain-soaked day touching weakly on her skin. She left the casement ajar despite the cold and damp, the coolness refreshing against her skin, occasional drops of rain blown in to darken the fabric of her gown. The breeze gently buffeted the casement in short bursts, its soft, hollow howl curling around the castle.

He had come. She was still stunned by all that had happened the night before, all that she had *allowed* to happen. She had talked to a demon, the creature lying on her bed with all the familiarity of a bosom friend.

Even more shocking, she had allowed that demon to invade her dreams and . . .

A clenching shudder of desire and pleasure went through her, even as she shut out the memories of what had happened in her sleep. It was too shameful. She had been without modesty, without honor. She had let herself lie exposed to him with only the slightest of coaxing. And she had felt such a wonderful burst of feelings and sensations . . . Her cheeks heated, and she shied away from the images each time they came to her mind.

It might have only been a fantasy, but to her body it felt as if it had been real. Worse yet, her body wanted to do it again. Desperately.

There were more questions she wanted to ask the demon. She wouldn't be able to do it while in a trance again, though—not with Mara in the room. She'd have to manage to do it while asleep, taking control of her dream no matter what that demon tried to do to her.

She shivered in delighted anticipation of just what he might come up with, and as quickly was flooded with shame for her reaction. He was a *demon,* she reminded herself.

Yes, but he had talked to her. He had told her she was beautiful and perfect. He had touched her, and made her feel things such as she had never imagined. And it had all seemed for her benefit.

Just as Sister Teresa had warned: The Devil would have a handsome face and shower her in flattery. The warning was but a sigh against a storm of temptation.

A thought of Vlad flitted briefly to the surface of her mind, and a feeling that she was betraying him in the most wicked of ways. He would never know, though, that while she might be virgin still in her body, her mind was far from pure.

Another rush of shame went through her, that she should have such a deceitful streak within her.

But even as she felt it, she knew that neither guilt nor threat of damnation would keep her from once again removing the necklace. She tried to persuade herself that she *had* to find out what the demon wanted from her, that it was critical.

She wasn't fooled. She was Eve, and now having had one bite of the apple, she wouldn't stop until it was devoured in its entirety.

Theron stepped up onto Lucia's bed and stood astride her sleeping form, looking down at her with a roiling mix of emotions he could not wholly decipher.

She wasn't wearing the amulet. Neither was she sitting up, attempting to confront him while in a trance. It looked for all the world as if she was again inviting him into her dreams. She *wanted* to dream of him, even though she knew he was a demon.

It was just her sexual hunger urging her to it, he told himself. It had nothing to do with their conversation last night. She didn't like *him;* she only liked what he had made her feel.

But still the hope trembled in his chest: foolish, crazy desire that she might want more from him than that.

He tried to shake off the thought, and to remember why he was here. To make good his threat to Vlad! To sully Lucia's purity and teach Vlad a lesson! To make the sun-blasted mortal give in before Nyx put Theron in her harem and thus took away any chance of his ever escaping the Night World and the ennui he'd found there.

He wasn't here to get soft about Lucia. It was time to re-establish some distance between them, and to take Lucia another big step down the stairway to depravity. He would prove to both himself and to her that it was the *sex* she wanted, from whoever could give it to her. Then he could stop this nonsensical wondering about what she felt about him.

He stepped weightlessly onto her chest and squatted down, his sex hardening as her hungers coursed through him. He reached out and touched her brow.

In her dream she was on horseback, galloping across a vast plain of green, her hair snapping in banners behind her, the wind cutting in cool exhilaration through her clothes. She rode astride, the chestnut mare beneath her floating smooth as a cloud above the ground, missing not a step.

The plain reminded Theron of the inner wilds of Asia, and the mongols who rode in such graceful ease over its vast steppes. Waves of such men had washed from Asia over Europe throughout the centuries, razing all in their path.

He used such history as inspiration, and on the horizon toward which Lucia rode he created a horde of riders.

He felt the alarm flush through Lucia. She turned her horse in a wide arc and galloped away from the invaders, bending low over the horse's neck, panic tensing all her muscles. "Faster, faster!" she urged the horse. "Oh dear God, faster!"

The panic kept her from thinking; kept her from remembering that this was a dream. All her focus was on the horse between her legs, and the horde at her back.

The thundering of hooves grew louder, the horsemen gaining on her with a speed possible only in dreams. Lucia risked a glance over her shoulder, and screeched when she saw that the lead rider was but yards behind. The rider's face was covered by the guard of his helmet, and all that was visible was a shadowed jaw and the line of a hard mouth.

Lucia's heart tripped, and she poured her essence

into the dream horse, gaining for a moment a spurt of speed that pushed her beyond the reach of her pursuer.

Theron watched in stunned surprise for a moment as she put herself out of reach of his horseman, and then he fought again for control of the dream. His warrior surged forward, ahead of the horde, his stallion's hooves throwing up clods of dirt and grass with every hoofbeat. Lucia turned round to look again, her eyes wide with fear, but Theron felt as well a hint of sexual thrill running through her. *She was enjoying this.*

It *was* only the sex she wanted. A spurt of disappointment went through him, and was as quickly replaced with anger. He'd give her all she could take, then!

The horseman came up even with her, and with one sweep of his strong arm swept her off the back of her mount and in front of him on his. Lucia clung to his leather-armored body, the pace of the stallion and her precarious position putting her in fear for her life.

The horseman turned away from the mare, arcing off in a different direction, his horde following at a distance behind.

"What do you want of me?" Lucia cried. "Let me go!"

Theron made the horseman say nothing, only tighten his grip. Lucia's fear of falling faded away. She feared the warrior and what he had planned for her, but even so her body began to ready itself for what was to come. Theron felt a thrill of desire coursing through her, and gave to her the image of the warrior sliding himself home deep within her. Her inner passage contracted in response.

The horseman took her to a barbarian city built upon the side of a mountain. At the highest point of the city was a temple, reached by a hundred stairs. The horseman rode straight up to the top of them and was met by robed men at the door. He handed Lucia down to them, and she looked back at him in confusion. He was giving her away already?

"She will serve us well," the horseman said roughly, and rode off. *Ha! What would she think of* that? Theron thought in satisfaction.

Inside the dream, hidden from Theron's awareness, Lucia knew that she was dreaming, and knew as well that Theron was the one creating this adventure for her. She knew that she *should* exert her control and start asking the questions she had saved up for the demon. Instead, a wild curiosity about what would happen next was consuming her. She didn't *want* to be in control.

She wanted to be bad. She wanted to let Theron do as he would with her. In a strange way, she felt like this dream was his gift to her; a poem, a song, a painting that had been created just for her.

She was still in delightful ignorance of what would happen next, when the robed men led her into the temple. Its pillars were covered in scalloped designs in red and gold, the high domed ceiling painted deep blue with gems making brilliant stars in its depths. The floors were of malachite, the green clouds of color polished to a mirror-like sheen. At the end of an aisle of pillars was a dais, and on the dais an altar covered in a drape of soft black fur. It looked like a bed, with four posts of spiral gold at its corners. Gold straps of silk hung down from the posts.

"What do you want of me?" Lucia asked the robed men, an excited trepidation flooding her at sight of the bed-like altar. Again she was given no answer. She felt a moment of distrust of Theron's intentions, but then remembered that she *could* stop this whenever she wished.

Strange music began to play quietly from somewhere behind the altar; hollow sounds of horns and drums, and flutes without melody. An unseen male chorus lowly chanted a song without words, the deep tones vibrating in Lucia's chest. The sounds echoed strangely in her head, making her feel weirdly disoriented and unbalanced.

The men held her arms while assistants came and stripped her of her shoes and hose. And then, while she struggled feebly in their hold, they undressed her, strange hands touching her lightly as each garment was removed. In a moment she was stark naked, standing upon the cold stone floor with only her own long hair and her hands to cover herself. She blinked in surprise, not sure that she had wanted this.

Curiosity, and the knowledge that this was but a dream, were all that kept her from bolting.

The robed men stepped away, and then they and their assistants formed a line down either side of the aisle. They bowed their heads.

Lucia stared up the aisle to the black fur bed at the end, and as if of their own volition her feet started to carry her toward it. The music grew louder, filling her senses, distracting her from any sense of embarrassment at her nakedness. *Theron is here with me. He is creating this for me,* she reminded herself, and felt herself willingly submit to the story unfolding. *These dreams are the truest language Theron knows.*

As she reached the altar, two of the men came forward to pull forward a jewel-encrusted step stool that she obediently used to climb up onto the bed. She turned around and sat, the fur soft under her thighs, and just stiff enough to prickle against her tender sex. *Theron wanted me to feel that,* she thought, and felt a thrill go through her.

The robed men were still bowing their heads. The ones who had helped her onto the bed now stood at its head, waiting beside the posts, each one holding a silken strap. One of them held his hand out to her.

No, she couldn't . . . And yet she watched herself hold her hand out to him. A shivering excitement ran down her arm when he took her by the wrist and wrapped the silken band around it. The silent men tied each wrist and ankle to a post, until she was lying in the center of the black fur, her knees bent, her thighs parted. A flush of embarrassment went through her at being so clearly on display, and she tugged belatedly against her bonds, as if to reach down and cover herself.

Theron listened to the surface emotions flooding through Lucia, the embarrassment warring with a shame-filled thrill of excitement as she realized that any man could look upon her. It was the shame that Theron wanted to target; that, and the strange conviction she had that her sex was dirty and foul and something to be hidden even from a lover.

Vlad would like such twisted modesty, but to Theron it was only a hindrance to pleasure.

Theron had the robed men nudge Lucia to lift her hips, and when she obeyed they slid a thick velvet cushion beneath her pelvis, raising it up as if putting her sex even further on display. Lucia whimpered, and tugged again against the bonds that held her and to which she had so meekly submitted a moment ago. She lifted her head to see what was happening in the temple, but her own body blocked her view.

Theron made the music grew louder, increasing by increments, building toward some unknown climax. Lucia struggled harder against the bonds, trying to close her thighs, but then she felt male hands holding them apart, and a moment later there was the kiss of a cool mouth against her, taking the sensitive center of her pleasure between two lips and sucking. Shock made Lucia go motionless, staring up at the gem-studded ceiling far above.

Deeper in Lucia's mind than Theron could sense, she sighed in delight. *Yes, this was what she'd been waiting for. This wickedness of a mouth on her foulest parts was what she wanted, and it was what she could only imagine accepting from Theron. He knew her, and accepted every dark, depraved part of her and found it perfect.*

The unseen man's mouth released her and painted a long, flat stroke of tongue against her folds.

From the corner of her eye Lucia saw the horseman approaching. She recognized the character, even though he was no longer wearing the helmet. His dark brown hair was damp around his face as if he had just washed himself, his blue eyes glowing like flashes of sky against his swarthy skin. He had a large nose and rugged features, and a scar on his brow, and there was nothing of softness about him.

But the eyes gave him away. This was the face Theron had chosen to take in this dream.

A softer mouth lay itself against her sex, and her eyes widened as she realized that it obviously was not the horseman who touched her. A more timid tongue than the last one teased at her and then traced down to her core, lapping there against her entrance.

She tugged against her bonds, trying to cover her breasts with her hands, her knees trying and failing to close against the man laving her down there. The man who was *not* Theron. "What is happening?" she cried to the horseman.

The horseman—Theron—touched her lower lip with his callused fingertip, his voice gentle. "You are our living goddess." He traced a line down from her lip, over her chin, and down her neck to the spot just above her heart. Her breasts tightened at the nearness of his hand, her nipples begging to be touched. "My men worship at your altar, seeking your blessing before they return to battle."

"*Men?*" A new mouth replaced the timid one. This one thrust a tongue deep within her, swirling inside her as if seeking a reward. Hands slid beneath her buttocks, clasping her, raising her up as if the man sought to drink from her. Lucia half-closed her eyes, her body responding even as her mind shrank from the touch of so many men in such a wicked place. She tugged against the bonds that held her wrists, then gripped the straps in her fists.

"Make them stop," she said softly, even as a new mouth came and painted delicate tongue strokes upon her folds. Confusion swirled through her: Were all the men part of Theron?

Yes. As she remembered that this dream was all of his creation, her hips rose to meet each butterfly touch of the tongue flicking against her flesh, the sensation doubling.

"Your pleasure is the blessing they seek. Each drop of your arousal is a potion of strength and power."

"What drops?"

He reached between her legs, bending forward as he did so, his face coming closer to hers. Lucia stared into his brilliant blue eyes, knowing him for who he was.

Theron's fingertip replaced the tongue of the worshipper, dipping inside her. Lucia closed her eyes, the firmness of his touch as he slid the tip within her a dozen times more satisfying than the gentle play of tongues. She lifted her hips, urging him deeper.

Instead, he withdrew, bringing his finger up to his own lips and stroking it across them, leaving a sheen of wetness there. "*These* drops. To drink a woman's pleasure is to be blessed by her essence."

A new touch came to her sex, flicking against her and then lapping her at her slit, as if to catch the wetness that had been coaxed from her.

"Your pleasure flows from you like wine," he said. "They will drink of you through the night, only stopping when your climax is near. And then . . ." Theron looked intently at her, waiting for the question.

"And then?" she barely managed to ask.

He drew off his clothing and stood before her naked, his desire for her evident in the upward straining of the thick rod at his loins. "And then I will come into you."

"No." She shook her head, but didn't know if she meant truly to protest. "No! I am a virgin."

He untied one of her hands, and brought it toward his groin. "Feel the staff that will break through your locked doorway."

Her eyes wide, she didn't struggle as he brought her hand to his arousal and gently wrapped her hand around it. It was warm and hard, and velvety smooth. She imagined him kneeling between her thighs, pressing this deep within her, and as the unseen man played her with his mouth she hit her climax.

Her whole body tensed as the waves rolled through her. "Theron!" she cried out.

Theron jerked in surprise. He gaped at Lucia as her

climax calmed to distant rippling, leaving her afloat in a placid sea of satisfied desire.

"I know it's you, Theron," Lucia said, even as she took control of the dream and erased the remaining bonds from her wrist and ankles, and removed the other men from the temple. She held her arms shyly open. "I've known all along. Will you . . ."

She didn't complete the question, but he felt it in her mind, and felt too the fear that he would say *no*.

All thoughts of holding a distance from her fled, and instead he felt strong within him that yearning which had tortured him while watching the tribal bride hold her husband. He wanted to feel a woman touch him with tenderness, to feel her arms around him as she sought shelter within his embrace. He wanted to *matter* to someone.

It was a yearning utterly unlike what a demon should feel.

"You know it is me, and you are not afraid?" he asked her, speaking through the visage of the horseman.

She started to drop her arms over her chest, even that one question from him too much of a rejection for her.

Even though he could not feel her touch, he had the horseman climb up onto the bed with her, pulling her arms wide again and taking her into his embrace.

Lucia sighed and wrapped her arms around the horseman's neck, pressing her face close, her breasts flattened against his broad chest. Theron could sense how deeply she was luxuriating in the feel of a body against her own, as if her skin hungered for this type of contact even more than she hungered for the sensual touch of a man.

The amulet may have kept Lucia from the sexual release offered by dream demons, but it was her incarceration at Castle Rosu that had isolated her from the loving touch of family and friends. Theron began for the first time to get a sense of how painful a wound that isolation had wrought in her psyche. It had left a vast emptiness inside her, bordered only by yearning and incomprehension.

It was his fault, of course, for making the bargain with Vlad. He'd never thought that it could wreak this sort of damage on a person, though. Not that it would have stopped him six years ago, even if he *had* known. He wasn't one to feel guilt or compassion. And yet, with Lucia . . .

She clung to the horseman, calling the figure by his name, and Theron was overcome by guilt, and by a longing for something that could never be. "Don't, Lucia," he said hoarsely. "I am not truly touching you."

She lifted her head away from his chest, her hands loosening from around his neck. "I know that I am dreaming, but this feels almost as good as real."

"*Almost?*" He had thought she felt it exactly as it would be in reality.

She smiled a small smile. "Nothing in dreams feels as it does in truth. It is always . . . lacking something."

"Lacking what?"

She shrugged, rolling onto her back, away from him, and with a twitch of her mind garbing herself in a gown. "Intensity."

The casual, seemingly unimportant word was a shock to him. He remembered how it had felt to briefly be in possession of that girl's body, the one who had been with Vlad, and suddenly he knew that Lucia was right. It *was* different.

"Are you all right?" she asked, rolling onto her side and rising up onto one elbow.

He blinked in surprise. "Of course."

"You seem troubled."

She was asking after his well-being? "I just—I just didn't fully realize that your waking world was so different in its sensations."

"And yet I prefer the world of dreams," she said sadly. "So much more happens there."

An idea suddenly struck him. "Would you like to strike a bargain?"

She raised her brows, wary curiosity in her eyes. "What sort of bargain?"

"Knowledge for knowledge."

She shook her head. "I have nothing to teach you."

"Teach me what it is like to be human."

She laughed softly, the sound without humor. "There surely would be others better suited to such lessons. I know almost nothing of life."

"There is no one else who will talk with me as you do."

"But I know nothing!"

"You know the difference between a dream and reality."

"Do I?" she asked, and he felt her asking it of herself more than of him.

"You do. And in return I'll teach you anything you want to know."

"You'll teach me about your demon world?" she asked, a light of excitement flickering to life in her eyes. "And show me the history of mine? And most of all . . ."

He waited for her to finish. Her cheeks were coloring.

She lowered her voice to a whisper, as if they could be overheard even in a dream. "Most of all, tell me how a baby is made!"

His lips curled into a smile. "I can do better than tell you." He took control of the dream, and a moment later Lucia was pregnant, only a few weeks from giving birth.

Her eyes went wide, her hands going immediately to her stomach. Theron had been in the minds of countless women who were breeding, and he had felt their symptoms with unnerving frequency. There was one thing he wanted to be sure she got to feel: He made the dream-baby she carried give a kick.

Lucia jumped. "What was that?"

"It's the baby, moving."

Lucia's mouth shaped an O of awe. "Truly, this is what it feels like to carry a child?"

"As near as I can tell," he said.

She wrapped her arms over her distended belly, the movement protective and possessive both. *"I want one,"* she said, with all the force of her mind and soul. He felt a wave of desire for a child wash through her with a power far greater than any meager sexual climax.

And in that moment he felt the desire, too. Whether formed from Lucia's wants or his own, he did not know, but he looked upon her with her hands over her belly and imagined that it was *his* child that grew so safely inside.

A child. It was a new and exhilarating thought. A child, formed of him and Lucia.

A child, of flesh and blood.

He *had* to get Vlad's body.

Chapter Twenty

Lucia played her mandolin, the music but a backdrop as her mind went over the past five nights with Theron. In the light of day, she could barely believe any of it had happened. The strongest mark of truth was how weary she was: It was as if her sleep was no true sleep at all, and the world-wandering that Theron shared with her might as well have been accomplished on foot.

Such things he was showing her! So many people she had never dreamt existed; so many landscapes that were more exotic than anything she could imagine on her own.

Some would think she was insane to have let any of this occur. She was wicked beyond comprehension to enjoy spending her nights with a demon. He seemed so nearly human, though—with an almost human need for connection, however much he might pretend otherwise, and however hard he made it by appearing to her each night in a different guise.

He had kept his promise not to take her virginity, but

she had been more and more wicked and let him do much else to her.

She thrummed a chord on the mandolin, trying to chase the guilty thoughts away. She would not regret those touches. She would not! They were only dreams, after all. She could do what she wished in her own mind. And where was Vlad?

She heard knocking at the main door of the castle proper and stopped her playing. She was in the small courtyard in the center of the keep, and the main door was down a narrow corridor and steep flight of steps. The knocking echoed up that tunnel like a drum.

Someone answered the door, and Lucia heard male voices. The guardsmen? A heated discussion began with the servant who had answered the door, and Lucia put down her mandolin and went to the entrance to the corridor, listening intently, alarm creeping up her spine.

After a few more unintelligible barks of male anger, the female servant chirped something conciliatory. Heavy footsteps began to clomp up the stairs.

Lucia's eyes widened. A man, in Castle Rosu? What had happened? What was going on? Was it important news?

A few seconds later a mass of blackness began moving up the shadowy corridor. Her heart jumped up into her throat and she backed away, back into the sunshine, stumbling on one of the cobblestones and barely managing to right herself.

The shadowy figure emerged from the corridor and blinked at the bright light like a rat emerging from the cellars. And the man *looked* like a rat: a black, disease-ridden rodent with flesh melting off its face and its hair disarranged by its scratching at fleas. The beady, flashing eyes were sunk in purple-shadowed sockets.

It was only as the shock began to fade that she recognized his black robes as those of a priest.

"My lady," a servant girl said, running up to her. "This is Father Gabriel. He says he is the brother of Vlad Draco, your betrothed."

Lucia stared dumbstruck at the man. It had been six years since she had been this close to a solid, human male. The comparison to Theron, in all his dream perfection, was less than favorable.

Worse yet, this was the brother of her betrothed, and a priest. All her bravado of not regretting the past nights fled from her. The priest stood before her like a living accusation of her sins, sent to her at the very moment that she most needed such a reminder. Guilt for everything she had done flooded through her.

As Father Gabriel surveyed the courtyard and then rested his fitful gaze on her, she gathered her courage and stepped forward, then gave her best curtsy, rusty with disuse. "Father Gabriel. Welcome to Castle Rosu. I am Lucia of Maramures, sister of Prince Dragosh, and I welcome you to my home."

"So you're Lucia. You've grown into a fine thing— good breasts on you. Vlad will be pleased."

"Father?" Lucia said, taken aback.

He scratched at his face and his shoulder jerked, as if twitching involuntarily. "You're wearing the necklace Vlad gave you. Good. He said he asked you never to take it off."

She smiled sickly, guilt again swamping her. "That's right."

The priest smiled back, the motion quick and as

quickly gone. "Do you have a room for me?" he asked abruptly.

"Uh, yes, I'm sure we can ready one." Lucia widened her eyes at the serving girl. The maid nodded and ran off. "You are staying with us, then?"

"Why else would I be here?" he asked, fidgeting impatiently.

"I just . . . It's been a very long time since there has been a man inside the walls of Castle Rosu."

"That's how it was supposed to be, wasn't it?" he snapped. "But I'm a priest, and it's not the same thing as having soldiers bedding down in the hall. My escort will stay in the barracks with the rest of that filthy lot." He jerked his head back in the direction of the main door.

"Er, yes. Forgive my impertinence, but is there a . . . ah . . . a reason for your visit? News, perhaps?" she asked hopefully.

He blinked at her. "News? No. I have a letter to you from Vlad, though."

Her heart skipped a beat, caught between excitement and guilt. "A letter? Truly?"

He rooted through the leather satchel that was hanging over his shoulder. "It's probably in one of the bags. The guards will have to find it for you."

Lucia clenched her fists, trying to keep from tearing the bag off his shoulder and searching through it herself. *A letter from Vlad.* It was a greater gift than anyone could have brought her. She was shocked and pleased and confused.

"Is this it?" Gabriel pulled out a much-abused roll of parchment, flattened, creased, and stained from its sojourn in the bottom of the satchel. "Yes, this is it. Here." He held it out to her.

She took it greedily, appalled that he had let such damage come to the thing. If there was a single word that was unreadable due to his negligence, she didn't know but that she might have to toss him down the well, future brother-in-law or no.

"Will Vlad be coming soon?" she asked, the reality of this promise flooding through her, drowning out thoughts of dreams and dream lovers.

"Soon. Yes, soon. Soon enough. A few more weeks and Moldavia will be finished. He'll come for you then."

"He sent you to tell me?"

"He sent me to make sure you were ready, and to check that all is as it should be."

"As it should be?" she repeated, feeling another spurt of guilt.

Gabriel's restless, distracted eyes locked with hers. "He's concerned about your innocence. There's been no threat to that, has there?"

Lucia was too stunned to lie for a long moment, and then words came to her faithless tongue. "As I said, there have been no men within the walls of Castle Rosu for a very long time."

"No *nighttime* visits?" he asked pointedly.

Alarm raced through her veins. He couldn't know anything about Theron, could he? "Visits? What manner of visits could I expect atop this mountain in the middle of the night?"

"I didn't say *middle* of the night," he said. He sounded even more suspicious.

"You could say midafternoon and the answer would be the same: No living soul comes to Castle Rosu."

He studied her for a long moment, his eyes narrowed. "I see. Very well, then. I'm sure Vlad will be interested to hear that it is so. I'll go to my room now, shall I?"

"Yes, all right. Let me find a servant to guide you."

She went to fetch a servant, Gabriel's words unnerving her, and then told Vlad's brother she would see him at supper. As soon as his fidgety, fur-scalped, suspicious self was gone, though, she raced up to her room and threw herself onto her bed, the letter clasped tightly in her hand.

A message from Vlad. From Vlad!

She examined the seal, cracked from its rough journey, and picked out the symbol of a dragon with arching spiked tail and tongue of fire. As she began to ease open the seal, a spurt of guilt shot through her again. She hadn't been as true to him as she should have been; she had been welcoming Theron into her mind with immodest zest.

If she was so easily tempted that a demon could find himself invited into her bedroom night after night, it was no wonder she had been sequestered here. Living men might be far more than she could ever resist.

Gabriel's image came to mind, and she wrinkled her nose. She could resist some, certainly.

She gripped the flattened roll of parchment tightly in her hand. She would be better from now on: no more sexual play with Theron. She would be the wife Vlad had been waiting for, and he would be the father of her children. He deserved a faithful wife. After all, he had probably been faithful to her all this time. He might have been absent, but he'd been off at war—surely not for no good reason. And he deserved all that he'd been promised.

With that resolution set in her heart, she felt almost deserving of opening the letter. She carefully unstuck the seal, preserving as much of the precious wax symbol as she could, unfolded it, and began to read:

My dearest Lucia,

I trust that this letter finds you safe and well in your mountain fortress, and that you have been enjoying the benefits of a life in such pure air and quiet surrounds. I envy you the peaceful life you have been living.

Lucia made a face. Enjoying the air? Enjoying the quiet? She'd had enough air and quiet to last her a lifetime.

I am sorry that I have not been at liberty to write to you before now, but I had more important things to do. I had a kingdom to win for my beautiful bride! Everything I do, I do with the thought of you clasped tight to my happily beating heart. I think of you in my bed . . .

This was more like what she wanted to hear! He was fighting battles for her! His heart was thumping with love! And best of all, he was imagining her in his bed, waiting for him to come make passionate love to her.

in my bath . . .

Oh, in the bathtub, too! She'd liked that with Theron, at least until the turtle head had appeared and scared the wits out of her.

in my tent and on my horse . . .

On his horse? Wouldn't people see? He'd have to hold on to her tightly, else she'd be sure to fall off.

and even while eating my sausages.

Sausages?

It took a minute, but then she realized with a flush of shame that she had assumed a very different meaning than Vlad had intended. Of course he hadn't meant that he was thinking of having sex with her on his horse or in his bath. He was a good and honorable man and wouldn't write such things to his beloved.

She resumed reading.

I will win Moldavia for you, my love, my sweet mountain snowflake with honeycomb eyes. I will do this because I envision the day when the entire region will be united under my rule, and every lip will utter the name Vlad Draco with the respect due a god. Draco! Draco! Draco! they will chant, and throw flowers before me, kissing my feet as they beg for mercy. You will be there, too.

Lucia chewed her lip. Although it would be grand to have such a popular husband, she hoped he didn't expect *her* to kiss his feet and beg for mercy.

Then again, she *would* kiss his toes if he would like it as much as she had when Theron sucked on hers.

That thought reminded her of all she had done that was not innocent, and she felt another flush of shame. No, she couldn't suck Vlad's toes. It would remind her of her demon lover.

I look forward to the day when you will be mine, body and soul, and know that you must anticipate that day as eagerly as do I. It will be very soon; perhaps within the month.

Keep well, Lucia my darling, and always wear the necklace I gave you.

Your faithful and eager betrothed,
Vlad

Lucia lifted her pendant in the palm of her hand, and it seemed to wink back at her accusingly. She didn't think she was ready to give up Theron entirely, but perhaps tonight she could tell him that he could no longer touch her in her dreams. She winced at the very thought. She didn't *want* to give up those fantasies and touches. They had become as sustenance to her, and she feared she might starve without them.

It had to be done, however. Her beloved was coming. Vlad was real, and her future. Theron, as much as she liked him, was not her future and never could be. He couldn't even become substantial, see her in the daylight. No, he was not going to be the husband to whom she owed her allegiance. He could never be more than a dream.

And the time of daydreams was ending, the time of awakening beginning. Her life was going to start at last.

Chapter Twenty-one

Mara took a deep breath to try to still the shaking of her hands, and she rapped on the door.

"Enter!" Father Gabriel called from inside.

Mara opened the door and barely stepped over the threshold, keeping her hand on the latch as if she could turn around and flee. She had never met this priest, but she had heard of him in her brief time at Vlad's palace before she had been sent here. People said he was half-mad, but that the Church kept him in its ranks because he could see the Devil in people and chase him out. Some others said that he was more in league with the Devil than against him.

At the moment, though, Father Gabriel was sprawled in a chair, his body appearing boneless beneath his black robes. He loosely held a small clay bottle in one hand. As she watched, he took a sip and then winced as if at bitterness.

When his expression cleared, Gabriel gestured imperiously to her with one hand. "Come in. Shut the door."

Mara did as bade, and came to stand in front of him, her hands clasped tightly in front of her. "You asked to see me, Father?"

"You're Mara, Lucia's maid, aren't you?"

"Yes, Father," she said without meeting his eyes. It seemed safest to stare at the floor.

"Vlad said I should whip you for your laxness in your duties to your mistress."

She gasped, meeting his eyes. "Father?" she squeaked.

"I needn't do so, though, if I can count on you to help me."

She looked more frightened than pleased. "Yes, Father, of course you can count on me."

A yawn overtook Gabriel, his mouth gaping wide and a bellow of tired pleasure coming from his throat. "Damn, but that was a long journey. And I don't want to climb those stairs ever again. Good Christ, I thought my heart was going to explode."

Mara tried to hide her surprise at his profanity. He did not seem at all priestlike. "Er, yes, Father. There are more stairs than anyone would like to climb."

He set his little bottle on a table near the chair and focused his sharp black eyes on her. The pupils were so large, she couldn't see if there was any other color to them. "Do you know why I'm here?" he asked.

Mara shook her head, but she was afraid he was here to see how well she had—or hadn't—been doing her job of guarding Lucia's innocence.

"Do you love your mistress?"

"Yes, Father," she lied, assuming it was the right response.

"More even than you love your duty to your prince?"

She shook her head. "No! Not at all!"

Gabriel stuck a finger into his nose and rooted around. He found a treasure and pulled it out. "I need to know where your loyalties lie," he said, briefly examining the bit of dried mucus before wiping it on the chair and looking again at Mara. "Do they lie with Lucia or with Vlad?"

Mara tried to keep the revulsion from her face as her mind ticked through the possible answers, trying to decide which Gabriel would most like to hear. The truth was that her loyalties lay wherever was best for Mara. "I serve my mistress by deferring to her lord. He knows what is best for her."

Gabriel raised one brow. "A clever answer. Do you understand me, then, when I say that the best you can do for your own future is to remember what you've just said?"

Mara nodded.

"There will be no hieing off to Lucia, spilling into her ear all that goes on between you and me."

Mara shook her head and hoped that he didn't have any ideas about touching her. Her stomach roiled at the thought.

"Good. Now answer me this: Has Lucia ever taken off her necklace?"

A chill went down Mara's spine. How could he know? And if he knew that, he might know that she herself had probably been the one to take it off the first time. Gabriel's black beetle-shell eyes were watching her closely, and she was afraid to lie more than a little. "There have been a few nights when she has not worn it. I thought she did not want to get it tangled while she slept."

"These times when she did not wear it—did you notice anything strange happening during the night?"

Mara dampened her lips. She could feel sweat breaking out all over her body. She didn't want to be blamed for this! But she was afraid to hide it. Gabriel seemed to have ways of knowing things that he shouldn't. "There was one night . . ."

"Yes?" he asked, sitting up straight.

"One night almost a week past she did seem to be talking to someone, but there was no one there."

"Talking?" he asked, his surprise evident.

She nodded, worried that she had given the wrong answer. "Talking. She was sitting up and had her eyes open, but there was no one there. She was in a trance, but I was frightened for her so I shook her awake." Thank God she could say that, and have it be the truth. At least it would sound as if she had been taking some care of Lucia.

"You saw nothing else?"

"No."

"No sign of anything . . . demonic?"

Mara's eyes widened.

"What is it?" the priest asked sharply.

"She said that—she said 'demon' while she was talking to no one!" Mara's heart raced with fear. Had there been a demon in the room, right there with her?

"What else did she say to *no one?*"

"I can't remember; it didn't make sense. It was as if I was hearing only half a conversation." She'd never be able to sleep again. What if there had been a demon there, and what if it had come more than once? She suddenly remembered the night she had walked in her sleep and woken beside Lucia's bed, the necklace on

234

top of the furs. Had a *demon* made her do it? She shuddered in horror and crossed herself.

Gabriel glared at her, still waiting for more information, and she dug deeper into her memory, trying to find some tidbit to give him.

"She said something about being scared, and about truth. But when I woke her, she seemed angry with me and said there had been nothing to be concerned about."

"Did you believe her?"

"She seemed different than usual, but not as if any harm had come to her. I didn't know what to think, or what else I could do."

Gabriel nodded. "There wasn't anything else you could do, except *put the necklace back on her.*" He glared at her as if this should have been obvious, then smiled in a less than reassuring manner. "You've told me what I needed to know, Mara. I'm sure Vlad will amply reward you for your help."

Mara allowed a wary smile to touch her lips. She might come through this all right, after all.

"Of course, Vlad won't be happy to know that a *demon* has been visiting his betrothed's bedchamber, and that Lucia's maid was unaware of what was happening not ten feet from her lazy bones."

Mara felt her stomach drop into her knees, her legs going weak and wobbly. "But . . ." She could see her life's end, whirling up toward her in a storm of pain and darkness.

"If you're a very good girl, I may give you a chance to redeem yourself."

"Yes?" Hope fluttered to life inside her.

"You're going to help me catch the demon."

Her breath froze in her lungs. Catch a demon? She couldn't do that. He might as well have asked her to catch a wildcat with her bare hands.

There was nothing to do but accede, however. She was caught between a demon and a devil, and whichever way she turned, she would be torn to shreds. It was better to side with the devil she *could* see, sitting before her with his finger once again up his nose, than to side with the demon that she couldn't.

"Yes, I'll help."

She would have been better off as a farmer's wife.

Chapter Twenty-two

Under the cover of both semidarkness and her bed furs, Lucia removed her necklace and shoved it to the edge of the mattress. She pulled her sheet and furs up to her nose and huddled down into her pillow, hoping that anyone who might come to check on her—like her betrothed's hideous brother, Father Gabriel—would see nothing amiss.

Father Gabriel had appeared at the supper table more than halfway through the meal, and Lucia was grateful he hadn't been earlier. She supposed she should be more eager to befriend her future relation, but the man made her flesh creep. His demeanor at the table had been far more relaxed than at their first meeting, though; so relaxed, in fact, that he had followed Sister Teresa's lead at one point and dozed off.

He'd awoken with a start and fixed Lucia with his rat-eyed stare, then smiled as if trying to be affable. "Can you see the future, like your great-grandmother Raveca could?" he asked.

The question had stunned her, taking her completely by surprise. Her mouth had hung open, no response coming to her tongue as she tried to figure out how he could have known to ask that question.

Teresa had snorted awake right then, watery eyes blinking at the candlelight as she got her bearings. "Is it time for the sweet?"

"Almost," Lucia said.

"I was asking your young charge if she had visions of the future," Father Gabriel said to Teresa.

"Those trances are the Devil's work! You will have to tell her so, Father Gabriel. She does not listen to me."

"I believe such abilities to be a gift from God," Father Gabriel agreed. "I wouldn't want her to stop. On the contrary, I should like very much to know what she sees."

Lucia shook her head. "I don't see the future. They're just daydreams."

"No prophecies?"

"I'm not a seer."

Gabriel narrowed his eyes, staring hard at her. Lucia began to fidget under his gaze, her guilt bringing a flush of heat to her cheeks. "No vision of the future, ever?"

"They are so rare . . ."

He leaned forward, hands on the table, as if he would crawl across it and throttle the answer out of her. "What have you seen?" he growled, and she was suddenly too frightened not to answer.

"I saw Vlad arriving here at Castle Rosu to claim me."

"And?"

"And that is all. Vlad, arriving."

Gabriel sat back in his chair, still examining her.

"It says very little," Lucia apologized, still astonished that this priest would want to hear about her visions instead of advise her to pray for forgiveness.

"It says much. It says that he will be victorious in battle, and that he will survive to claim you."

"Oh. Yes, I suppose it does." She hadn't even thought of that aspect of the vision. All she had thought about was how sad she had been. Again, she wondered why.

The priest interrupted her musing. "You could be very useful to Vlad in ways other than forging an alliance with your brother if you put your mind to it."

Instead of being flattered by the suggestion, Lucia found herself feeling somehow *demeaned*. While she would indeed like to be of help to her future husband, she didn't like this feeling that visions or alliances were the only value she would have to him. Somehow, in all her romantic imaginings over the past years, she had forgotten that this was at its heart a political marriage.

But then she had remembered the letter from Vlad, filled with his eagerness to be with her, and she had shoved the worrisome thoughts aside. Of course Gabriel would dwell on the utilitarian aspect; he was not in love, like Vlad.

"I tell her that she needs to be a good wife to her husband," Sister Teresa put in. "She shouldn't spend all her time daydreaming."

"Then you're a fool, old woman," Gabriel snapped. "Haven't you been listening? Or is it just that you're stupid?"

Lucia felt her heart trip. She'd never known anyone to be cruel to Sister Teresa. The elderly nun was harmless and kind. "Father Gabriel, please," she said softly, feeling that she had to do something. There was no one else to speak up for the woman.

"What?"

Lucia shook her head, frowning at him.

"Is it time for the sweet?" Sister Teresa asked again, blinking at them both as if nothing had happened.

Gabriel rolled his eyes.

"Here it comes now," Lucia said, as one of the serving girls carried in a tray with almond pastries.

There hadn't been much said after that, and Gabriel had retired to his chamber soon after. Lucia had returned to her own room to find Mara acting strangely nervous, and several objects in the room had been moved slightly. A candlestick, a small silver mirror, a well-polished silver pitcher . . .

"Why are you moving things around?" she'd asked.

"No reason, really. Something to do."

"Is there something the matter?"

"What? No!"

"Are you sure?"

Mara had shrugged one shoulder, the movement jerky and awkward. "Just the excitement of a visitor."

Lucia couldn't help the grimace of distaste that crossed her features.

Mara's mouth had twitched into a strained smile. "He's a little . . . odd, don't you think?"

"A most unusual priest."

"Yes. Do you suppose he'll stay until Vlad arrives?" Mara asked.

Lucia hoped not! But she had only shrugged in ignorance. She was not going to share her thoughts with Mara. The maid had a long way to go before she would earn trust again. Lucia had only laughed softly to herself.

"My lady?"

Lucia shook her head, not answering. She'd just realized that she had a stubborn, distrustful, vengeful streak inside. Who'd have guessed?

Now Mara was lying on her pallet but not sleeping, given the shallow sound of her breathing. Lucia had no reason to suspect that Mara would go tattling to Father Gabriel if she saw her remove the necklace, but it wasn't a chance worth taking; she had to remove the necklace covertly. She couldn't risk trying to talk to Theron while in a trance state, either—she didn't want Mara to hear anything she said.

She closed her eyes and tried to relax, willing sleep to come quickly. The more desperately she wanted genuine sleep, though, the farther away it ran from her anxious mind. It was several hours before she finally slipped beneath the surface.

Chapter Twenty-three

Mara listened to Lucia's breathing deepen with true sleep, and after several minutes she rose quietly from her pallet, her nerves on edge and her heart racing.

Was the demon here, right now? Could he see her? She could see nothing but the darkness of the room, the edges of the furniture barely touched by the single candle that guttered in its own drippings on the corner table where she had carefully placed it.

She had placed many things that evening, following Father Gabriel's instructions. Silver mirrors and a silver pitcher, the candle, and a blown glass cup were arrayed in a loose circle around Lucia's bed, their placement appearing random to anyone who wasn't looking for it. The reflective surfaces of the silver and glass would substitute for actual lit candles, according to Father Gabriel. He had ordered her to come fetch him after Lucia had dropped off. The demon would visit her in her sleep, but if Father Gabriel was lurking outside Lucia's door all night, the demon would be suspicious.

Just as important, though, was that Lucia not be aware of what was planned. Father Gabriel thought Lucia might be in league with the demon, that she might try to help the creature escape.

With any luck, Mara herself wouldn't have to face the demon. God in heaven, she hoped not! After she fetched Gabriel, the priest would enter Lucia's chamber, quickly place a candle in the one spot that would complete the circle, and then the demon would be caught. There was a heavy earthenware jug under Lucia's bed—placed there by Mara—and Gabriel would recite a spell to capture the hellspawn within it. If all went well, the night would be over almost before it began.

But first Mara had to fetch the priest.

Her heart beating wildly, aware that the demon might even now be sitting on the bed, Mara made a shaky show of yawning and stretching, and then of going to the chamber pot. She lifted her chemise with shaking hands and squatted, her knees knocking, and with great effort forced herself to tinkle into it. When she was done, she made a face at the pot as if it were too full. She lit another candle and then picked up the chamber pot and took it and the candlestick toward the door. The hairs on the back of her neck rose as she turned away from the bed, her imagination telling her that the demon was watching and was not fooled, and that it would leap upon her at any moment.

Emptying the pot was the only excuse she had been able to think of for getting up and leaving the room in the middle of the night. The demon might be suspicious of her purpose if she didn't have something so obvious in her hand.

A flash of white startled her, making her slosh the pee in the pot. It illuminated the room around her for a brief, vibrating moment. She looked over her shoulder at the windows and saw another flash. Several seconds later, distant thunder rumbled through the air.

A storm was coming, rolling in over the mountains.

Mara barely contained a whimper. Demons and lightning and the middle of the night. Could this get any worse?

She opened the door and gladly escaped the room, feeling a small measure of safety as the door shut behind her. She made her way down the long, dark halls, the candle flickering in the drafts and almost blowing out. She stopped by the privy and set the chamber pot on the floor to one side. The wooden privy, its door hanging open, creaked in a growing wind, and Mara swore she'd never subject herself to the terror of using it. If the privy fell, it would mean a very long drop from nearly the top of the castle walls to the trees and rocks and dangerous slope below.

Lightning flashed, its burst of white light visible through the hole in the privy seat.

Mara shut the door. She'd come back and deal with the pot later. It was time to fetch Father Gabriel.

Chapter Twenty-four

Lucia dreamt. She found herself on a raft covered in plush rugs, rocking gently on the surface of a glassy sea. The setting sun steeped the western sky in pinks and oranges, and painted fiery trim onto distant thunderclouds. Above her the twilight had deepened the sky to violet, and the stars burned silently like the distant fires of gypsy camps.

Lucia turned and saw a green island, its lush, exotic growth bathed in golden light. "Where am I this time?" she asked.

"A place thousands of miles from Castle Rosu," Theron's voice said.

Lucia turned around again and saw a man lying on his side, wearing nothing but a colorful piece of cloth wrapped around his hips and legs. He was dark-skinned this time, with thick black hair and brows and a slightly hooked nose. His lips were full and almost brown, and while his eyes were black, there was at their centers a hint of blue fire shining through.

"Why do you always appear in a different guise?" she asked.

"Variety is the spice of life, or so they tell me."

"But I always know it's you."

"No, you don't."

"I do," she said lightly, with a confidence she shouldn't have had but did. "It may take me a little while, but I always know."

She then realized that she, too, was wearing only a piece of cloth, although hers was red and covered her breasts, leaving only her shoulders and arms bare. She wasn't wearing anything underneath, and her hair was loose. She reached up and felt a large flower in her hair, then rubbed the cloth of her wrap between her fingers, fascinated by the texture. "What is this?"

"It is what the people here wear."

"Why are we here?"

He sat up and propped an arm on his bent knee. "It is one of my favorite places and I wanted to show it to you."

They had never been to sea before, and she had never imagined a place such as this existing. "What a miracle, to be able to travel thousands of miles from Transylvania with the shutting of an eyelid in sleep."

"The people here do not even know that Transylvania exists. They have never heard your language or even seen a person with your pale coloring. They are all dark, like me, and they spend their days in the sun and water, and in the shade of huts made of the leaves of trees."

"Are they a happy people?"

"For the most part. But even they have their share of bad lovers; otherwise I would never have had reason to come here." He grinned.

She frowned.

"You don't like to be reminded of the other women I've visited, do you?" he asked.

"It's nothing to me."

"Isn't it?"

"Of course not. And it's going to have to mean even less." She gathered her courage and met his eyes. "You can't touch me again in these dreams we share."

Sister Teresa slowly and carefully undressed, preparing for bed. She dimly remembered sitting in her chair at some time earlier in the day, but then she had woken up cold and stiff, lying on the floor, and her room had been dark.

Now she couldn't seem to think straight. Her hands were stiff with cold, and half her body felt faintly numb. She didn't know what was happening to her.

Her cold hands made it difficult to deal with the small pins in her black wimple, so she left it on for the moment and took off her gown instead.

Her chemise needed changing. It was a struggle, but she managed to get it off while still wearing the wimple. At least the wimple's length kept her shoulders warm. She was nude except for it and her black stockings, tied by worn garters around her knees. Was there something more she was supposed to take off before getting into bed? She didn't think so.

She looked down at her breasts. They were slack and droopy, nothing like the fine, full breasts she had had at Lucia's age. Sometimes her youth felt as if it was a thousand years ago. At other times it was as if events had happened only yesterday, they seemed so clear in her mind. Clearer, really, than anything that happened in the present.

She frowned, remembering that a priest had arrived today. She should talk to him about Lucia's trances . . . although she had a vague memory of him saying that he thought they were a gift from God. He did not understand. She needed to tell him that such trances were the Devil's work.

He was staying in a room at the other side of the castle. The east room, was it? Or was it the west? She ought to go talk to him before he went to bed for the night.

She opened the door and stepped out into the dark hallway, neglecting to bring a candle to light her way, only vaguely aware that she was chilly and not at all aware that all she wore was her wimple and her stockings. What little attention she was capable of was focused solely on finding the priest.

A small bubble of delight formed in her heart. It had been so long since she had truly talked with another religious person. Surely Father Gabriel would welcome a visit from a sister, no matter the late hour. He would be delighted to see her.

Chapter Twenty-five

"I can't touch you again? Why is that?" Theron asked, raising his brow.

Lucia shook her head. "It's not right. Vlad's brother, Father Gabriel, has arrived and brought me a letter from Vlad—"

"Gabriel is here already?" Theron jumped up to his feet, agitated, looking around them at the calm sea as if the blue water hid the priest.

"Already? You mean you knew he was coming?"

"I knew. He's a pestilence upon the earth, as you've probably discovered for yourself. Keep your distance from him."

"I try. He seemed to suspect that I had had dealings with you, though—or at least with a demon."

Theron cursed under his breath. "You didn't tell him the truth, did you?"

"No, of course not. It's hardly the sort of thing I would admit to the priest brother of my betrothed!"

"I didn't see him lurking about when I arrived. Has he made any suggestions about trying to capture me?"

"What? No! Not that I know of, anyway. But forget Father Gabriel for the moment. Vlad will be coming for me soon, and it is not right that I do such intimate things with you when I am betrothed to him."

"It is hardly being unfaithful to share a dream with me." He sounded more disturbed by her words than she had expected and was at least distracted from the topic of Father Gabriel. But why would Theron care whether he could touch her? There were thousands more women who would let him.

"Faithfulness is in the heart and mind, as well as in the body," she said.

"It is not as if Vlad was doing you the same courtesy."

She blinked. "I beg your pardon?"

Theron crossed his arms over his chest. "You must know that Vlad has taken women to his bed at every opportunity."

"That's not true," Lucia protested.

Theron laughed—not entirely kindly. "Lucia, I've seen it myself."

She didn't know whether to believe him. She didn't *want* to believe him, but . . . "Even if that was true, I'm sure he will be faithful as soon as we are wed."

"Your romantic notions have nothing to do with reality." Theron lowered himself back down to the rug and lay on his side, head propped on his hand. He was closer to her this time, and she felt the physical pull of his nearness. She didn't think she'd be half as affected if she didn't see that blue fire in his eyes that told her this was Theron and not just any demon.

How could she be growing so fond of a demon? It was insane. And yet, there it was. "What do you know of human reality, or of love?" she asked. "I thought you deferred to me as the authority."

"I have had four thousand years to watch humans. I am not completely without understanding."

"To watch, and to learn nothing," she said, not meaning it. She was just angry with him for speaking ill of Vlad.

"Do not talk as if you know whereof you speak, Lucia. You have never even kissed a man except in your imagination."

"Nor have you ever touched a woman."

He winced. "And yet I would wager I know more about both love and sex than you could ever dream."

"But do demons love?" she asked.

She saw a muscle flex in his jaw. "No, they don't," he admitted. "But that probably makes it far easier for me to think rationally about the emotion than a mortal ever could."

"I don't want to be rational. I just want to enjoy. I want a chance to love my husband without guilt."

"And if it proves impossible to love him?"

"Why should it? From everything I hear, Vlad is a heroic, handsome, kind, and tender man."

Theron guffawed. "Kind and tender? Vlad Draco?"

"He is, isn't he?" she asked worriedly.

"Lucia, you're going to have to wake up from your dreams of love if you are going to endure a marriage to Vlad. Do you have any choice about it? Can you refuse the marriage?"

She shook her head. "No, and I wouldn't want to. Oh, I could always refuse to say my vows, but my life would be worth nothing if I did."

"It will be worth nothing if you do."

"Why do you say that? Are you just trying to upset me? Why don't you want me to be happy?"

"That is exactly what I *do* want: your happiness. And I know you will find only misery with Vlad. He is not the gentleman you imagine, Lucia. He is a vicious, lying, violent man."

"You lie."

"I promised you I wouldn't."

She shook her head. "I won't believe it. I cannot base my decision on the words of a demon! What has he done that is so terrible?"

"You don't think that invading Moldavia for no other reason than a hunger for power was terrible?"

"Moldavia is an enemy of Maramures. Why would I weep over Moldavia being under Vlad's rule instead of Bogdan's?"

"You might weep if you knew all that Vlad had done to get as far as he has," Theron said.

"What do you mean?"

"You asked last night whether I had met Vlad before or after meeting you. I met him before, because he had cast a summoning spell in hopes of gaining a demon's aid."

"Aid to do what?"

"To break your engagement to Nicolae of Moldavia, and to take you for himself."

Lucia sat stunned for a long moment. A dawning sense of comprehension—and betrayal—slowly rose inside her. Nothing was quite clear yet, but she sensed that she was about to be given the answers to a hundred questions she had been asking herself over the past six years. "Tell me everything," she said softly.

Chapter Twenty-six

Gabriel opened his chamber door and let Mara come in. "Is she asleep?"

"Yes."

"Did you see any sign of the demon?"

She shook her head. "Not unless the storm has something to do with it."

Gabriel muttered under his breath and went to the small table where he had been re-reading demon lore, preparing for the battle ahead.

The sooner he captured Theron, the sooner he would get his hands on the poppy juice Vlad had sent with the captain of the guard. Thank the good Lord that Gabriel had thought to hide a separate supply in the lining of his bag, else he would have gone mad by now. That captain was as stingy with the juice as if he were a woman with twenty children, doling out milk.

He flipped through the pages of the tome on demons, looking for information on storms and how they might affect the capture of one. His hand shook as he turned the pages.

Damn. He had been holding off on his nightly dose of juice, wanting a clear head when it came time to spring the trap on Theron. He hadn't counted on it taking half the night for Lucia to go to sleep. He was well past needing the juice, but he had better continue to hold off until this task was done, else he would fall asleep.

He was feeling jittery. And he kept thinking he saw things move out of the corner of his eye. It was probably just the lack of poppy juice, or his imagination.

Although it could be the demon. . . .

"Who is that?" Mara asked, pointing at the open page of the book. There was a drawing of a hideous old hag, shriveled breasts hanging down to her belly, long scraggly hair dripping from her loins. She had dark fur on her lower legs, and great black wings rose from her back.

"It's the queen of the demons."

Mara crossed herself, her eyes round with fear.

"She scares you, does she?" Gabriel asked with pleasure. "Would it scare you even more to know that she comes in the night, seeking souls to eat?"

Mara gaped at him.

"She rips open human bellies and sucks the souls from the entrails as her victims scream in agony."

"Mother Mary save me," Mara whispered.

Gabriel grinned, enjoying the maid's reaction. "The demon queen and her ilk are what is visiting Lucia. God only knows how many of them are walking the halls of this castle even at this moment. This is a damned place, Mara, and you'd best hold tight to your entrails. Now go on back to your mistress's room and set your candle where I told you. They mustn't suspect that anything is going on. I'll follow in a moment and spring the trap."

"I have to go back alone?" Mara cried.

Gabriel slapped her lightly with the back of his hand, just enough to get her attention. "Go! Don't think about your own damned skin when it's your mistress who is at greatest risk."

"Yes, Father," Mara whimpered, and crept out of the room.

Stupid bumpkin, Gabriel thought. The ignorant were so easy to frighten.

A shadow moved in the corner of his vision, and he whipped his head around.

Nothing.

Lightning flashed, and a rumble of thunder made the small glass panes of the window tremble in their casings. A wind was picking up and beginning to howl around the corners of the castle like the damned souls of Hell. Rain began tapping on the windows like the bony fingertips of the dead, begging for entrance.

Gabriel looked back down at the drawing of the demon queen and shuddered. Perhaps Mara wasn't so wrong to be frightened.

He picked up a candlestick and followed in her footsteps into the dark hall.

Chapter Twenty-seven

Lucia stared at Theron in disbelief. It wasn't his words that she could not accept as true; it was, instead, his apparent belief that the story he'd just told her made Vlad look worse than Theron himself did.

She had let this, this . . . this power-mad inhuman creature—she had let this thing invade her mind and touch her in her most intimate places? She had let this *thing* find a place in her heart? She had betrayed her betrothed in her mind for a soulless, greedy, ambitious, utterly heartless demon from the depths of Hell, one who had come to her only in order to wreak a revenge on her betrothed?

"Since I can't get Vlad to hold up his end of the bargain—"

"A bargain which you yourself intended to cheat him on, in the worst way!" Lucia interrupted.

"Yes, but he deserves it. Since I can't get him to hold up his end, I was thinking—perhaps after he comes for you and you are wed to him, you could help me remove his soul so I can take over his body. I don't know how yet, but there must be a way to—"

"No! No, of course not! Are you mad?"

"You *know* me. You don't know him, and believe me, you don't want to."

"I wish I'd never met you! Do you realize what you've done? You've started a war. A war! Hundreds, maybe thousands of men have died because you interfered in what my brother had planned for me."

"You didn't want to marry Nicolae of Moldavia, anyway."

"I was fourteen! I would have adjusted! I wouldn't have been stuck here in a damned empty castle on top of a demon-haunted mountain with only a bunch of lonely, angry, dried-up women for company if *you . . . hadn't . . . interfered!*"

"It could have been worse."

"How?"

Theron shrugged. "You never know. Maybe you would have died in childbirth by now."

"Maybe I would have had a child of my own by now!"

"I really think you should consider my plan. You would stand a much better chance of happiness with me inhabiting Vlad's body than with Vlad himself in residence. He really is a vicious bastard, Lucia. I have not exaggerated that."

Lucia shook her head. "I have been a fool. A deluded fool. Sister Teresa was right: It is time I stop dreaming and wake up." Theron truly was a demon. A creature of the darkness. How had she let herself forget that? No one else but a damned monster could so coolly suggest taking over a living human body.

No one but a demon could treat so lightly the utter disaster he had made of her life. *Her* life. All her brother's coldness, all these years of loneliness came right back to Theron. And he didn't seem to grasp the enormity of it.

She met his eyes, and for a moment her heart clenched in her chest. Despite all she'd just said, despite all he had told her that revealed him as less than the human companion she had begun to think him, despite the knowledge that there could never, ever be anything between them . . . despite it all, she didn't really want to say good-bye. Yes, he was a monster, but in their short, strange acquaintance he had been the closest thing to a friend she had ever known.

"You've been as kind to me, Theron, as you knew how. You've been gentle. I know you could have been much more frightening at the beginning, especially since you wanted to hurt Vlad through me. So I thank you for that, and I hope you find some other way to get a chance at a mortal life, if that is still what you want." She paused, hurting. "But we cannot see each other again. I'm going to wear the necklace from now on."

"What?"

If she didn't know better, she would think he was hurt too. He didn't have a heart to hurt, though. He had no soul. He did not love. He had told her so himself. She shouldn't feel a pang at causing pain to a creature who could not feel the way a person did.

"What else is there for us? You are not who I thought you were. And perhaps I am not as good as I thought myself, either." She should have broken off their entanglement as soon as it began.

He didn't say anything for a long moment. And then, almost curtly, "Can I have one kiss good-bye?"

She should have been relieved at such an easy capitulation. She wasn't, though. Her fickle heart wished he would protest, that he would put up a struggle. She didn't want to so easily disappear from his life. To be dismissed. She knew that she'd be thinking of him for years to come.

"One kiss? Yes, all right," she said, as if she did not care. If that was all he wanted of her, that was all she would give him.

He leaned forward.

Chapter Twenty-eight

Mara crept slowly down the hall, the candlestick shaking in her hand, its tiny flame sending leaping shadows up the walls. She passed a window alcove and jumped as a burst of wind hit the glass, rattling it angrily as if the wind wanted to burst in and steal her soul.

Or maybe it was the demon queen, seeking entrance to the castle. Mara whimpered and hurried her step, the hair rising on the back of her neck as she became more and more convinced that she was being pursued by a demon. When she could stand the suspense no longer, she turned around in a sudden whirl and thrust the candle out before her, daring any creature of the night to step into the light.

The hall was empty.

Mara backed slowly to the foot of the narrow stone spiral staircase she would climb to return to Lucia's part of the castle. Her eye firmly on the darkness behind her, she climbed the stairs by feel.

As she neared the top she heard a noise . . . and it was

ahead of her. It sounded like raspy breathing. Her whole body trembling, she slowly turned to look.

She caught a glimpse of bare gray flesh and hideously sagging breasts, and then the candlestick dropped from her nerveless hands.

"The priest!" the beast cried. "Where is the priest?"

Mara gurgled in terror and fell more than ran back down the stairs, clinging to the rope rail, her muscles so weak with fear that it seemed they could barely support her.

Certain that she was about to feel the clawed hand of the demon queen on her at any moment, Mara stumbled and ran back down the hall toward Father Gabriel's room.

She turned a corner and saw the light of a candle and the dimly lit face of Father Gabriel. She stumbled the last few steps toward him and collapsed at his feet as if she had just crossed a hundred miles of desert.

"The demon . . ." Mara rasped.

"What? What about the demon?" Father Gabriel asked in alarm.

"The demon *queen!*"

"Yes? Yes? What? Speak, damn you!"

Mara pointed back the way she had come, still panting with terror. "The demon queen is *here*. And she is looking for you!"

"Holy mother of God," Father Gabriel swore, and Mara saw his slack face go sweaty and pale with fear.

Chapter Twenty-nine

Lucia opened her mouth to the kiss and let her tongue slide against Theron's, as he had taught her. His was wetly rough and warm, and tasted faintly of spice. As their kiss deepened, she felt the familiar hunger rising inside her. She reached her hands around his neck, her fingers splaying up into the cool hair at his nape.

She opened her eyes as they kissed, and knew that she didn't want him to look like a stranger while they kissed good-bye. She took control of the dream and changed him—changed him to the Theron who had sat on her bed in the middle of the night, with pale skin and black hair and eyes of blue fire.

He must have felt the change, for he broke the kiss and pulled back, and looked in surprise at his own hand. A moment later he changed into the warrior.

Lucia let a sly cat's smile curl her lips and forced him back to the true Theron. His image wavered between the two.

"Why do you want me like that?" he asked.

"I want to know to whom I am bidding adieu."

He changed then fully to Theron, although she didn't know if she had forced it herself, or if he had merely granted her wish.

She held his face between her hands and looked into his eyes. "Can you see me through those eyes? Or have I always been only looking into a picture of you?"

"I'm not really there, beneath your palms," his voice said in her head, while the dream Theron before her said nothing. "The Theron you believe you touch is only an image in your dream."

"So you truly feel nothing when I kiss you?"

"I feel an echo of the pleasure you feel; the more you enjoy it, the more I enjoy it."

"Then what do you feel when I do this?" She kissed the dream Theron again, gently sucking his tongue into her mouth and sliding her own along the side of it. He kissed her back, his mouth greedy on hers, and then slid his lips down the side of her neck and sucked at the place where neck joined shoulder. She felt a rivulet of pleasure run down her body from his mouth to her loins, pooling there in warm desire.

"I feel that one kiss is not going to be enough," he growled, speaking from the dream Theron. He scraped his teeth against her neck. "You can't say good-bye to me, Lucia. You love this too much."

"I don't," she said—knowing she was being untruthful, knowing that she wanted to taunt him into trying to make her change her mind.

"You cannot lie to me, not about this. You will keep taking that necklace off every night, even when you don't think you want to, because your body knows that this is what you need."

"Maybe it is you who needs me," she said, as his

mouth moved down her chest. He pulled her wrap loose, and she gasped as he took her nipple into his mouth, his tongue swirling around it. "Maybe you need someone who knows who you are. Does it feel better with the other women?"

"Pleasure is pleasure."

"Is it? Truly?" She almost reached for his loins, but then remembered that it was her own pleasure that he felt. She lay back and he followed her downward, one broad palm under her buttock, his lips still at her breast. "So it feels the same to you when another woman does *this*." She reached down and, gingerly, without experience or knowing how, touched her fingertips to her own nether lips. A tingle of pleasure ran through her flesh like the vibration of a plucked mandolin string.

He lifted his mouth from her breast and stared at her. She touched herself again, lightly brushing her fingertips over the sensitive folds. She was shy of it, but it felt good, and she wanted to make him feel pleasure. She slid her fingertips down lower and gently stroked the entrance to her core, her own touch rousing desire inside her.

"Lucia . . ." he rasped.

"Does it feel the same when other women do this?"

He shivered, as if unable to control the reactions of his dream self. "I give women dreams where they do that for their own pleasure . . . but they never do that for *me*."

She felt slick wetness on her fingertips and instinctively drew it up her folds, using it to glide her touch over the small, hardening peak of her desire. He was still frozen above her, as if prisoner to the pleasure she was making him feel. "You will never find this with someone else," she said. "Be sorry that you will never visit my dreams again."

"But I'm going to. You will call for me in the night, when you cannot stand being alone any longer." He brushed his hand down over her bare thigh, then back up and across her lower belly. "You'll call for *me*, the first to know your body, the first to bring you to climax, the one who took your virginity in your mind, if not in fact."

She let her hand fall away from herself. "But you haven't."

"I will."

She shook her head, even as his hand brushed down her inner thigh and then back up, his long fingers drifting over her sex and then trailing away again, leaving sparkling desire in their wake. "No!" she said, and did not know if she meant it. "That is for my husband, not for you."

"Try to resist me."

"I can erase this dream at any moment I wish."

"Perhaps, if you wanted to. And perhaps not." His fingers brushed again over her sex.

She mentally tried to shove him away, but he did no more than flinch. So she closed her thighs tight together and rolled onto her side, forcing him to pull his hand out from between them as she pulled her knees up toward her chest. "You can force anything on me."

He grazed his hand over her hip and then down her buttocks and to her exposed folds beneath, her feminine flesh pressed tight together by her thighs and helplessly open to his touch from behind. When his fingers brushed over her, it was twice as intense as when her thighs had been parted.

"I do not have to force anything on you," he said. "I will only do what at least some part of you wants me to do."

His fingertips brushed her again, and she closed her eyes and drew her knees up higher, exposing herself even more. Yes, she *did* want him to do this. It would be her last chance until she was married. It was only a bit of pleasure, harming no one. . . .

He gently nudged her to roll onto her back, and then he scooped her up in his arms and carried her to a bed covered in rich fabrics, sitting in the middle of the raft where there had been nothing before. He laid her gently upon it, her hips at the edge.

He dropped to his knees before her and then lifted her legs together until she had bent them up toward her chest, her knees and ankles pressed tight together. She held her knees with her hands.

Again, she was exposed to him from below, but when she looked down all she could see was her own legs blocking her view. A scolding shame whispered through her, that she should reveal herself so boldly and crudely, her body balled tight while her sex was out in the open for him to do with as he pleased.

Yet she knew it was as *she* pleased. She wanted him to touch her. She wanted—

His tongue licked the length of her. A cry of pleasure caught in her throat, and Lucia rocked her hips, begging for more.

He licked her again, harder, and then so lightly that she almost could not feel his touch. He put his hands flat on the bottoms of her thighs and rocked her against his mouth, his tongue hitting her with short flicks that were almost slaps against the peak of her folds. He slowed and then lay his open mouth over her, sucking gently, his tongue swirling slowly through her hills and valleys.

She felt herself rising toward the climax, where she had lost herself before, and she clung tighter to her knees, her legs tensing and her hips again rocking of their own accord.

He lifted his mouth away, and when it did not return she whimpered. She opened her eyes and saw that he was standing now, the violet velvet of the night sky behind him, the stars surrounding him as if in adulation of his beauty.

"Now, Lucia. I will give you what you've always wanted."

She released her knees and slowly lowered her legs to either side of his body, there being nowhere else to put them. As her line of sight became unobstructed, she saw that he was no longer wearing his cloth wrap. He was naked. His sex was pointing upward, rising thick and bold from a base of dark curls. It looked *right* to her now, as if it was exactly how it was meant to be. This was what a man was, and she, a woman, was made to accept it. Only—

"This isn't what I've always wanted. What I've always wanted you haven't the means to give me," she said, with the sadness of truth in her heart.

"I can give you anything within the world of dreams."

She shook her head. "You cannot give me love, in this world or any other. Nor can you give me a child. You cannot be a husband to me. You cannot truly hold me in your arms. I can only dream of you."

He leaned forward, bracing his arms to either side of her, the head of his sex touching her folds with the same careful caress as his fingers. "Isn't this almost the same thing?" he asked, and she heard an echo of her own sadness in his voice. He knew it, too.

She blinked against tears of longing for love. "No, it's not. And you won't be able to take my virginity, even in this dream, because it's not what I want."

He rocked against her, the length of his shaft sliding over her and back, once, twice, three times, until she started to rock with him, her body responding to this touch, so much in keeping with what it wanted. Then his head stopped at her opening and pressed against it, the pressure dull and strangely pleasant.

"You won't be able to," she said. She could feel her nearly perfect control over what happened to her own body. He wouldn't be able to force his way into her. "I've grown stronger, Theron, stronger perhaps even than you, in my own dreams."

"But are you stronger than your own desires?" he asked, almost in desperation, as if he thought only by doing this could he keep her with him. His hips rocked, and the pressure against her entrance doubled.

She closed her eyes, her body tingling in pleasure at the blunt, gentle force pressing against her.

"It's what you want," Theron said. "Tell me it is what you want."

Chapter Thirty

Gabriel puckered his anal sphincter to keep from fouling himself, his bowels loosening in fear. "The *demon queen*? Are you sure?"

"She was more hideous than the drawing! I was as close to her as I am to you. I could have touched her!" Mara's voice lowered dramatically. "Death-gray skin, hanging belly, and breasts like great empty sacs—with nipples pointing toward the ground to better suckle her demon young."

Gabriel shuddered, the she-beast growing larger and more hideous in his imagination. "Where was she?"

"In the hall outside Lucia's room, at the top of the stairs. She said, '*Where is the priest?*' She's looking for you!"

He felt the candlestick slip in his sweaty palm. God help him!

"What are you going to do?" Mara asked, grabbing the hem of his robe. "You'll capture her, won't you?"

"Yes, surely . . ." God in heaven, how was he supposed to do that? He pretended to know much more than he actually did about the world of demons and how to control them. "We must find a bottle or jug."

They hurried back to his room, and he set about frantically looking for something in which to capture the demon queen, knowing all the while that he was doomed. Doomed! One male demon in a circle of candles he could perhaps capture, but a demon queen roaming free?

Doomed!

"Here, this will work!" Mara said.

He turned around just in time to see her emptying one of his precious vials of poppy juice into his chamber pot. "No!"

She blinked at him in surprise, vial still upended.

He rushed to her and snatched it from her hand, his fingertips trying to catch the last precious drops as they dribbled out of the top. He licked a faint trace off his finger, but it was nothing. Nothing!

He'd use it, then. There was nothing else to do. He grabbed a few more candles and motioned Mara toward the door. "Take me to where you saw her."

Together they crept through the halls and back to the stairs. They looked up the dark staircase. Lightning flashed and thunder rolled, and Gabriel's unwieldy handful of candles slipped and slithered in his sweaty grasp.

They heard a voice echoing in the hall up above, and both froze. Mara's wide eyes met his own. "Did she say—"

The voice came again, fainter this time, calling its single word. "Faaaa-ther . . ."

"I don't want to go up there!" Mara whined, and she started to cry. "Don't make me go up there!"

Gabriel felt urine dribble down the side of his leg. Limbs shaking, he put his hand on the stair rail and began to climb.

Chapter Thirty-one

Lucia opened her eyes and met Theron's own, and even though she knew it was just a dream image of him at which she gazed, she saw in the fiery depths a truth about herself: She was falling in love with him. It was neither right nor wrong, it neither made sense nor was without sense; it simply was.

As the realization hit her she hid it deep in her heart, where he would not be able to find it. Her body knew the truth, though, and the wall she had been trying to build against him melted away. The head of his cock parted her flesh, and she gave a cry of pleasure and despair as she felt him stretching her, filling her, entering her with a few short thrusts to ease his way, then sheathing himself entirely within her, until she could feel his loins pressed up against her flesh.

She had had no control after all; her heart, body, and soul wanted what her mind had forbidden. She hadn't known that the mind was the weakest of them all and the first to give way.

He pulled back and then filled her again, her inner passage gripping him as if she could not get enough. With each withdrawal she pushed herself toward him, helpless to do otherwise, her body craving the completeness he gave with each thrust.

Her heart craved a different fulfillment, but it would have to survive on this substitute, taking what it could from his determination to be with her and to bed her, even if it was only in her own mind.

He reached down between them and splayed his hand over her pubic mound, his thumb reaching down and rubbing the peak of her sex. She felt herself climbing toward climax—each thrust taking her higher until she lost all sense of herself, all sense of him, all sense of where she was or what she was doing. All she knew was the pleasure radiating outward from the joining of their bodies.

She was almost there; the edge of the chasm was beckoning her and she wanted nothing more than to throw herself over it.

Chapter Thirty-two

Gabriel reached the top of the stairs. All was in darkness in the passageway, and the sounds were of the rain and the howling wind, circling the castle like wolves around a lame sheep.

He took one faltering step forward and then another, knowing it was a matter of kill or be killed. The lit candle he carried made the hall look all the darker and blinded him to the far reaches, but he hadn't the courage to extinguish it.

A sound different from the wind and rain caught his ear and he froze. Was that a rasping breath he heard? He felt the hair on his arms and neck rising, his gaze frantically searching the darkness.

A bolt of lightning cracked overhead, and the brilliant glare of white light broke through the windows and revealed, not twenty feet in front of him, the hideous demon queen.

She saw him at the same moment he saw her, and she raised her open arms toward him, her gruesome visage breaking into the smile of the damned, her mouth like a portal to Hell. "I have found you!" the she-demon cried gleefully, and started toward him.

Darkness descended once again as thunder rolled through the castle, and his last shred of courage dissolved. He dropped his candles and vial and turned and fled.

"Father!" the beast cried behind him.

Gabriel felt his heart almost stop in his chest and threw himself down hall after hall, searching for some escape, somewhere to hide.

He bumped up against a small wooden door and jerked it open. A burst of cold air hit him in the face, tinged with a faint stench of human waste. *The privy.*

He ducked down under the lintel and plopped down onto the wooden seat, jerking the door shut behind him. A brief moment passed, and then there was a loud, creaking groan all around him, audible even over the howling wind and the rolls of thunder.

His eyes opened wide as he felt the seat beneath him shift, tilting back. He grabbed for the door frame, but it was suddenly out of reach, and a sickening understanding of what was about to happen hit him.

"Oh, *shit.*"

The privy ripped away from the castle wall and fell toward the trees and rocks far, far below.

Chapter Thirty-three

"Open your eyes," Theron whispered.

She obeyed, and it was while gazing bare-souled into his flame-blue eyes that she went over the edge, her body contracting in wave after wave of greedy satisfaction, her passage clenching him within her. She tightened her thighs against his hips, her ankles crossing behind him as if she could hold him inside her forever.

As the waves died away she relaxed, and he lowered himself down on top of her, then rolled them both onto their sides, still joined, her top leg up over his thigh. He brushed her hair back from her damp face and kissed her brow with a strange solemnity. "'Set me as a seal upon your heart, as a seal upon your arm,'" he quoted to her.

She tilted her head to look up at him, puzzled. "That's from the Song of Solomon. How do you know it?"

"I heard it in your thoughts. Set me as a seal upon your body and heart, Lucia. You are mine and shall never belong to Vlad. Even if you marry him you will still be mine. I shall never let you go."

Lucia lowered her face and tucked it against his chest, closing her eyes and trying to keep him from sensing what was flowing through her mind. His words did not comfort or please her, for all that they were what she had wanted to hear. As the hunger of desire faded from her blood, guilt came washing in its wake.

She had reneged on her own promise to herself, to at least save her virginity for Vlad. Her body remained untouched, but the joining lived in her mind with as much vividness as if it had been real. Vlad was not going to get a pure bride on his wedding day.

She was a foul and wicked creature, to enjoy mating with a demon. Her soul was surely damned thrice over for falling in love with him at the same time.

May God help her, because she knew now that she could not help herself.

Chapter Thirty-four

Sister Teresa woke early, as the first light touched the horizon. She hadn't slept well, not well at all. She had vague memories of bad dreams, but fortunately they flitted from her mind even as she tried to capture them.

Her bladder was full and her gut was making unpleasant gurgling sounds; her dinner hadn't settled well last night and was begging to exit. She pulled a wrap around her chemise-clad shoulders and hurried down the hall to the privy.

When she got there and opened the door, though, she was met with empty space where the privy should have been. A few broken, rotted beams showed where the wood had given way.

Fortunately, someone had left a chamber pot sitting on the floor, and Teresa squatted above it in great relief.

She wrinkled her nose. No, dinner had *not* settled well.

When she was finished, she opened the privy door once more and lifted the chamber pot.

* * *

Anton, the captain of the guard sent by Vlad with Father Gabriel, yawned and scratched his buttocks, and made his way around the side of the castle. There was a wonderful view of the mountains and the sunrise, and as he peed the morning sun caught his urine stream, turning it into shining droplets of gold.

It had been a wild night in the barracks. The soldiers stationed here were a rough lot, and boredom had taught them how to entertain themselves. The scorchingly fierce local plum brandy had put them all in a good mood, and the Maramures and Transylvanian soldiers had gotten along with the Wallachians like long-lost brothers.

Anton grimaced in guilty amusement as he remembered what the spirit of camaraderie had prompted him to do. When the brandy had run out, he'd been far enough gone in his cups that he'd lifted the satchel of Father Gabriel's poppy juice onto the table. "Forget the plum brandy," he had said. "Take a look at what the good priest drinks!"

Anton shook off the last drops and started tucking himself back into his braies.

A moan drifted to him on the breeze. What the hell?

He looked around but saw nothing. The moan came again, this time sounding as if it was from slightly above. He looked up.

At first he couldn't make sense of what he was seeing. It looked like an impossibly enormous crow had somehow gotten itself entangled in one of the pine trees that clung to the side of the mountain at the castle's base. Then the breeze picked up and the black feathers moved, revealing pale, misshapen lumps of flesh.

The thing moaned again, and Anton realized with a start that it was human.

"Are you all right up there?" he called.

The moaning stopped, and then after a moment of silence came an angry voice. "Do I *look* like I'm all right? Get me down from here!"

"Father Gabriel?" There was no one else who would answer a plea of concern with such bad temper. Bastard. There had been a dozen times on the journey when Anton had been a hair's breadth from letting the man go it on his own. Doubtless he would have come to a fittingly bad end in short order.

"Yes, of course it's me, you manure-brained idiot!"

Anton ground his teeth. "The soldiers want to thank you for the poppy juice."

"*What?*"

"I hope you have more of it hidden away somewhere, because I think we may have gone through the lot."

Incomprehensible screeching met this announcement, and a wild struggle in the pine branches, yielding no change except to shake loose a few pinecones. At last the priest panted to a stop.

"How'd you get up there?" Anton asked.

"If you value your soul and your career, you will shut your mouth and get me down!"

"Yes, of course." In good time. It seemed a pity not to leave him hanging a minute or two longer.

Anton looked from the priest to a piece of wood also stuck in the tree, then up the castle wall. There was a small wooden door opening onto nothing except for a few stumps of timber that might once have supported a privy. Anton grinned, comprehension dawning.

As he watched the privy door opened, and for a brief

moment he thought he saw a wimple-covered head. Then there was a motion as of a pot being emptied, and a discolored slush of waste flew through the air.

"Hold your breath," Anton called to Gabriel.

"What? Hold my—"

A moment later there was no need to explain.

As Anton went to get help, Father Gabriel's outraged howls filled the golden morning air and echoed down the deep, peaceful valleys of the mountains.

It was, Anton thought, a beautiful day to be alive.

Chapter Thirty-five

"My lady, your gown is finished," Mara said, holding out the amber and green gown that Lucia had asked to be completed. The one she had seen herself wearing in her vision.

"Thank you, Mara," Lucia said with hardly any voice. She didn't want to look at it, nor to think what it meant. Vlad would be coming for her, perhaps sooner rather than later.

"Are you well?" Mara asked with a faint trace of genuine concern, laying the gown over a chair.

"Tired, is all."

"You have been tired much of late."

"I don't understand it. I sleep through the entire night." She slept, and Theron visited her in her dreams, and the whole night through they continued to explore each other's bodies and he taught her more things that she would never have imagined could happen between a man and a woman. Her earlier resolution to not wear the necklace had been for naught.

And she always woke with a feeling verging on exhaustion. When she'd looked in the mirror today, she'd seen a shadow-eyed reflection with cheeks that were beginning to hollow.

She had no appetite during the day, nor interest in what was going on around her. Father Gabriel had been confined to bed for a week and a half now, recovering from his tragic fall from the privy. He had cracked a few ribs and cut himself in several places, besides being very badly bruised and dislocating a shoulder. She hadn't even been to his room to check on his welfare.

In addition to the sex, she and Theron talked. Again and again he brought up how vile Vlad Draco was, and she almost believed him.

Lucia looked at Mara, puttering around the room. "Mara, you knew of Vlad before you came here. You met him yourself, didn't you?"

The maid stopped what she was doing and looked warily over. "Yes."

"I have heard rumors that he is not the gentle, noble man I believed him to be."

"Who told you such things?" Mara asked, turning away and fussing with a pillow.

"Mara . . ." Lucia repeated.

The maid turned back to her, a frightened look on her face. "My lady?"

"I will not hold it against you, nor will I repeat what you say to a living soul. Is Vlad Draco the man I was led to believe, or is he a murdering tyrant and rapist?"

"There is no question but that he is a great leader of men. He is much feared and respected in battle."

"That is not what I asked. From your knowledge of him, is he a good man?"

"My lady . . ." Mara said softly, a plea in her voice. "Do not make me say bad things about him."

"Even if they are true?"

"It would be as much as my life is worth."

Her refusal to answer was more disturbing even than a description of foul misdeeds could have been. And the look on her face. "You are that scared of him. What of Father Gabriel? Is he as wicked as Vlad?" Lucia asked.

"He is a priest."

"Again, you do not answer."

"I know that he has sought to conquer evil, when and where he has found it," Mara offered.

"Has he found it here?" She thought with alarm of Theron's visits. She had been taking Theron's safety for granted while the priest was stuck in bed, but surely Father Gabriel would be rising soon.

"He has seen it, yes. It is evil that threw him from the privy that night."

"Oh, I don't think so. That privy was rotten; you'd noticed that yourself. We all had."

But Mara shook her head. "I saw the creature myself. It was the queen of the demons, come to take Father Gabriel's soul."

"*What?*"

Mara nodded. "It's only by the grace of God that Father Gabriel was not killed by the she-beast."

"Why didn't you tell me this before?"

Mara shook her head and met Lucia's eyes. "Must you ask me that?"

Lucia could only hold her gaze for a moment, and then she turned away in guilt. So Mara knew or suspected about Theron. "Leave me."

"Yes, my lady." The maid quietly exited the room.

Lucia sank down into a chair.

What was happening to her? How had she become this enervated shadow of herself, existing almost entirely in her dreams? The hours of the day had become nothing more than a dreary obstacle to overcome as she waited for the night.

It was sapping her strength. It was as if all her vital energy went to her time with Theron, with none of it ever replenished by innocent sleep.

Was this what love was supposed to be? Although she had no experience of it, still she sensed all was not right. This was unnatural, what she had with Theron.

And yet she could not help herself. She could not stop herself from removing the necklace each night, and each night when he appeared in her dreams she greeted him with open arms.

As weary as she was during the day, she had been stronger each night in her dreams. She now had as much control as he did, if not more; it was, after all, her own mind in which they played.

Almost better than the sex with Theron were the places he continued to show her. He had been to all inhabited corners of the earth, and had watched the past four thousand years unfold. In her mind he could recreate images of any of it. Any time, any place. She had seen great pyramids in a desert; she had seen pyramids in a jungle; she saw people who lived in a land of ice; she saw people who lived in a swamp, their homes woven of the rushes that grew there. She had seen ancient Greece, and the great land of China to the east. The places and people seemed a fantasy, but Theron assured her they were—or had been—as real as she herself, and that to them she would be as exotic and unimaginable as they were to her.

It was an education such as no monastery full of books could ever provide, and she felt as unable to give up those adventures as she was unable to give up her teacher.

She looked at the green and amber gown lying across the other chair. It was a reminder of what was coming. Who was coming. Vlad *would* arrive.

How could she marry him? She couldn't—not only because of Theron, but because everything Theron had told her led her to believe Vlad was a monster.

Theron had kept her glimpses of Vlad's work brief, out of courtesy to her sensibilities. The small views of the violence he wrought was enough to make her ill, but even worse was the memory Theron had shown her of one of the girls Vlad had raped.

She *couldn't* marry Vlad. And yet she had no choice, not truly. Theron would not be able to help her; he had no substance in this world, and had already failed to steal Vlad's body. She was on her own.

There was only one person she could think to talk to. One person who always listened.

Chapter Thirty-six

Lucia found Sister Teresa in the garden, on her favorite bench in the sunshine. Lucia recognized that the nun was no longer quite herself, old age having robbed her of half her wit, but Teresa's heart had not been affected. She was still there if and when Lucia needed her.

Lucia sat down at the old woman's feet, the feel of the light on her skin soothing and warm, the faint scent of Sister Teresa's clothing bringing back memories of the many times she had sat just this way.

How many more times would she? Precious few, she feared. Her life was about to change, and Teresa's was closing in on itself.

The nun woke from her doze with a snort and blinked at the garden around her, gathering her bearings. She patted Lucia on the shoulder. "Have you been studying your Latin?"

Lucia shook her head.

"You look as if you have been up all night studying.

Were you reading that history? I shall test you on it, but you may have more time, if you wish."

Lucia smiled sadly. "No, I haven't been reading. I've just been thinking."

"Not daydreaming?"

"Thinking. And wanting your advice."

Sister Teresa stroked Lucia's hair. "You look troubled."

"I'm scared."

"Of what?"

"Marriage."

"That's nothing to be frightened of. It is not a bad thing, and even has its pleasures."

"You talk almost as if you know," Lucia said.

"It was a long time ago that my husband died, but I was happy enough with him while we were together."

Lucia turned around and stared up at Sister Teresa, slack-jawed. "You were married?"

"When I was very young. But he died, and there was no one else for me. Our child died, too." Teresa's gaze turned inward. "It was a very sad time."

"Was your husband a good man?"

"He was a simple man, but good in his heart, yes."

"Did you love him?" Lucia asked.

"I grew to love him, in my way. It happens like that sometimes, when two people live together and take care of each other."

"But what if the man is bad and has a wicked heart? Can you still grow to love him?"

Teresa blinked. "What is troubling you, child?"

Lucia's weariness and worries all seemed to rise to the surface at once, spilling over in the face of Teresa's simple kindness. She felt her lip trembling. "I . . . I have been hearing some very bad things about Vlad Draco. I fear he is not a good man. How am I to wed him, and to be the wife at his side, if he is cruel and violent?"

"Ah, child." Sister Teresa pulled Lucia against her, holding her gently as she shook and wept. She stroked Lucia's hair and made murmuring sounds. "There is always choice. Perhaps not the choice you wish, but there is choice."

"What choice do I have?" Lucia asked, lifting her head and wiping at her tears with the palms of her hands.

A strange light of clarity seemed to illuminate Sister Teresa's visage, and for a moment Lucia thought she could almost see the face of youth in the old nun. When she spoke it was not with the trembling uncertainty that had been so often her mode of late.

"You have the choice of how you are to be his wife," Teresa said. "You can cower in your chamber and walk in fear, and jump at the sound of his voice. You can let him know with every word and gesture that you fear and hate him.

"Or, if you are strong, you can take your place beside him and stand tall and unafraid, even when your heart trembles. You can use your gentleness to calm him in the dark of the night and soften his harshness. You can win his respect, and perhaps then win his ear, so that he will listen when you counsel mercy."

"But will I *love* him?"

Sister Teresa shook her head. "You are to be a queen, Lucia. Great responsibility comes with such a position, and the wishes of your own heart will forever be of less import than your duty to your people.

"Or you could be a selfish queen," Teresa continued

after a moment, "and dress yourself in finery, and feed yourself sweets all day and count your jewels, and never give heed to those who suffer under your husband's rule. There is always choice."

Lucia swallowed back the last of her tears, stunned by Teresa's words. They were not the gentle sympathy she had expected; they were not the comforting, *"He will love you and be tender, and you will be happy,"* she had hoped to hear.

"There is always choice," Teresa said again, and the old woman stared off into the distance. She blinked, and then the light of clarity was gone as she looked down at Lucia. "Child, have you been studying your Latin?"

Lucia returned to her chamber, Teresa's words echoing in her mind. She sat down again and stared at the amber and green dress.

She thought she understood the meaning of her vision now. She would touch her necklace and be sad because she had sent Theron away forever. She would weep because she must give herself to a man she did not love, and likely never could. And she would wipe those tears and go to him because it was her duty. Because she alone might be able to temper his violence and bring mercy to those who lived under his rule. Because she was meant to be a queen, and a queen worthy of even a single head bowed in respect was a queen who put her subjects before herself. And she needed to do this because she was no longer a child, and because it was time to put away childish dreams and wishes.

"'For now we see through a glass, darkly; but then face to face,'" she recited softly. It was herself she had not seen clearly, and it was herself she now saw face to face, the veils of dreams and wishes finally lifted. She knew what was right and had to do it if she were ever to bear looking at her own face in the mirror again.

She was no longer a child, but she knew she hadn't the strength to act alone. She saw that truth in the shadows under her eyes, shadows that spoke of a woman who could not refuse herself pleasure.

Lucia rose, and before she could think twice about it she made her way to Father Gabriel's chamber.

Chapter Thirty-seven

Theron checked to be sure Father Gabriel was still stuck in his bed, then made his way to Lucia's chamber, thinking all the while about what he would show her this time. The desert nomads, perhaps, with their camels? Or maybe the savannas of Africa, thick with animals such as Lucia had never seen.

Yes, perhaps the savannas. He came to her room and stepped up onto her bed, pausing to look at her as she slept.

" 'Thou art all fair,' " he said softly. He didn't understand how he could ever have thought her boring. He obviously had known nothing about her.

The hours between their meetings were torture for him. He hadn't visited other sleeping women, the thought of tasting their dreaming pleasure repulsive to him. He only wanted Lucia.

She filled his thoughts. All his energies were focused on her. When he was not with her, he thought about her, and he planned their nights together. He remembered things he wanted to tell her, and questions to ask her. He thought of music he had heard, music that he would re-create for her while he brought her to climax again and again and again.

As dawn approached each morning, he would reluctantly tear himself away from Lucia. It was as he left her each day that he cursed Vlad for breaking their bargain, fruitlessly seeking a scheme that would at last force Vlad from his body. His time was running short: It would not be long before Nyx would demand his presence and his wings would be clipped, his energies forced to serve her pleasure.

But he only wanted Lucia's pleasure. He wanted her solid in his arms, wanted to father a child by her. He wanted the life he saw imagined in her own mind, where together they could build a family, and watch their flesh and blood grow and prosper.

What was an existence in Nyx's harem when compared to that? It would be hell.

But each morning, when he once again failed to come up with any answer for how to step into the Waking World and claim Lucia for his own, he would turn his thoughts back to her, losing himself in preparations for their next night together.

He'd become a slave to her happiness, as much a lapdog as Samira had become to Nicolae. He saw that, and he did not care. There was nothing that mattered to him now but Lucia.

He reached forward and touched her brow.

Lucia felt Theron's arrival in her mind and let him change the scene around her as he wished. He put them atop a tall tower open to the sky above. A bed was in its center, covered in pale green silks. She walked to the rail that went around the circumference of the tower and looked out over the landscape below. Vast grasslands appeared as she watched, and a herd of small horses painted in black and white stripes. Farther away, enormous gray beasts lumbered slowly forward.

"Where are we?" she asked.

"Africa, far, far to the south of your homeland."

"What are those creatures?" She pointed to the black-and-white horses.

He explained, and went on to tell her more about the creatures and peoples of the grasslands. She listened with only part of her mind, the rest of her—hidden from where he could sense—heartbroken over what she was about to do, and second-guessing the rightness of her actions.

Still outwardly asleep, she gained control of her physical hand and forced it to raise one finger, tapping it on the covers of her bed. She tapped until she felt Mara lay her own hand over it, letting her know that the signal had been received.

Now Mara would go to fetch Father Gabriel, and Lucia would gain control of the dream and of Theron's attention. She would blind him to the true physical world, creating instead an illusion of it where they were alone in the room except for a sleeping Mara. The real Mara and Father Gabriel would thus be able to complete a candle circle around Lucia's bed and capture Theron.

She had strong misgivings, though. How could she possibly do that to Theron? How?

But how could she not? As Father Gabriel had pointed out to her, there was no other way to be certain Theron could never approach her again. All she could do was cut him from her life completely; it was obvious that she could not limit herself to conversation with him.

And there was no telling how violent Theron's response might be if she simply tried to stop his visits. He had, after all, first come to her in a quest for vengeance. He might have a violent response to such rejection. He was, as Gabriel reminded, a demon.

Although her head told her that it was right to do this, that it was the only way to step safely into her future, to be an adult and act responsibly, her heart wept and accused her of betrayal. This was beyond cruel, and almost more than she could bear. She didn't know if she would ever be able to forgive herself.

It was what was meant to be, though; she had seen the vision and knew that she would touch the necklace and weep at what it meant.

It was time to wake, and to be a woman fully in the world. No matter the heartbreak it caused.

Theron noticed that Lucia wasn't paying her full attention to the zebras and elephants and felt a spurt of disappointment. He'd failed her with his choice of entertainments. Perhaps she was even growing bored with these tours of foreign lands. Was he talking too much? Lecturing too much? *Son of the moon*, he hadn't had any practice at entertaining a woman by a means other than sex. He didn't know what he was doing.

He took her hand. "The animals don't interest you."

"What? No, they're fascinating, really. Thank you so much for bringing me here."

"Would you rather see someplace else? Name the place. Name the time. I'll show it to you."

"No, really, Theron. This is lovely. I'm just feeling a little tired."

He scooped her up in his arms, taking her by surprise, and carried her to the bed. "Then come lie down, my fair one. I will awaken you in the best way I know." He laid her down on the bed, then lay down beside her, on his side. He trailed his fingers over her breastbone.

She lay her hand over his, stilling his touch. "Is it all right if we just talk?"

Alarm went through him. Had she tired of him already? Was she bored with lovemaking? Was she having second thoughts about being with him? He feigned nonchalance. "Of course. What did you want to talk about?"

She shrugged listlessly. "I don't know."

"Something's the matter."

"No, everything's fine."

"Please tell me. What's bothering you?"

"Nothing."

"Did I do something?"

"No, it's not you. It's me," she said.

Another, bigger jolt of alarm went through him. He'd seen this speech in the minds of thousands of women, either being given or being received. It was the breakup speech. "You want to leave me."

The slight widening of her eyes betrayed her.

"Goddess of the Night," he swore softly, as he felt a cold, sinking dread wash over him. It settled in his belly, making him feel ill. For a moment he couldn't even see straight—the real room where Lucia slept blurred before his incubus eyes. He closed them, and concentrated on the dream.

"Why?"

"I don't think this was meant to be."

"What does that mean?" he asked, although he suspected he already knew the answer. As hard as he had tried to make each of their meetings perfect, he had felt an increasing hollowness. It was like rot at the core of a tree, leaving the branches green until all at once it fell over in the slightest of breezes.

"It means . . . it means I have to marry a real man, not a phantasm of my imagination."

"I *am* real. Maybe not tangible in your world, but I am *real.*"

"It's not the same."

He knew it wasn't. That was where the hollowness came from: They touched in dreams but did not touch in flesh. They did not talk of a future. They could never have a child, and Lucia deserved to have a child.

He hadn't told her about Nyx and the threat of the harem. It shamed him; he didn't want her to ever know that he would be made a sex slave to his queen, with no choice in the matter. It was emasculating.

"No living man could ever know you as well as I do, or give you as much pleasure," he tried. "No one could show you the world as I can."

She shook her head. "I need a daylight life, Theron. I need to do real things, with my real body. I need to leave Castle Rosu. I want to have children. Can *you* give me children?"

"That's not a fair question."

"Of course it is," she said.

Of course it was. He couldn't stop himself from protesting, though. "But why stop now? We could keep going until Vlad comes for you." From what he had seen in his spying, Vlad's success against Moldavia and his arrival at Castle Rosu might, indeed, happen not too far from the moment when Theron's reprieve from Nyx was over.

Again Lucia shook her head. "This is not working."

"Please, Lucia. Listen to reason."

"What reason is there to the heart? If there was reason, I would never have fallen in love with you."

He stared at her, not sure if he'd just heard what he thought he had. "Have you?"

"Have I what?"

"Fallen in love with me."

She sat up and drew her legs up to her side, turning away from him and looking out over the savanna. "I can't love a demon."

"Are you saying you don't love me, or are you saying you don't want to admit that you do?"

"What is love? You said yourself that I do not know. You, obviously, do not know. Is love supposed to be exhausting? Is it supposed to sap the enjoyment out of daily life?"

"That's how you feel?"

She nodded, looking down at her hands.

"I didn't know."

"How could you? You cannot love."

He shook his head, sensing that something was not right. "The women I have visited in the past, the ones who have been in love—they have been miserable half the time but ecstatic the other. They are never exhausted, though. They seem to have twice the energy of anyone else."

"Perhaps they had hopes for a happy ending to their romances. What hope have we? This, right now, is the best we can hope for. This is not the way I want to live my life."

"You won't want to live it with Vlad once you meet him. You'll wish for this back. I have seen so much more than you, Lucia. Trust me when I say that, incomplete as this may be, it is a hundred times better than what most humans can ever hope for."

"What would you know of that? You can't know, Theron. You can't truly understand. I was not created to live my life through my dreams, much as I have tried to make it so. It is time for me to wake up, and to become a woman. A *real* woman, not a pretend one. And that means ignoring the childish pleas of my heart and doing what is right." She sighed. "And I had best do it while I still have the energy."

He put his hand on her back. She didn't pull away; she only bent her head forward as if defeated. "You *are* tired, aren't you? Perhaps that is affecting the way you feel."

She changed her position, turning fully around to face him. She held his hand between both of her own. "I grow wearier and wearier with each morning. It is as if this dream existence is draining my life away. I don't think it's good for me."

As she spoke, Theron felt a cold nausea go through him. "Lucia . . . oh, good goddess. Lucia, I didn't realize . . . Your exhaustion—it's my fault. *Blast!*"

"It's *my* fault, for not saying no to you."

He shook his head. "No. I forgot— How could I forget? Of all the stupid— My only excuse is that I was so caught up in seeing you in your dreams, I completely forgot."

"Forgot *what?*"

"Dream demons are forbidden from visiting a specific human night after night. It's a rule I've broken, but I didn't stop to consider the consequences to you: With every visit, with every climax you feel, I take some of your energy. It's as food to us, you see."

"No, I don't see," she said crossly.

"All that frustrated sexual desire you had—to an incubus, such is the scent of . . . well, of a roasted pig to a hungry mortal."

She crossed her arms over her chest. "I'm flattered."

He shook his head. "With one visit from an incubus, or even two, a mortal woman is left feeling relaxed and happy. The extra tension is taken away.

"But with more visits, there is no extra tension left. The incubus starts to drain the woman of the energy she needs for daily life.

"That's what's happening to you. I've been taking too much of your energy."

"What happens if you don't stop coming to me?" she asked.

"Eventually . . ." Good goddess of the night, how had he let this slip his mind? He'd been so engrossed in his own need to be with her, he'd completely forgotten about her welfare. She was right: He knew *nothing* about love. *Nothing.* "Eventually, you would die."

"And you *forgot* this?" she asked incredulously. He saw tears start in her eyes. "You've been draining me of my life's energy and you didn't even *notice*? You could have killed me, and all you would have done is stand there and wonder what happened. Do you see now? Do you see that this is wrong? It is so wrong, it will kill me if it continues."

"I just need to give you time between visits. It will be all right, Lucia. If I give you a few days, you'll be back to normal."

"No, Theron. No more. If you care for me at all, do as I ask and leave me be."

He didn't want to leave her. He couldn't.

307

He shook his head. "You're just tired. I'll give you a week's rest, then come back. We'll talk about it then. You'll see, you'll feel differently."

"Leave me, Theron."

"I can't."

"You must leave me. Leave me *now.*"

Something changed in his vision, and for a brief moment he saw that all was not as he'd thought in Lucia's chamber. There were candles almost all the way around the bed. Candles, and Father Gabriel was chanting.

His real self sprang away from Lucia, leaping into the air and out of the circle just as the final candle was put in place. He hovered outside it, his body flushed with panic, and watched as Father Gabriel finished his spell and then pulled on a cord, dragging a clay jug out from under the bed.

"I've got you now!" Father Gabriel cried in triumph and slammed a cork into the neck of the jug. A moment later he poured red wax over the cork, then pressed the seal of a signet ring into it. "Neatly jugged and ready to go home to Vlad!"

Lucia stirred and woke, sitting up in bed. "Did you get him?"

Father Gabriel lifted the jug high and slapped its side. "Right here."

Lucia closed her eyes for a long moment, then opened them again. "It's for the best."

Theron felt the words pierce through him like a beam of killing sunlight.

She had planned this. She had known that Father Gabriel was going to capture him. She had known, and had kept him occupied while the circle was completed.

Something shattered within him, ripping him apart with shards of pain.

He flew out of Castle Rosu like a bat out of Hades, filled with rage and grief, and a feeling in his chest as if he was being rent apart by a greedy giant, his chest gnawed off and swallowed in one hungry bite.

Theron sought someone to blame for his pain; anyone. He wanted to pour it out on another, relieving his own agony by causing some deserving soul to suffer the torments of the damned.

One name came immediately to mind.

Chapter Thirty-eight

Theron streaked across the sky like a meteor of doom. He would land on Vlad Draco like a ton of rocks and smash the bastard to a bloody paste. Lucia would never have to marry the fiend, for he would not exist after Theron was through with him.

Beneath the rage, grief tormented him more cruelly than any demon ever could torment a mortal. *She did not want him.* He would never go inside her mind again. She would never speak to him again, would never share her pleasure with him. He was alone again, as he had been for four thousand years.

She did not want him. She would have him captured in a jug rather than let him touch her again.

He couldn't comprehend what his existence would be now; if he had had a soul, he would have said it had been torn from him, all his purpose gone, all his will to continue his existence gone.

Where had he gone wrong?

He couldn't even guess at the answer. All he knew

was that she would not give him the chance to make it right.

It did not stop him from caring for her, or from being horrified that Vlad would marry her and make her life a living hell. She could reject him and try to capture him until another thousand years had passed and Theron still would not want any harm to come to her.

If he could do nothing else for her, he would stop Vlad from claiming her. He didn't care if he himself was destroyed in the process. He was destroyed already, nothing left of his former self. The only thing worth existing for was saving Lucia from Vlad.

After that, he'd gladly stake himself to the ground and let the sun rise upon him. It would be a merciful release from the grief that devoured him.

He found Vlad in a tent, encamped with his army south of Galatsi. The bastard was discussing strategy with his generals: The tide of war had taken a turn against him, as Bogdan's son Nicolae had come to lead the family troops. From the sound of it, the bumbling magician had learned a thing or two since Theron had last seen him, and Bogdan's forces were reinvigorated. Vlad's, however, were struggling.

Theron drifted through the camp, most of it bedded down for the night, though a fair number of soldiers still were awake and hunkered around their fires, talking or cleaning weapons. Theron listened with great interest to the conversations among them. Rumors were rampant of monsters and great unnatural beasts; of demons from Hell and evil spirits, all under the rule of Nicolae of Moldavia and brought to arms in aid of Bogdan's forces.

The men were losing the will to fight, their concern

more with their own skin and their eternal souls than with invading a country with such damned inhabitants. Nicolae and his generals rode enormous wolves as their mounts, it was said.

The soldiers whispered of going home, to familiar lands where one never worried about giant ogres coming to bite off one's head.

With their courage shattered, the men did not fight with ferocity; and without ferocity, they were vulnerable to the swords and arrows of Bogdan's mortal army. The Moldavians were cutting a swath through Vlad's forces, pushing him back toward the Wallachian border.

Good, Theron thought. He was glad of it! It was best that Vlad suffer defeat and ignominy before Theron destroyed him.

He was glad, too, for Nicolae, for Nicolae's success must be pleasing for Samira. He didn't know if her month as a human was finished yet, but he was sure she must be rejoicing in Nicolae's victories, wherever she was.

Theron found the tents where the wounded were being tended. Behind one of those tents were the men who had not fared well under the care of the surgeons. Their bodies were stacked three deep, soaked in blood, flesh ripped and bare, bodies broken.

They were just what he needed.

He couldn't inhabit a living human body without the permission of the owner. But with a corpse, the owner had already left. He didn't personally know of any demon who had ever attempted to animate a corpse, but he had heard the tales and was desperate, willing to give anything a try.

He looked through the piles as best he could without

being able to move any of them, trying to gauge which were in the best shape.

He found a likely candidate at the top of a heap, dead of a gash to the belly from the looks of it. All the limbs appeared to be in one piece, although the face had been smashed. Still, one eye looked all right, and there was a mouth that might work. Theron threw his fate to the winds and dove into the body.

All was blackness. He felt a jolt of panic, and wondered if he'd just killed himself. As quickly as the panic came, it went—if he had been destroyed, he wouldn't be wondering about it.

He tried to lift an arm, and after a long moment of straining he felt it shift. He concentrated on opening the one good eye and after several seconds was rewarded with a bleary view of the camp. He used the arm he'd gotten moving to help push himself into a sitting position—and promptly fell off the pile of corpses, banging his head painlessly on the ground.

The body felt numb, and it was only with great effort and much lunging about on hands and knees that he managed to get it up onto its feet. He swayed and stumbled and ran with clumsy feet to keep up with the torso as it fell forward.

He staggered away from the pile of corpses, heading for Vlad's end of the camp.

"Gheorghe?" a soldier asked, stopping in shock and gaping at him.

"Muhhh-wuhhh," Theron said, the smashed mouth having trouble using what was left of lips and tongue. "Murrrrr . . ."

The soldier, eyes wide, staggered backward as Theron stumbled toward him. He didn't mean to give chase, but he was falling over that way and trying to stay on his feet. He lifted his arms, trying to grab hold of the soldier to keep his balance. "Muhhhhh . . ."

The soldier bolted.

"Muhh!" Theron called after him.

A fading scream was his answer. Soldiers were stirring around their fires and out of their tents, their attention caught by their running, screaming comrade.

Theron stumbled off in the other direction, still heading for Vlad's tent.

The one working eye showed him only a small, blurry picture of what was around him, with no depth. He stumbled over a tent rope and collapsed onto the canvas side. The whole thing listed, then slowly fell over, arousing a burst of curses from within.

As Theron flailed amid the canvas and ropes, the soldier inside managed to worm his way out, emerging with a face fiery with anger.

"Muhhh!" Theron said, caught on his back like a beetle. "Muhhh!"

"What in— Oh, Christ, what happened to you?"

Theron's hand slipped in something, and he craned his head to look. *Sun-blasted* . . . His entrails had come out. They were spilling out of the gash in his gut.

He lifted his hand toward the soldier, asking without words for help getting up.

The man backed away, shaking his head.

"Muh!" Theron said angrily. The bastards—why wouldn't any of them help him?

The soldier darted to a neighboring tent, speaking rapidly to its occupants.

Theron rolled over and eventually managed to climb off the tangle of canvas and ropes. As he did, he found himself atop the soldier's sword. Perfect! He used it to help lever himself back up onto his feet.

The soldiers in the other tent emerged and gaped at him. Theron looked down at himself again, and saw that his entrails were dragging on the ground. Well, that wouldn't do. He'd trip. He slowly gathered up a slippery loop of them, his numb hands having a hard time of it, and draped the loop over his neck.

"You need to get to the surgeon," one of the braver of the soldiers said.

Theron tried to say *Vlad*: "Bwad!"

"What was that?"

"Bwad! Bwad!"

"Stay here; we'll send for the surgeon."

"Muhhhh!" Theron said in disgust, and lumbered off again.

"Hey, that's my sword!"

Theron turned half-round and swung the blade in a drunken arc. "Muh!"

There was angry discussion among the soldiers, and as Theron staggered onward he heard, "I don't care, it's my sword! I can't let him have it, even if he is half dead."

A moment later the soldier was upon him, trying to wrest the sword from his grip. It was hardly a struggle, the soldier easily taking it from Theron's corpse's weak grip.

It made him mad.

"Rrrr . . ."

"It's nothing against you, fella, but you can't take my sword. Get yourself to the surgeon, for Christ's sake."

"Rrrr!"

The soldier turned and started away. Theron lurched after him and threw himself on the man. The soldier staggered under his weight but remained on his feet.

Just then the first man Theron had seen arrived with several of his comrades. "See, it's Gheorghe!"

"Good Christ," one of the others said, and crossed himself.

"You know this freak?" said the man to whose back Theron clung. The soldier tried to toss Theron off, but he got his arm around the fellow's neck and held on.

"It's Gheorghe, who died this afternoon."

"Who—what?"

"He's been dead all day."

"Rrrr!"

"Get him off me! Get him off me!" the soldier screeched.

Theron tried to chew on the back of the soldier's neck but mostly just gummed the man with his slimy mouth.

The soldier shrieked hysterically, again and again, spinning in circles like a dog after its own tail.

"What in God's name is going on here?" a voice of stern authority demanded.

Theron released the soldier and stumbled, then found his balance and was face-to-face with Vlad. Theron grinned.

Vlad grimaced in disgust.

"Bwaaaaad," Theron said.

"What was that?"

"Bwooo chee ah." It was supposed to have come out *Lucia*.

"What is going on here?" Vlad asked the group at large.

Theron stepped up right into Vlad's face and tried to say his own name. "Tair-on."

Vlad scowled. "Eh?"

317

"Tair-on. Bwoo chee ah."

A flicker of panic came into Vlad's eyes, as if comprehension was dawning. "Someone explain! Why is this man not being tended by a surgeon?"

"Your lordship, this man died this afternoon."

Theron grinned again. "Bwad."

Vlad stepped away from him and drew his sword. "This man is dead, you say?"

"He was this afternoon. Maybe the surgeons were mistaken."

"Don't be an ass. He shouldn't be moving or talking. A child could see that. You're a sorry lot of soldiers if you can't deal with something this simple."

With a single stroke of his sword, Vlad lopped off the arm Theron was holding out to him.

Theron frowned at the stump. It did not bleed. "Bwad! Muhhh!"

"Shut up!" Vlad demanded, and with a second stroke of his blade he cut Theron's head from his shoulders. It landed a yard from Vlad's feet.

"Bwad!" Theron said from the head. "Bwad!"

One of the soldiers collapsed in a faint. Others backed away. Mutterings of evil spirits and witchcraft moved around the circle.

"It can't harm you!" Vlad said, and lifted Theron's head by the hair. He held Theron's borrowed face in front of his own and said in a low voice, too low for the others to hear, "Is this the best you can do?"

"Bwoo chee ah. Muhn."

"She's not yours. She's not!" Vlad swung back and then threw Theron's head off into the darkness.

Theron left that part of the body and dove back into the headless corpse. He crawled toward Vlad.

"You're dead!" Vlad screeched in fury, and hacked

away at the corpse's limbs. "You're dead and you can't hurt anyone!"

Theron put himself into one of the lopped-off arms and grabbed Vlad's ankle.

Vlad bent down and yanked on the forearm, then used his own fingers to pry the dead ones off. "Go back to Hell, where you belong!"

Theron abandoned the hacked-up body and went to find a fresh one.

The next night Theron found a much fresher body, free of obvious signs of damage. He carefully concealed the rotting wound that had poisoned the soldier and tried like a drunken man to make his steps straight as he went in search of Vlad. The limbs were impossibly stiff, though, and he could not unbend his arms. His walk was a tottering, bent-legged odyssey across the camp.

He spotted Vlad, who was returning to his tent, a meeting with his generals just finished. His personal guard was milling around but had not yet taken up duty around their prince.

"Vlad Draco!" Theron said as sharply as he could through the lock-jawed mouth of the corpse. He gave himself a clumsy punch to the jaw, loosening things up.

Vlad's attention snapped to him.

Theron affected as relaxed and casual a stance as he could but feared he looked instead as if he'd been frozen while climbing a tree. One of the guards crossed his arms over his chest and blocked the way.

"What is it?" Vlad asked.

"A message, sir!"

Vlad narrowed his eyes suspicious. Theron stood stiff and bent-legged, one arm raised, his hand reaching for his head as if to scratch for lice. Vlad came close, and drew the dagger from out of Theron's belt before Theron could stop him. "This is a poor disguise, demon."

But good enough for an audience with you, Theron thought. "You will have no prize in Lucia. I have taken all the innocence that I threatened, and I have felt the convulsions of her orgasm as I plunged myself within her. She is ruined, Vlad. Ruined. Your virgin page has been smeared with ink."

Vlad's face turned dark red with fury. "You have *not*. She wore the necklace!"

"She removed it for the promise of the pleasure I could give her. I have licked at her loins, Vlad Draco, and drunk of her pleasure. She has no innocence left and has given her heart to me. If you take her now, it will be my leavings you are having."

A vein bulged in Vlad's forehead. "Your *leavings?*"

"Your brother tried to capture me, but you can see how well that worked. You should know that the amulet worked even less effectively."

Vlad's nostrils flared. "If she *is* ruined, then I just won't need to show any care with her, will I? She'll still be my wife—the ties with her family are too valuable to renege on *that* deal."

Theron's stiff hands clenched, and he wished he had that dagger in one of them.

"If Lucia is ruined, I can take her through her back passage and not care whether she likes it. I can whip her crotch with a switch until it is bloody and knows who is its master. Yes, if Lucia is ruined, I can take pincers to her nipples and thrust a needle through her folds, sewing her closed. I can hang her by her hair and let her spin from the rafter while I drink my wine.

"And when I tire of all that, I can tie a rock to her ankle and throw her in a river, and blame the murder on my enemies."

Vlad stepped back. "Kill it," he ordered.

The bodyguard drew his sword.

For seven nights Theron animated the corpses of Vlad's army, terrorizing the soldiers and pursuing Vlad with a single-minded intent: to kill him.

The trouble was, Theron in a corpse was no match for Vlad with a sword. As the week wore on, the soldiers started burning the corpses, and Vlad surrounded himself with an armed guard, with instructions to hack to pieces any walking dead who approached. The terror that Theron caused in the first few nights began to fade as the soldiers got used to bodies that spontaneously reanimated. If anything, their respect for their leader grew, as the story went around of how coolly Vlad had dealt with the gruesome Gheorghe.

"Bwuck," Theron cursed, as a sword once again chopped a head from its possessed body.

The army was still in retreat, though, still being forced back into Wallachia. From his spying in incubus form, Theron knew that Vlad was considering calling for a truce and agreeing to an orderly retreat back to his own lands.

Although it would not be the victory Vlad had wanted, it would still be an end to the wars. And that would mean he would go to Lucia, and visit upon her all the heinous atrocities he had threatened.

Theron had only a single night left before he must go to Nyx. Only a single night to protect Lucia from the tortures Vlad held in store.

Theron went in incubus form to Vlad's tent and

perched on the back of a folding chair, watching Vlad study a map and sweat over the routing his forces were getting. The man's mind was plainly far from fears of Theron.

It was as if the bastard had no soul. Nothing fazed him for more than a few minutes. Vlad was pure, cold, calculating confidence. He plainly knew that he would always win. No one had ever bested him, and no one ever would.

Theron watched as Vlad finally lay down to sleep, still clothed and ready for action at the slightest alarm.

As the hours slipped toward morning, Theron watched and tried to wrap his mind around what he planned to do. But how did one, even a demon of the Night World, ever completely prepare for suicide?

For he'd seen it now: There was no stopping Vlad. There were no threats that could scare the man; there was no way to fight him physically, and he could not be tricked out of his own body.

It didn't mean Vlad would win, however. Theron had one thing that Vlad did not: someone who was more important to him than existence itself.

He tried for a time to sift through his centuries of experience, looking for something to savor one last time; something to review, and be pleased with; something that might make his having existed at all mean something.

Every thought came back to Lucia. Nothing mattered but her. His original plans to be a king on the earth were but a child's fantasy, and one ignorant of all that was important.

It was only Lucia who mattered. Lucia who must be given a chance to live a happy life, which she would never have if Vlad got his hands on her.

Lucia.

With that single thought in his mind, Theron stretched out his wings, lifted himself off the back of the chair and hovered in the air for one long moment; he stared down at Vlad, anticipating the annihilation that would come to them both in a moment, when he forced himself into Vlad's body.

The end was here.

Lucia.

He let himself fall.

Chapter Thirty-nine

"Open your eyes," a deep female voice said.

Theron obeyed, opening his eyes to a soft darkness studded with tiny, twinkling lights like distant stars. He was lying down, and his body felt strangely heavy. Something rough was against his skin, but at least it was warm.

Warm. He'd never felt a sensation quite like this before. He blinked into the soft darkness. "Have I done it, then? Is this what comes after?"

"For demons, nothing comes after," the voice said.

He turned toward it, squinting as he tried to make out the face or even the figure of the speaker. The star-like pinpoints of light shifted, and in the movement he caught a sense of her outline.

His mind cleared in a rush, and he struggled to sit up. "Your Majesty!" It was Nyx.

"Rest easy, Theron." With a touch he could not see, she gently pushed him back down onto his back. "You will need your strength."

"You don't still want me for your harem, after what I tried, do you?"

She laughed softly. "I wasn't sure you would do it, you know, but then, you've always been different from the others."

"Your Majesty?"

The stars coalesced a bit more, and now he could make out the shape of her face. Stars gathered together to form the whites of her eyes and the white of her teeth. Her substance was the night itself, her flesh a dark swath of eternity swirling with distant galaxies.

"Vlad is no more," she said. "He had only the shadow of a soul, and it did not put up much of a struggle before departing for the afterworld of the Day Gods."

Relief flooded through him like a rush of warm water. Lucia was safe. Safe! He had done it. A sense of peace filled him.

"Do you not wish to know about yourself, then?" Nyx asked with a laugh in her voice.

"I assume you will feed me to the Day Gods as well."

"You don't think I want you in my harem?"

He shook his head. "I would be no good to you. I have lost the magic of it. I have lost the will for it. It is fitting that the Day Gods have me and rend me to pieces."

"Ah, Theron. It is not quite time for your end. You did it, you see."

"I did it," he repeated, not understanding. "Did what?"

"You took Vlad's body."

He shook his head. "No. I forced myself into it. I will be destroyed."

"And yet you have not been."

"You saved me?"

She shook her head. "No. You found the catch in the natural laws. You found the one way to get what you desired all along."

"I don't understand." Was she saying that he was in Vlad's body *right now*? He moved his hand over his body, feeling the rough thing that covered it. Was it *clothing*?

"I know you don't. It's a matter of love, Theron. And of self-sacrifice. The beings of the Night World do neither. They have no souls, they do not love, they do not put the welfare of another above their own.

"But you, Theron, have somehow learned to love, and have grown yourself a soul. For the soul of a mortal being is made of the love he has for others.

"When you fell into Vlad, you fell purely, with love in your heart. You had no wishes for yourself, no hopes of gain. All you wanted was to protect the woman you love.

"If Vlad had loved her—if Vlad had loved *anyone*— this would have ended differently. But here you are, and Vlad is gone, and I have a new story to entertain Darkness the next time he visits."

"Thank you," Theron said, too stunned to think of anything else to say. He still didn't believe it.

Nyx laughed and stood, and began to move away. "I didn't actually want you in my harem, you know. I knew from early on the mischief you did with Vlad and Dragosh. I grew impatient with waiting to see it remedied, and thought you needed a reason to hurry things along." She grinned at him, wicked as only the daughter of Chaos could be. "Enjoy your stolen life, Theron. It will go by all too quickly."

The darkness followed her, stars swirling in her wake as she went. As she disappeared and the darkness faded, light began to fill the tent where Theron lay.

It was the soft light of morning, glowing through the canvas walls. He lay still, and watched in silence and in awe as it touched his skin and did not burn.

He was human.

He had become Vlad Draco.

Chapter Forty

In Castle Rosu, Lucia woke well before dawn. She didn't know how long she had been asleep but guessed it could have been no more than a few hours. She had not slept the night through since the aborted attempt to capture Theron two weeks ago.

Her restless slumber was not from fear that he would return. It was from knowing that he would not.

Father Gabriel gloated over his jug like an old man with a chest of gold. He was convinced that he had captured Theron inside, although Lucia was certain he had not. She had felt Theron pull away before the final candle was in place and knew he had not been caught.

But even though he had escaped, she knew he would not be returning to her dreams. He would not want to, after such a betrayal.

And she would be afraid to face him even if he did, her shame too great to bear. Her self-loathing outweighed her longing, and so she wore the necklace day and night.

How long until dawn? She lay in bed and stared into the empty, lonely darkness. She sensed no presence but her own and Mara's, no waiting lover, no promise of distant lands and indescribable pleasure.

Theron had been right: After a couple of nights of dreamlessness, she had regained her strength and energy, enough so that she once again longed for his touch. She knew it was wrong to do so, but knowing that could not stop her from wanting him.

She threw back the covers and got out of bed. She didn't want to spend the rest of the night lying there, wishing for things that could not be. Better to dress and distract herself with reading, or the mandolin, or even sewing. Anything.

"My lady?" Mara asked from the floor, woken by Lucia's movements.

"I want to get dressed."

Mara got up and went to light a candle. Lucia had noticed a change in the maid since the night of the candle circle. She seemed more subdued and willing to obey; subservient, even. As she should have been all along. Mara seemed to have gained a respect for Lucia that had not been there before.

It came too late, though. Lucia no longer cared what Mara thought.

The maid combed and arranged Lucia's hair, brought water for her ablutions, and then took a gown from the garderobe. "You have not yet worn this one, my lady," Mara said. She was holding out the green and amber gown.

Lucia stared at it, and a sense of inevitability came over her. Was it to be today, then? "Yes, all right. That one."

She felt almost separated from her own body as Mara helped her dress, pinning her sleeves on and lacing up the back of the gown. The life for which she had been waiting for so long was finally about to begin, and she could not have been less excited.

The boring sameness of Castle Rosu seemed precious in its peacefulness, now that the time to leave it was almost upon her. She looked around her room, at the furniture and walls that had become so familiar to her over these past six years, and felt as if they were already only half her own. Her heart was taking leave, detaching itself from this place, unable to hang on now that it knew she would soon be gone from it. She couldn't imagine spending another evening here, cozily passing the time next to the fire while dressed only in her chemise and a wrap.

"Begin packing my things, Mara."

"My lady?"

"Vlad comes today."

Mara stared at her but did not ask how she knew. "As you wish, my lady."

Lucia went out into the hall and toward the stairs but stopped at the sight of the window seat alcove with the east-facing windows. She went to it and opened the casement, pushing the panes wide.

In the distance, a star shone brightly above the horizon, a lone light in the lavender, twilit firmament. She sat on the seat and watched as the first hint of orange tinged the sky, and then pinks and golds, as the sun crept over the mountains, the light diffused by morning dampness and distance. The mountains themselves were silhouetted, their dark green slopes looking black against the golden light.

Amid the birdsong of the forest another sound came: the far-off echo of male voices. Just a word here or there, a command or the rhythm of a sentence, but it was enough. Vlad and his men were climbing the 1,490 stairs up the mountain.

She waited where she was, listening as the voices came nearer, the drifts of sound on the wind more frequent. Without even thinking of it, she touched the pendant over her breast.

A tear slipped from her eye, as she thought of all the girlish dreams she had had for this day; the high hopes for romance and happiness. For six years she had looked forward to this day of deliverance.

Now that it was here, she knew it was the day on which the old Lucia must die forever, and the new one—feet firmly on the ground—must be born.

She stood and leant out the window, looking down at the great drop below. Enough to kill a person. How long would it take? Half a minute? The vast empty space drew her. It would be so easy, so quick . . .

A pounding came at the great doors below, the sound echoing in a faint, penetrating drumbeat down the corridors of the castle and up the stairs to her alcove. And then there were voices echoing in the cloistered halls of Castle Rosu.

Lucia closed her eyes for one long moment, feeling the coolness of the morning air on her face, and then closed the casements and latched them shut. It was time to meet her groom.

Chapter Forty-one

Gabriel heard the noise of the arriving men and over-
came his stomach cramps long enough to crawl his way
to the window that looked out over the courtyard. He
pushed open the casement and stuck out his sweating
head. Unfamiliar soldiers were milling below, wearing
the colors of Wallachia.

Thank God! Vlad was here at last.

Gabriel had consumed the last rationed drop of his
poppy juice two days before and had been suffering the
torments of the damned ever since. Sweats, stomach
cramps, muscle cramps, vomiting, diarrhea—it felt as if
he was dying.

The sickness was bad enough, but foul fiends from
Hell had chosen to torture him as well, doubtless called
down upon him by the demon queen. Giant spiders
crawled up the walls of his room, but no one else could
see them. Squatting creatures with enormous teeth and
skin like toads hid in the shadows in the corners of his
room, but when he called one of the maids to come

chase the things away, the maid would say that there was nothing there.

Tired of rushing to his aid when there was nothing they could see amiss, the servants had stopped answering his calls for help, and he was left alone with the beasts of the darkness. He barred his door and huddled under the furs on his bed, daring to venture out from under the covers only when his bowels demanded it.

But now Vlad had come: his brother, whom nothing could frighten. Gabriel would like to see the demon queen try to work her evil on Vlad Draco—she would lose that battle in a hurry.

Best of all, though, when Gabriel showed Vlad the jug holding Theron, Vlad would reward him with all the poppy juice he could swallow.

He whimpered and grew faint at the thought; it was so beautiful.

Gabriel grabbed the jug and wrapped his arms around it, huddling over it as he rushed to his chamber door. He batted away giant spiders that dangled from the ceiling, trying with their hairy legs to snatch the vessel from him.

"No, go away! It's mine!"

He managed with one hand to get the door to his chamber unbarred, and dashed out into the passageway. He hurried down the stairs and through rooms, heading for the grand hall meant for formally greeting guests.

"Juice, juice, juice," he panted under his breath, weeping softly with relief that it was almost his. "Juice, juice, juice . . ."

He was still chanting in a murmur when he finally reached the hall and saw his brother, standing a head taller than the rest of the men, his dark eyes watching everything and missing nothing. They lit on Gabriel, but there was no spark of welcome.

Gabriel slunk forward, the jug cradled in his arms. "I did it, Vlad! I did it! Look, I caught him!"

Gabriel caught Vlad's gaze and looked up at him with the eagerness of a dog waiting for a scrap.

A small smile curled Vlad's lip, and then a blue light flared in his eyes. "You're going to need a bigger jug, priest."

The voice that came out of Vlad's throat was not the one Gabriel had heard all his life. Confused, he held out the jug. He was falling back on the one thing that made sense, and that would please Vlad. "He's in here."

His brother leaned forward and whispered. "I'll tell you a secret."

"Yes?"

"He's not in there."

Gabriel frowned down at the jug. "But I put the seal on it."

"He's not in there," Vlad repeated. "He's in *here.*" He tapped his own chest.

Gabriel met Vlad's eyes again, and this time the blue flame was steady in Vlad's pupils.

Gabriel dropped the jug, the earthenware shattering on the stone floor.

"I am going to make you pay for what you tried to do to me," Vlad—who was *not* Vlad—said.

Gabriel looked wildly around him. The soldiers were idly watching him, faint sneers of disgust on their faces. He saw no friend, no aid. He heard a noise on the stairs and spun around.

Giant spiders were stepping elegantly down the stairs, their ebony bead eyes all looking at him.

"Vlad?" Gabriel asked in a plea, not quite able to believe that his brother, who was standing right in front of him, was not who he seemed to be.

"Vlad is gone," his brother whispered. "It's only Theron here now."

Gabriel grabbed for the crucifix hanging around his neck, and thrust it out in front of him, his hand shaking. "In the name of Jesus Christ, leave this man!"

But Theron only smiled and said, "This is *my* body now, and you cannot force me from it. So run, priest. Run down the mountain and far away, before I decide just what, exactly, I'd like to do to you."

Gabriel looked again for help from the people around him, but no one met his eyes. The only things watching him were the spiders, creeping now over the walls and ceiling. One dropped down on a thick strand of webbing and landed on his head, clinging to his scalp.

Gabriel shrieked. Again he looked to Vlad, and again he saw the blue flames in his eyes. Nothing made sense; nothing was as it should be; all was damned, all haunted. He ran out into the courtyard, barreling through the group of soldiers, and then out of the castle, down the 1,490 stairs, and out into the wilderness.

He ran until he could run no more, but even then he could not outrun the demons that chased him.

Chapter Forty-two

Theron's heart beat as if to fly from his chest as he waited for Lucia to appear on the staircase. He was glad of the encounter with Gabriel, which had given him an outlet for some of his tension. In truth he would have liked to have bodily thrown the priest off the mountain, but that would have meant leaving the hall and delaying his meeting with Lucia. Sending the priest screaming off into the woods would have to do, and was not ungratifying.

He watched the staircase, waiting, remembering how this scene had been already in Lucia's mind when he came to her dreams, and changed it to suit himself.

How would she react when she saw just how much he had changed things this time? There was a cowardly part of him that didn't want to let her know he was Theron inside Vlad's body; that wanted to play this role of Vlad Draco and start anew with her, pretending to be the man she had dreamt of since her betrothal.

As tempting as that was, he knew he could not do it. It

would not be fair to her, and she deserved the chance to make her own choice. No one else had given that to her, but he would. He was here to love her, not to own her.

If she would let him.

Lucia reached the bottom of the stairs and raised her gaze to that of her betrothed.

Brown eyes even softer than those in the portrait looked back at her, from a face stronger than art had depicted. His dark auburn hair was pulled back and tied by a leather thong, and his skin was tanned by the sun. The dirt of travel was upon him, and he looked as if he had traveled many miles in a great hurry in order to reach her.

He was a handsome man, even more so than in her imaginings, but if tales were to be believed, his heart was as cold as his face was beautiful.

"Welcome to Castle Rosu, my lord," she said, and curtsied deeply. As Sister Teresa had told her, there was always a choice. She chose to please him as best she could, and to win his respect. She would not cower. She would not weep. She would put away childish things and become a queen.

Even if it broke her heart to do so.

He strode slowly toward her, closing the distance between them. The soldiers and servants who had gathered in the hall stood still and quiet, watching.

She was still on the bottom step when he reached her, the added height keeping her from being overwhelmed by his size. He was a tall man, broad-shouldered and finely built. Once upon a time, she would have counted herself a lucky woman.

He picked up her hands and held them loosely. "Lucia."

She felt a sudden prick of tears in her eyes, for his voice in that one word was so like Theron's. "My lord."

He met her eyes and looked so intently into them that she found she could not look away. His dark gaze looked upon her as if she was much beloved, and known to him for years, not moments. His hands gently squeezed hers. " 'Rise up, my love, my fair one, and come away,' " he said.

Her lips parted in wonder. It was her favorite verse from the Song of Solomon. How had he known? And his voice . . .

"Are you ready to leave this place, my fair one, even if it be with me?"

There was only one person who had ever called her his fair one. She felt the tears fill her eyes. It couldn't be him, it couldn't, and yet . . . "Is it you?" she whispered.

A blue flame seemed to burn for a moment in his eyes. "It is I, if that is who you wish me to be."

She closed her eyes and felt a tear spill down her cheek. When she opened them again, he was looking at her with anxious worry.

She laughed softly, released his hands, and put her own on either side of his face, holding him gently, not wholly believing she was not dreaming. How could this be? She was afraid to accept it as truth. "Am I awake?"

"You tell me," he said.

"I do not know."

"I have dreamt of you, Lucia. For the first time in four thousand years I have dreamt, and each dream has been of you."

"Can you ever forgive me?" she asked on a breath of tears.

"There is nothing to forgive."

She put her arms around his neck and held him close, her face in his neck.

"Only tell me," he whispered, for her ears only, "do you wish to be my wife? It is your choice."

She lifted her head, her lips parted in wonder. "My choice."

His dark eyes met her own. "I will not force you, even if it *is* what you want."

"Theron." Perhaps this was real, perhaps it was not. She was living in it, either way. "It is what I wish, more than life itself." She smiled. "But let this be the last time you change your face, my beloved. I should like to know the one I shall forever be seeing in my dreams."

"In your dreams and on waking. It is time for both our lives to begin, together." He tenderly lay his lips against hers, the touch gentle and unsure, and together they shared the first true kiss they had either of them known. He wrapped his arms around her waist and held her close, and his touch was more precious to her than a thousand dreams of passion.

She broke the kiss and brought her lips close to his ear. "I am my beloved's, and my beloved is mine."

He lay his cheek against the side of her neck, his lips against the place where her neck met her shoulder, and she held the back of his head with her hand, knowing that she had woken to a life more beautiful than any dream.

"Are you going to have them send up a bathtub and hot water?" he asked softly. "There are so many things I have been looking forward to trying in the flesh."

She laughed and pulled away just long enough to give the order to a servant.

Yes, life was beautiful upon waking.

Chapter Forty-three

Theron tried to undress Lucia with hands made clumsy by desire. "How do your sleeves come off? I can't see how—"

"Pins."

He found one of the straight gold pins and tried to pluck it from the fabric. "Ow! Sun-blasted—" He looked at the injured digit. "I'm bleeding!"

She grasped his hand and examined the wound, then laughed and put his finger in her mouth, sucking it. He felt a jolt of desire go straight to his loins. His cock, already hard, seemed to thicken yet more and strain against his braies and hose. He shifted, trying to free his erection from a fold of fabric.

"You do it," he said hoarsely. "I'll die of frustrated lust if you make me fumble my way through all those ties and pins."

She pulled his finger from her mouth. "Yes, all right. But do you want me to undress you, too?"

He was already jerking on the ties of his *pourpoint*, un-

341

willing to wait on that score either. Finesse and seduction were being trampled on his way to Lucia's bare body.

"This was so much easier as an incubus," he groused as he found that one of his ties had worked itself into a knot. He pulled the dagger from the sheath at his waist and cut the thing, then used it to cut the rest of the ties as well.

"But was it as much fun?" she asked.

He looked up from his clothing mutilation and saw that she had her bodice off. Her nipples showed darkly through the fine linen of her chemise. She reached her hands behind her back and worked at the tie of her skirt, the movement thrusting her breasts forward and making them jiggle as she struggled with the fastening.

"No, it wasn't as much fun." He threw the dagger to the side and grabbed Lucia around the waist, his hungry mouth going down to her breast and sucking her nipple through the cloth.

"Theron?" she squealed.

He sucked hard, then managed to gain a moment's control over himself and released her. "Sorry. It's this body of Vlad's."

She looked down at her chest, lifting the neckline of the chemise away from her body to examine the pinkening flesh and the erect tip of her nipple. He growled.

She quickly covered herself back up, a hand over her breast. "What about that body?"

"It has a will of its own. And *this*," he said, gesturing downward at the cock that fought to be free. "It's like that horse I've had to ride. It wants to go where it wants, when it wants, and no one had better try to stop it."

"And where does it want to go, right now?"

"In you." His eyes went to her chest, and he remembered how she had looked naked, in her dreams. "I want to toss you onto your bed, hike up your skirts, and have at you."

She bit her upper lip. "I see."

"I'm not going to. I'm going to take a bath first. You deserve a better bedding than a dirty warrior rutting between your legs like a beast."

She pursed her lips, eyebrows raised. "It doesn't sound completely unappealing."

He shut his eyes and took a deep breath, trying to control the involuntary flex at his groin, as the one-eyed beast tried to reach her. "Lucia, don't *say* things like that! I won't be responsible for what happens if you do."

"Oh dear me. What a shame."

He growled again and made himself turn away and continue undressing, ripping fabric when it would not come off his body as quickly as he wished. The tub was waiting for him, but it was only a quarter of the size of the one in the dream he had shared with Lucia.

He got the last of his clothing off and stepped into the bath, lowering himself into it in a squat.

He shot right back up again, an unmanly screech squeaking from his throat. "What in the name of Night—"

Lucia, her skirt off now, came and squatted down to put her fingers in the water, the neckline of her chemise falling away from her and revealing a perfect view of her breasts. They formed a deep valley of cleavage that, if he pressed together and thrust into . . . "It's quite nice. You just have to go in slowly," she said.

Oh, good goddess of the night . . .

"No, thank you. I'll stand as I am. I'm not putting my cock down in that boiling water. It might be damaged."

She stood and looked at his offended appendage, the thing still stiffly erect and looking none the worse for its dip in the water. "I'm guessing it would fare just fine. Do you want me to wash you?"

He groaned. "Yes." *Oh, yes.*

She dipped a rag into the water and sudsed it, then began to work over his chest. The water from the rag dripped down her arm and up her sleeve, and he watched its path with hunger. She pressed her front against him for a brief moment as she reached behind him to scrub, and when she pulled away again her chemise was soaked, the fabric gone transparent and clinging to her nipples.

"Rinse," he groaned, the one word all he could manage. As an incubus he had been capable of speech and cajoling, poetry and refinement; sensitive, elegant seduction.

As a living man, he was lucky to do more than grunt while desire was upon him.

It had been upon him since he first fully accepted that he had become Vlad Draco and was free to claim Lucia as his bride. The moment that thought had hit him, his new body had become a beast impossible to tame. It dragged him across the countryside, a hound on the trail of a deer, unwilling to stop for anything until the prey was found.

He wondered that human men ever accomplished anything at all, if this was the state of their minds. He wanted to do nothing but rut, for hours, for days. He wanted to sheathe himself in Lucia and stay there the rest of his life, and then some. He had looked at the men around him and wondered that they could go to war when there were women who might part their legs to them and let them rut. Rut rut rut.

Lucia used a pitcher to pour water over him, and when the soap was gone from the important places he stepped out of the tub, scooped her up in his arms, and carried her to the bed. He dropped her there with something less than the grace he would have managed as a dream demon.

She helped him to remove her chemise and then lay back, one knee raised, her arms stretched above her head. "I know you're eager, Theron. I think I'm ready, if you are."

He tried to hold back. "It won't be so easy as in the dreams, Lucia. You are a virgin, still. It will hurt."

"So are you virgin."

"It's not going to hurt *me.*"

She raised her other knee, her thighs parted, giving him a full view of her. "I think I'm going to be all right. We have practiced so long and so well in my mind. Please, Theron. Let's not wait."

It wasn't an offer he could refuse. He climbed between her legs and tried to position himself at her entrance. She was wet and slippery as he nudged himself against her, looking for the right spot, and so deliciously warm against the head of his cock that he was afraid he would climax right then and there. He had to pull away for a moment to regain control of himself.

"Is there a problem?" she asked, worry in her tone.

"I've never tried to control one of these," he said, looking down at his wild bit of manhood. "I've never been on this end of things. I know what to do from *your* perspective, but . . ."

She reached down between them and gently grasped him, guiding him into place. "Here. Put it here."

He felt her flesh part around his head. "Oh, goddess, Lucia . . ."

He felt her muscles tighten against him and he forced himself to hold still, only the tip of his head inside her. "Are you all right?" he asked from between clenched teeth.

"It's a little uncomfortable," she said, strain in her voice. "I'll be fine, though. Come, demon, let's do this thing."

"No more demon," he gritted out, eyes closed, still holding back although her flesh was calling to him with each slight movement she made.

"Beloved," she said. "My beloved."

He opened his eyes and looked into hers. "I love you, Lucia. I only exist to love you."

She smiled. "And I love you, against all my attempts not to." She rocked her hips up then, forcing him into her, and he was powerless to resist. He thrust deeply inside her, even as she gave one sharp cry of pain. He was powerless to pull out, though, his senses overwhelmed by the wonder of the warm envelope of damp flesh that surrounded him.

He lay partly on top of her, his hips on hers while his arms supported him above her. "Are you all ri—"

She rocked against him in answer. He thrust again, and once more, and then his climax took him over. He called her name and pressed hard into her, his whole body tightening, his eyes rolling back as the waves hit him, carrying him to a place he had known existed but had never truly felt for himself.

"Never," he groaned.

"Never?" she questioned, holding still beneath him.

"Never have I felt or imagined anything like this." A climax stolen from a dream, he discovered at that moment, was nothing as compared to the reality of flesh upon flesh.

"I'm glad," she said, sounding possessive and satisfied. "I'm glad I could be your first, no matter how many thousands of women you have visited in their dreams."

He collapsed on top of her and rolled to the side with her, his satisfied beast still inside her. He felt like an animal. "I'm sorry."

"Sorry for what?" she asked, looking into his eyes and stroking his cheek.

"Sorry that I made such a sorry job of taking your virginity. Good goddess, I finished in under a minute."

"Perhaps half a minute."

"Oh, goddess," he groaned in embarrassment, and turned his face into the furs upon which they lay.

She laughed softly. "We have a whole lifetime to get it right, Theron. A whole lifetime."

He turned his head slightly, just enough to look at her with one leering eye. "I won't need that long. Give me twenty minutes."

She laughed again and kissed him. "I'll be ready."

He grinned. "Make it ten."

He was going to like being human.

Epilogue

Sighisoara, Transylvania, One year later

Lucia stood in the window of her and Theron's home in the center of town, holding her newborn baby boy in her arms and watching the people go about their business in the cobbled street below. She and Theron had been living in this citadel town for several months, as Theron cemented ties with Transylvania, ensuring that Wallachia would have a powerful ally across the mountains.

There was an uneasy peace between Wallachia and Moldavia. Theron had not met face to face with either Bogdan or his son Nicolae, who now commanded Moldavia's armies and had married a mysterious woman with no known family named Samira. Lucia had been shocked when Theron had told her that Nicolae's wife had actually been a succubus, and his friend. *Had* been. He didn't know now whether Samira might consider him more enemy than friend, and he was not yet prepared to let Samira and Nicolae know that he had succeeded in taking over Vlad's body.

Rumor had it that Samira and Nicolae were expecting a child of their own. When Lucia had heard the news, a chill had gone through her, and she had lain a hand over her then-large belly as the words of her great-grandmother flashed into her mind: *Not until a whelp and kit bear young will lands again be one, and peace and prosperity come to the children of Raveca.* She and Nicolae had not been the kit and whelp to join and bear young together; might that thankless task fall to her own child, and to Samira's?

She pushed the unwelcome memory aside, and turned her attention back to the present, and the fragile joys it held. "You see, my love?" she whispered in her baby's perfect, seashell ear as she watched the burghers below. "People, living their lives in peace. Never take this for granted, sweeting. It is good to be among one's fellows, and to live fully in the light of day."

"What troubles are you filling our son's head with?" Theron asked lightly, coming up behind her. Putting his hands on her shoulders, he bent down to kiss her neck.

She smiled and half-turned so that she was leaning against him and he could see the face of their child. She lifted her own lips and kissed Theron's cheek.

His large brown eyes met hers, warm with love.

It had taken several months, but she had finally grown familiar with him in Vlad's body. Sometimes she thought she saw a flash of blue fire in his eyes, but she never knew for certain if it was more than just her imagination.

"I'm reminding him that the people in his life matter more than anything else," she said.

Theron gently touched the baby's cheek, his own expression one of tenderness and awe, as if he still could not believe he had a son. "I'm sure he understands. If he doesn't, he could have no better parents to teach him."

"Do you understand, little Vlad?" Lucia asked, nuzzling the baby's head. They had named him Vladimir more by tradition than choice, it being a long-standing tradition in the original Vlad Draco's family. She didn't mind, though—in public life Theron was called Vlad, and since she'd never known the real Vlad, she was happy enough to associate the name with both her husband and her son. The original Vlad might as well have been only a bad dream.

Her brother Dragosh she had seen only once, when he had come to congratulate her and Theron a few months after their wedding. Dragosh had not been as she remembered him: He had looked old and broken, not the energetic, all-powerful figure of her childhood. He had seemed uncomfortable in her presence, and even more so when she told him she was already expecting a child. Whatever bond they had once shared seemed lost forever, and they had become as strangers to one another. It saddened Lucia, but having Theron and a child of her own to love had softened the ache.

There was a knocking on the door.

"Enter!"

Sister Teresa came in, guided by two serving maids who were her constant attendants and caretakers. While Lucia had wanted to keep Sister Teresa with her, despite her deterioration, she had been glad enough to give Mara a dowry and let her marry a pig farmer.

Of Father Gabriel, no one had seen or heard anything for certain. There was a rumor going around, though, that gypsies had killed a lunatic priest in the forest, having in the middle of the night mistaken him for one of the dark, ravening demons of their mythology.

The light of sanity was almost never in Sister Teresa's eyes these days, and Lucia feared that there was little time left for the frail nun. She was grateful, though, that Teresa had lived long enough to see baby Vlad born. Lucia carried the baby over, holding him so that the nun could see.

Teresa's eyes brightened at sight of the baby, a rare clarity briefly coming to them. She lightly lay her withered fingertips on his head. "Oh, precious baby. Beautiful baby."

"He's our little dragon," Lucia said. "Our little Draco."

Teresa smiled and touched Vlad's cheek, the baby turning into the touch, his mouth working as if seeking food. "Not Draco," she said tenderly. "*Dracula.* 'The son of the dragon.'"

Lucia felt a chill go through her, for what reason she did not know. She held Vlad close and kissed his forehead, feeling a sudden need to protect him. "Darling baby, you will have a long and wonderful life," she said, as if the words could be a charm against any evil that might befall him.

"Dracula," Teresa said again, smiling.

"Dracula."

LISA CACH

Come to Me

Samira is the lowliest creature of the Night World: a mere succubus, a winged spirit bringing dreams of passion to sleeping men. She knows every wicked wish that lurks in their hearts, and yet she has never felt the touch of a man's loving hand. Nor has she wanted to...until now.

Shattered by war and banished to a crumbling fortress, Nicolae turns to the dark arts. He plans to use Samira as a tool to find a means to oust the invader from his lands and regain all that he's lost. When she arrives on his doorstep in human form, his long-sought vengeance is lost. What happens next will change their worlds forever.

LISA KLEYPAS
LISA CACH * CLAUDIA DAIN
LYNSAY SANDS

Wish List

Dear St. Nicholas—
What we'd really like for Xmas this year is:

An Irish Estate
A Family
~~Mountains of Sugarplums~~ (Too fattening)
A Quiet Elopement
Someone to ~~burn~~ close down all the London clubs (like White's)!
Marriage to a Man who is Honest, Loving, Sexy, Handsome, and Titled.

But we know there aren't enough of those to go around...
are there?

—Respectfully,
Four Hopeful English Ladies

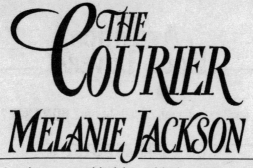

THE COURIER

MELANIE JACKSON

In the alternate world of the Wildside, earth is populated not only by humans but creatures of dark, seductive magic—pookas, sylphs, goblins and more. This wonderland is in delicate balance. And the goblins are always plotting.

Lyris knows all about goblins. But is Quede, the strange owner of the plantation Toujours Perdrix, the biggest threat in New Orleans? Or is it Romeo Hart, the fey who laughs at death and quickens Lyris's blood? This courier mission she's just been assigned is trouble. No question. Lyris is in danger of losing her life, her soul, or her heart—but by the time she discovers which, it will be too late.